Jenny Ackland is a writer and teacher from Melbourne. She has worked in offices, sold textbooks in a university bookshop, taught English overseas and worked as a proofreader and freelance editor. Her short fiction has been published in literary magazines and listed in prizes and awards. Her debut novel *The Secret Son*—a 'Ned Kelly-Gallipoli mash-up' about truth and history—was published in 2015.

Little Gods is her second novel.

LITTLE
GODS

JENNY ACKLAND

ALLEN&UNWIN
SYDNEY·MELBOURNE·AUCKLAND·LONDON

Allen & Unwin
83 Alexander Street
Crows Nest NSW 2065
Australia
Phone: (61 2) 8425 0100
Email: info@allenandunwin.com
Web: www.allenandunwin.com

A catalogue record for this
book is available from the
National Library of Australia

ISBN 978 1 76029 711 4

Internal design by Sandy Cull, gogoGingko
Set in 11.5/17 pt Scala by Bookhouse, Sydney
Printed and bound in Australia by Griffin Press

10 9 8 7 6 5 4 3 2 1

The paper in this book is FSC® certified.
FSC® promotes environmentally responsible,
socially beneficial and economically viable
management of the world's forests.

For my mother, Pamela Ackland.

Though she be but little, she is fierce.

William Shakespeare, *A Midsummer Night's Dream*, Act 3, Scene 2

Little Lamb, who made thee?
Dost thou know who made thee . . . ?

William Blake, 'The Lamb'

OLIVE MAY LOVELOCK had always felt the tree was hers. The family told stories about finding her asleep out there, a small child curled up asleep among the roots. She used to say it was the place where the orange felt strongest.

The great hulking peppercorn was a monster of branches and broad roots that pushed out of the earth like the rolling backs of porpoises and formed small caves where young children would dig and find treasure. Old shards of pinky-grey slate, white rabbit bones and, once, a bullet casing. When older, Olive took to the air to escape the anguish of the ground, climbing the tree as if it were a ladder.

Now, when she holds still and puts down her pen to bring her mind inwards, she can see there are many versions of her past self concertinaed within like a string of paper dolls. There she is six years old, then nine, then eleven. A repeating pattern of girl children, thoughts fluid yet certain. She is grown but what separates her from them? She may not sit astride a purple Dragster, toes digging deep into runners whose insides smell like wet cheese, lacing shiny plastic handlebar streamers between her fingers. She may not have bony knees or determined hair that's too much. Eyes that sweep terrain and cloud and clear as rapidly as the sun drops beyond a country horizon. She was no longer a girl bombing off the high board but still there are snapshots of herself, images frozen in time that appear randomly, overlaid with words that could be borrowed from fairytales: *beeswing, gidgee, fiddleback*.

As a child, trapped in the savage act of growing up, Olive had sensed she was at the middle of something, so close to the nucleus she could almost touch it with her tongue. But, like looking at her own nose for too long, everything became blurry and she had to pull away. She'd reached for happiness as a child, not yet knowing that the memories she was concocting would become deceptive. That memories get you where they want you not the other way around.

Thoughts circle and pull at her. No matter how often she walks the city beaches, her mind finds itself back at Serpentine. A person can try, but old sorrows travel with you and perch on your shoulders like fraternal twins, and try to tell you things. You carry your past with you and along the way it repeats indigestibly, lodged like a rock in the belly, the gullet, the bowel, wherever it is a person carries their messes and shame. As the years started to pull behind her like toffee, her mind always managed to find itself at her uncle and aunt's farm. And whenever she returned to those dark sticky years, it was still surprising how it all unravelled so quickly, the summer she turned twelve.

BEGINNERS

EVEN AT TWELVE Olive had known that others thought her family odd. Those Lovelocks, people would say, their looks loaded with meaning. They said it in the butcher, the supermarket and the haberdashery. They said it at the milk bar and in the playground at school.

'They say her wedding dress was made of wool,' one woman said to another in the newsagent.

'And there's the haughty one.'

'And that Thistle.'

Silence then, and knowing nods, as Olive watched from behind the newspaper rack with a lemon-lime Chupa Chup in one hand and thirty cents in the other.

Her mother was one of the Nash sisters, a clutch of prickly women who'd grown up in Stratford. Three girls maturing behind a high hedge with neighbours on both sides who strained at fences and peeked through holes. Their mother, sensing all those opened ears, made sure transgressions were dealt with inside the house, windows and doors shut tight. As if that weren't enough, there were the Lovelock brothers, in sheep not wheat. The way people said it made it sound like a mistake.

When the two families had merged matrimonially, things had become complicated and not just for the leftover sister. It was a truth Olive Lovelock also struggled with as she stood in front of her grade six class on a Friday afternoon early in December.

In her hands was her family tree chart and she was trying to explain how the people fitted together. She told the class her mother was called Audra and was a housewife and shy, and that her father was Bruce and worked in some unclear way for the Wool Board. She told them that sometimes her dad talked about 'fribs' and 'wefts' and that he had a wall of shelving in the shed at home where he poked grading samples from different breeds.

The other children sat on the carpet with their simple drawings on their laps. Linear, vertical, neat. Olive squinted at her hand-drawn diagram. All the lines were crisscrossed with wild loops and arrows that flared in the direction of explanation keys she'd put in boxes down the bottom. Some of the children were looking at her, some at the ground. Bosco Scully was in the first row and punched the arm of the boy next to him. The teacher was sitting at the back, at one of the student desks. Her eyes were closed.

Olive knew she didn't have much time so was racing to finish, but Mrs Barton interrupted her and placed a fingertip to the side of her head.

'Time to finish up,' she said. Olive nodded, but it was hard. She had more to say. She was excited because as well as the family tree presentations it was the day of her twelfth birthday. She'd brought a chocolate cake for lunch to share with the other children—not that any of them deserved it. She and her father had made it after dinner the night before, trying to keep quiet in the kitchen. The cricket had been on the radio with the volume down low. They'd stood side by side in front of the cooling rack and agreed they'd done a pretty good job. Then her guts had twisted as the cake sank in the middle.

'Oh.'

'Don't worry, big girl. We'll just build it up a bit.' Bruce pointed at the centre. 'With extra icing, here and here.'

But Olive had put too much food colouring in the icing and it had turned blood red. It dripped down the sides and collected in a viscous puddle in the concave centre and it had been this evil confection that made Bosco Scully spew. The emphatic red hurl had landed on the carpet right in front of Mrs Barton's shoes, making her drop the metre ruler. After the vomit had been cleaned up, standing in front of the class to do her talk, all Olive could be certain of was that two sisters had married two brothers with one of the sisters and one brother left over.

'It's a bit tricky,' she said. 'You see—'

'That's fine, Olivia,' Mrs Barton said. 'You can sit down now.'

But Olive planned to tell the class how her uncles said 'flock' for the very rude word and that birthday cards in her family were always written 'Happy Birthday to Ewe'. She was going to show that bit on the board because otherwise they wouldn't get it. Also, she was going to tell them that her aunt's wedding dress was made of silk, not wool, like some people had said. But mostly, she wanted to remind Mrs Barton that her name was Olive.

She went and sat down. The children on either side lifted their knees and it was Snooky Sands who made the most fuss about shifting backwards to make room.

Olive had asked Snooky only once why she was being so mean.

'My mum said not to play with you. It's because you're a bad influence.'

Olive watched Snooky walk away feeling the distance grow as if a real thing. She began wearing her grandfather's old binoculars around her neck.

'For seeing birds better,' she told the adults.

'For spying on people,' she told Peter.

She'd found the binoculars in the shed at the farm and her aunt had told her she supposed she could have them. Rue always said 'supposed' in a way which meant she preferred Olive didn't, but she took them all the same. She liked the feel of the strap around her neck, the weight of the glasses as they bumped against her tummy. They gave her power to know whether a person was smiling or serious, to see how their mouth stretched as they talked. If she wanted to, she could count how many times a person blinked in sixty seconds, and whether they chewed their lip while thinking about what to say next. She looked at birds with the binoculars and she looked at clouds. The binoculars made her feel she could see anything in the world that she wanted to.

SHE HEADED HOME, scraping her runners on the footpath. She stopped for a while at Miss Alexander's gate to try to get the orange cat to come for a pat, but it rolled on the driveway and ignored her. She called to it, keeping an eye out because the old lady was crazy. She had long grey hair that fell out of her bun, bushy eyebrows and no front teeth. She hissed like a goose at children if she ever caught them at the front of her house. Once she had scared Olive as she walked home from school and had pushed her up against the hedge asking her what her name was. Olive scratched the backs of her legs trying to get away. She waited a bit longer at the end of the driveway watching the cat.

She wanted a cat or a dog, she didn't mind which, but her mother had said no.

'What do you want to have pets for?' her mother had said. 'They just die, and then you get sad.'

She was almost at her house when she saw Peter waiting for her. On the footpath she stood in front of him and swung her binoculars to her eyes.

'Where were you?' she asked him. She rotated her body in small increments. 'Bosco threw up.'

'The high school? My mum wanted to go and talk to the principal.'

'What even for?'

'Who even knows. I think she wanted to look again. I don't know, she doesn't tell *me* why.' He made a noise that sounded like *chuh* in the back of his throat.

'But there's only one high school around here and we did the visit already.'

'I know.'

'Maybe she'll send you to boarding school.'

'As if.' He shook his head back to get his hair out of his eyes.

Like Olive, Peter Stonehouse was an only child and from the beginning he had adhered to her with commitment even though she always picked her scabs and sometimes her nose. He liked how pointy her chin was and didn't care that she could be ferocious in her extremes of emotion. To stand by and watch her cool interactions with others—even adults—was thrilling for a boy like Peter. He was someone who listened to the grown-ups and did what they told him. He'd realised the adult way was not a choice but a rule until you were a grown-up yourself and got your own turn. But Olive May Lovelock, she was taking her turn now. The only thing he didn't really like about her was how she could be opposite sometimes. He couldn't remember the word but it started with 'h'. It meant that she didn't always do or say things the same way all the time. She was always changing her mind. He thought the 'h' word also described someone who was always sick and complained about it like his aunty Mol but he wasn't sure.

'Why did he spew?'

'Probably the cake. It was really red.'

'I'm going to the pool. Coming?'

'I can't. We're going to the farm for the weekend, for my birthday.'

'You can come for a while, it's only—' he raised his wrist and looked at the watch that had been his grandfather's '—quarter to.' He gave the watch a dry kiss.

'You're going to marry that watch.' Olive lifted her binoculars in the direction of the lady across the road who lived with another lady who wasn't in her family. The story was that one of them had

fed her husband glass and gone to prison. No one knew which of
the two women it was.

'I *told* you, it's been near Germans,' Peter said.

It looked like just an ordinary watch to her. The face was round
and had a heavy brown leather band. The inscription on the back
read *PDS 26 May 1935*—Peter had the same initials as his pop,
Phillip—and his grandparents' wedding date. Peter had made the
mistake of telling Olive that he put the watch to bed each night in
a square box with cotton wool.

'You can come for a quick swim. I've got snakes.' He touched
his pocket.

'I don't have my bike or my things.'

'So get them.' Peter started riding slowly beside her as she walked.
'I've got mine already.'

They stopped by her place then set off again. Peter was talking
about the new high school uniform and the booklist but she wasn't
listening, she didn't care about any of that. She was thinking about
whether she had any coins in her pocket. If she did, she thought
she might get a Razz or a Glug, maybe both. She rode down the
footpath with Peter behind her. Overhead there was a thin line of
white cloud that hung above them, hard-edged against the pale
blue sky. Perhaps it was a trail from a plane but Olive didn't think
so. It looked more like a cloud that didn't realise what shape it was
meant to be. They turned left at the end of the road and continued
on to the Stratford Memorial Pool.

HEAT RADIATED OFF the black pitch in the car park and they pushed through the turnstile, the noise of shouts carrying across the space. The pool complex was filled with children and adults, some lying on towels on the cement, others on the grassed slopes which rose in waves around the perimeter. Olive looked at the small kiosk with the big clock over it. Four o'clock. She had an hour or a bit more.

They got into their bathers in the change rooms that smelled funny and walked across the grass to find a spot where they dumped their things and walk-ran to the fifty-metre pool, increasing speed once they hit the hot cement. They jumped in from the edge—Peter with his legs tucked into a sitting bomb and Olive in a silent-scream safety jump—and began to cycle through their usual activities. Handstands down the shallow end. Getting on each other's shoulders in turn. Swimming underwater and making it two-thirds of the way across.

Once, when getting out and running along to the shallower end, Olive knocked over a small child. The girl sat on the concrete, howling, saliva swinging from her open mouth. Olive bent over and tried to pick her up but the girl just sat and cried. Then the mother was there.

'I didn't mean to,' Olive said. 'It was an accident.'

'It's fine, don't worry,' the mother said, smiling. Olive looked at the little girl who had stopped crying and was getting up. Olive straightened and walked to where Peter was waiting and jumped back into the water.

'What happened?' he said.

'Nothing. It wasn't my fault.'

She and Peter sat a while on the bottom with their arms crossed, shouting messages to each other, and then climbed out and lay on their towels to eat sherbets and suck Razz tetra-paks.

'Gary Sands,' Peter said.

Olive sat up and shaded her eyes. Gary Sands was standing in waist-deep water with his mates. He was holding someone under the water and laughing. An older girl, Liz, struggled to the surface and broke free. Gary lurched back, head snapping, and whinnied like a horse.

'He's mental,' said Olive.

'Takes special medicine my mum said.'

'Yeah. Mental-case medicine.'

She picked up her towel. 'I have to go.'

'Let's do the boards, just quickly? Only a few times, like ten?'

'Alright.' She didn't really need to go. Her father wouldn't be home yet and her mother would be still lying down.

The diving pool was a place where you spoke in a whisper, like at church. Older boys flung themselves off the platform with frenetic, back-arching horseys and plummeted from the high boards, their thumping bombs pushing spray high into the air. The teenage girls gathered in hard-hipped broods nearby, standing with one leg straight and the other bent. Olive didn't know why they stood like that but they did. They were the girls who had pierced ears, sleepers which they rolled in their lobes as they watched the boys. If they ever went in the water, they kept their heads out so that their fringes stayed flicky and Olive didn't understand that either. What was the point of going to the pool if you didn't even go in, and if you went in, to not go under all the way?

If the older girls weren't beside the diving pool, they lay on their towels up the back of the mound along the fence, smoking, and with their oily hands on each other's shoulders, leaning, merging, laughing. They didn't eat anything, not even one hot chip, rather chewed gum and spoke with their hands over their mouths and propped themselves up on their arms, stomachs flat. They turned their heads when the lifeguard walked past, thongs snicking against his hardened heels.

Olive climbed the few steps up to one of the small boards. She walked to the end and stood. The surface was gritty under her bunched toes. She always delayed the jump, like the last scrapings of neapolitan in the bowl. The boys behind her shouted, telling her to stop taking so long, but she waited a moment more before making a small bounce and stepping off the end, her fingers pinched at her hips as if holding the edge of a dress.

The smack of cold was revelatory as she went down to the other world and back up to the surface made choppy as more and more bodies plummeted from the other boards. She swam to the ladder as quickly as possible and went and jumped again—*ker-plish-plosh*—and rose, wiping the hair from her face once she breached.

'Move, idiot!'

An older kid was looking down at her, shouting from the board above. His tummy tubbed over his shorts. 'Get out of the way.' He waved his hands and then he was coming. She swam to the edge and behind her came the sound of his body slamming the water and the push and pull of it against her legs as she hauled herself up the ladder. She was scared that one day someone like him would jump on her and crack her bones. If that happened she would be lost and sink to the bottom, where she'd drift in the deep and it would take too long for anyone to find her.

She did five more bombs off the low board then got out and sat on the edge watching Peter do pin drops off the high board. Then he climbed out and sat next to her.

'Still no?'

She shook her head.

'Maybe after Christmas?'

'Maybe,' she said.

They watched the older boys doing horseys and both saw it when Gary's brother Luke Sands landed wrong, hitting the water with a flamboyant belly-whack. He shot up and swam to the ladder, his face reddened against the blue tiles. His eyes met Olive's.

'What's so funny, binocular girl?'

He climbed out and walked over to them. He stood behind her, dripping water down onto her upturned face. She got up and Peter got up too.

'I reckon your boyfriend's pretty funny if you ask me.'

Olive looked at Peter, then back at Luke.

'You're a dickhead, Luke Sands, and your brothers are rapers, everyone says so,' she said.

'What did you just say to me?' Luke Sands cupped his palm and batted at the side of his head. 'Say it again?'

'I said you're a dickhead and your brothers are rapers.'

He took a step closer, grabbed her by the shoulders and shook her hard. Her teeth clacked and she expected to be let go and fall backwards into the pool but he stopped and she was still upright. She looked at his face. He had a small scab near his bottom lip. He let go.

'I know about you,' Luke Sands said. 'And your cousin, the dwarf with a tail.'

'It's not true,' she said.

'What's not true? What about your sister then?'

He was smiling at her. One of his teeth looked grey and it was very small. 'Yeah, we're not supposed to talk about it but everyone knows.'

Olive stepped forwards and placed both of her hands in the middle of his chest. She pushed and he windmilled, righted, wobbled again and went backwards into the diving pool. The lifeguard blew his whistle and came over as Olive stood on the edge. She looked down on Luke Sands as he trod water, ready to push him back in with her foot if he tried to climb out.

'You're dead meat,' he shouted. The guard blew his whistle again and told Luke to get out.

'Let's go.' Peter pulled at her arm. They walked away. Olive could hear Luke's high voice protesting that it wasn't his fault but she didn't look back. She and Peter were almost at the towels when she spoke.

'I'm not your girlfriend, you know.'

'*I* know—God, Ollie, me neither. He just said it and I didn't say anything back because if I *did* he would only say it *more*.'

Peter kept looking over his shoulder. He was right but sometimes his big teeth bugged her and the way he always put extra pressure on some words when he got upset.

'It's not true about Archie.'

'I know that too.'

'Did you hear what else he said?'

'So what? He's an idiot.'

Peter bent down and tied his runners.

'You made it worse.'

'Why are you even angry at me?' Peter asked. 'You shouldn't of pushed him.'

'What?'

He stood up.

'You shouldn't have done it.'

'Why not? He was saying those things. Besides, he would have pushed me if he was quicker.' She lifted a leg and raised her arms slowly to what they called the stork position. 'I'm like the wind, though. No one can catch The Olive.'

'I don't know, you just should have been scared. I just think that.'

'Well, I'm not scared. Not of him and not even of Gary.'

'Well, you should be,' Peter said. 'Of Gary especially.'

Olive put her dress on over her bathers. She held out a hand and clicked her fingers.

Peter gave her three snakes and she shoved them into her mouth.

'Do you want to come around tomorrow?' he said.

'I'm not here, which I did tell you about. I'm at the farm.'

'What?'

'For my birthday. You never listen properly.'

They were walking to the bike rack. Olive balanced her towel in a sheik roll on top of her head and Peter flicked his fingers in a way that made them crack. He counted under his breath each time he did it: *Whone, twhoo, thuree, foah, fahv.*

He was always doing things with his body. Jumping on things, climbing things, skipping over or under or trying to walk in funny ways, kicking his legs up high or bent so far over that his palms touched the footpath in front of his feet. Olive thought it was stupid and they'd had an argument. He tried to say she used to like those things, that she used to laugh, and she told him she never had. Never.

At the entrance, people were pushing out through the gates, families going to their station wagons in the car park, weary but happy as if a good day's work had been done. For Olive, it was more than that. Being at the pool, she was real. Her body was real in the water, the way it enclosed her with its vivid blueness.

Her fingers were real as they opened the plastic wrapper of a smooth-bottomed pie or pulled an icy pole out of its sticky paper sheath. She was real lying on the hot concrete with her stomach and leg tops almost burning, water outlining her body in small warming puddles. The pool was one of the places where she came into her body and she wished she could stay there forever. She always held back in the real as long as she was able, whether at the pool or in Peter's backyard or astride her bike at the park. She tried to stay as long as she could in all of those other places but eventually she had to leave the real. She had to leave those places and go home.

Olive and Peter rode away from the pool, Olive in front until Peter, without comment, peeled off at his house with the jasmine bushes along the drive. She went the extra three blocks, down Violet Rise turning left at Kellda. This was her street, where the houses were all neat. The nature strips mown short. The neighbours clipping bushes and pushing hand-mowers, the burring sound of the rotating blades clipping across the grass. The scrape of a rake at the edge of the footpath, metal on cement.

She went in at the driveway to her place, braking hard on the gravel so that she skidded sideways to a stop. She checked the cast-iron letterbox and dropped the lid hard. The noise of it slamming into place was so particular and marked the end of another afternoon.

Entering the house, coming in from the brightness of the day to the orderly dim of the interior, was like a shrinking. She went up to her room to wait for her father to get home. She sat in the little window nook and looked out. Down on the street, a green Charger rolled past the house and turned right at the end near the walkway that linked the tennis courts with the back of the Catholic church.

Jethro Sands.

She could see his sunglasses, the ones with the wire edges. Jethro Sands was driving his car around the streets. She sat in the little window nook and watched the car as it turned the corner and disappeared.

JETHRO SANDS WAS the oldest of five brothers from a family that had leaned hard on a spread of generations. Sands brothers rode their bikes in baleful posses through the streets of Stratford. They loafed against the milk bar window, glaring and powerful. Assorted brothers gathered beneath the diving board ladders at the pool each summer, forming groups of thinly muscled boys that pushed ahead in the queue and pulled at the ties on girls' bikinis. They were responsible for the abandoned shopping trolleys by the freeway entrance and the broken bottles smashed outside the scout hall. Sands boys had also been behind a destructive rampage that saw the systematic shredding of the memorial plants along the main avenue with plant matter strewn along a length of a hundred metres or more.

Snooky was the youngest and the only girl. Olive used to feel sorry for her but not anymore. Snooky and the triplets were in Olive's year and she had tried to work out how it was possible.

'It has to be because they're stupid—the triplets, that is,' Olive had said to Peter and so far, no one had come up with anything better than that.

Gary was the next oldest down from Jethro, four years older than Olive and Peter. People said he'd been dropped on his head as a baby. He was sly and hands-on, a kid who would stop you on the street and twist your forearm until you cried and gave him whatever you had in your pocket. The year before he'd tried to do it to Olive but she'd stood there unblinking, glaring at him until he let go.

'You think you're better than me?' he had said, his face nasty, his nails digging into her arm.

She had wanted to say yes.

Gary Sands was missing half of one of his fingers. Some people said it was chopped off by an axe in a game of chicken but others said it had been caught in a door—whether car, house or garage, no one really knew. A final theory was that he'd been on a flying fox and had fallen off but that somehow the bit of finger stayed behind, hooked into the handle, continuing on to the end of the ride. However it happened, it was Gary Sands's finger—or his *not-finger*—that intimidated other kids the most. He would hold it up, stand with the stump of his index finger raised, palm facing backwards. What he was saying with that not-finger was: *Look. I am a kid who lost a finger and survived.*

Luke Sands, who was a year older than Olive, was one of the triplets. The others were called Mark and John. Adults called them the Apostles but Thistle said that there had never been a good Sands. Olive thought John was the best of them. Once he'd played with her, Peter and her cousin Sebastian for a day. It had been summer-time and they were riding to the blackberries near the highway. John had gone with them, dinging his bell on the street as they flashed past on their bikes, and he'd ridden fast to catch up and be absorbed into the group. No one had remarked that he'd appeared, and for the afternoon they'd wandered the bushes, John wordless among them, as they ate berries and made jokes about teachers at school, shopkeepers and television ads.

John Sands had long yellow hair and freckles that spread over his entire face. He even had some on his lips, small brown flecks. When he talked, his tongue was visible between his teeth, pointed and pink. He laughed often and as he did so held his slender belly with both hands, rocking backwards, eyes closed, astride his motion-less Dragster.

Olive had spoken the truth when she told Peter she wasn't scared of Luke Sands or even of Gary. But Jethro Sands was different. Jethro Sands was a man with a thick neck and black hair. Everyone had a story about Jethro Sands, the oldest brother, and rumours had circulated about him for as long as Olive could remember. People said he had started a fire in the rubbish bin at the petrol station when he was thirteen and that he went to juvie.

Jethro had a scar near one of his eyes, an angry tear that scraped through his eyebrow and reached up to his forehead where it disap-peared beneath his hairline. In winter he wore black motorcycle boots and a checked sheepskin jacket that was orange and brown. He had sideburns like a man's and the other kids said his eyes were like laser beams in comics, that your face would explode if he even looked at you. That was why he wore those steel-rimmed reflective sunglasses, they said, as he cruised around in his car with his hairy arm out the window, fingers spread wide on the door.

Jethro Sands was like the scariest crackers on Guy Fawkes Night. He was the loudest thunder, the meanest dog. Out of everyone she was scared of Jethro Sands the most. She imagined buildings and trees bursting into flame on either side of the road as he drove along, turning his head slowly from side to side. He was threat-ening, noxious. Dark.

OLIVE WAS LYING on the couch imagining what it would be like to be Heidi when her father got home from work. As her parents moved around the house, carrying things to the car, she stayed on the couch. She wondered what goat's milk tasted like, and how it would be to live on a mountain. Heidi had been taken away from her grandfather, from the mountain, and was so upset by it psychologically that she started to sleepwalk. She felt trapped in the nice house in the city, where she had been taken to be a companion to the sick girl. Olive thought about how it would be to be trapped like that, in a house where you didn't belong and that you hated so much it made your brain go different and you started to do things you couldn't remember. Like walking while asleep.

'Are you ready?' her mother said. 'Do you have your things?'

Olive nodded. She always had her things ready to go to the farm. Once she had told her mother she would like to live at the farm with her cousins and had been surprised when her mother seemed angry.

'But it would make sense,' she said. 'I can catch the bus to school with the others. Rue wouldn't mind.' Her mother shifted her shoulders in a way that let Olive know it was a very bad idea, and told her it was time for bed. Olive had wondered what it was about her suggestion that had been so wrong.

•

They drove out to Rue's place from Stratford. Once they were past the church, Olive sat back and closed her eyes to wait for the buttery

23

flashes inside her eyelids to deepen to reddish-black. The shift in colour meant they were almost at the highway. With her cheek resting against the window, even without peeping, she knew they were driving through the war trees. She could see in her mind how their knobbly branches tried to embrace across the top of the road. Stretching but never touching.

Her mother looked out the window and her father's head swivelled left to reveal his profile, the Lovelock nose, his lips pressed together. Olive knew it even with her eyes closed. She turned her face left too and opened her eyes and lifted her binoculars to the landscape as it blurred, the light and shadows blending to brittle greens and greys. She couldn't wait to see Grace.

Once they reached the highway she put the binoculars to the side and sat up. She checked the seat pocket. The plastic bags were there. The nail scissors too. She leaned forward and scanned the road ahead, alert to the animal forms that might appear, in front or to the sides of the car. Wherever they might appear, she was ready. She knew that you had to check the pouches of struck animals and always made her father stop so she could run back along the road. The first time she'd done it her mother had been appalled, saying it was disgusting. Olive sat in the back with a wombat infant, the dismembered teat still in its mouth. The next time they'd seen a fallen animal—a kangaroo—Audra had told Bruce to keep going, but Olive emitted a noise set at such a drilling pitch her father had been forced to turn the car and go back. There'd been maggots that time and a barely alive joey. As they drove on to Rue's, Audra had ordered her daughter to touch nothing. Olive had sat like a gruesome surgeon, her hands held aloft all the way, the tiny thing shifting on her lap. Once they got to the farm she was goosestepped inside the house and her manky hands scrubbed puce by Audra.

Olive kept a record of animals saved, written inside the cover of her diary, and Audra kept a supply of plastic bags and thick rubber bands in the glove box so she could bag up her daughter's hands. They'd arrived with several native rescues over the years, Audra walking in stiff-backed and glowering, Olive smug and golden, her hands mittened in plastic, being steered from behind by her mother's finger in the middle of her back.

'I'll put the kettle on,' Rue would call.

'Bring the Pine O Cleen first,' Audra would call back.

The joeys were repatriated by a local woman who wore tea cosies as hats and Olive's campaign to keep the babies at the farm was swiftly smothered by Rue, Audra and even Thistle.

'They need to go back to nature,' Thistle said. 'You've done your part.'

No matter how much she begged, she wasn't allowed to keep even one.

•

They pulled off the road into the driveway and Olive looked for her first glimpse of the house. She loved the house at Serpentine. She never visited her own place in dreams yet wandered the rooms of this building, passed through its doors and around its corners as if her feet were floating above the polished wooden boards, the old floral carpets, the linoleum.

It was broad and weatherboarded in white, with a flowerbed running around its perimeter on three sides and a hard-won, foot-sharp lawn on the wings. People dropped their boots with a thud at the main arena of action: the wide verandah located at the front of the house. All kinds of properties were scattered across the rattan chairs and couches, in announcement that *here resides a family*. Books, plates covered with toast crumbs, Olive's abandoned craft projects. Straw hats, dented and rusted cans of insect repellent. A discarded plaster cast from when Archie had broken his arm.

The pit-like space underneath the verandah was enclosed with white latticework and it made the perfect spot for children to lie on their backs and eavesdrop on adults, waiting in the dark for secrets to be revealed. It was just Olive under the verandah doing the listening these days, though. Sebastian didn't want to climb under there, he didn't like getting dirty and complained that they never found out anything interesting.

Another good spot for listening in was behind the thick drapes in the Green Room. Olive had stood there, motionless, waiting for someone to come in and reveal a secret, waiting so long it made her legs shake. Only once had anyone come and said something, but it hadn't been interesting. It had been about Thistle, and how she had made something happen on purpose. But William and Rue hadn't said what it was that she made happen, so it hadn't been very useful *at all*. At least under the verandah Olive could lie down and relax. Sometimes she played her harmonica, but at other times she simply lay rigid, eyes closed and ears straining, only to emerge covered in cobwebs, which caused the sisters to start and clasp their throats, florid patches of pink on their cheeks as if here in front of them was a phantom, materialised from the underworld. Olive liked the idea of being a ghost and sometimes wished she could wander the earth at midnight listening at doors and passing through walls to stand beside the beds of sleeping people. She would reach into their brains and know their dreams and then she would write them down.

•

She had seen a ghost. Once, on a winter night, a little girl had sat on the end of her bed. Olive had lifted her head to look and in the moonlight could see the girl's eyes were open. From behind the walls came the sound of an organ, like in church. Deep and spooky. Olive had lowered her head to the pillow and gone back to sleep. During the night though she lifted her head once more and the girl was still there. In the faint morning light, she watched as the ghost disappeared as fingers of cold sun stretched into the room.

•

They stopped in front of the house and Olive looked for her aunt Rue.

'There she is.'

Rue had heard the car and risen up out of her flower garden, a gloved hand at the brim of her hat, the other hand holding clippers. From the house came the three cousins, Sebastian, Archie and Mandy, all with birthdays in April. Archie was there at her door, shouting something about a magazine, his t-shirt collar pulled wide. He was a year younger than Olive and with a permanent cold that blocked his ears so he said 'what?' all the time. Just behind him was Mandy Milk, who was five and couldn't sneeze without snot flying out of her nose. Mandy was pale and small and permanently startled, and when the sun caught her ears it made them glow a transparent pink. Whenever she could get close enough to Olive, Mandy clung to her waist, as she did now. And behind the two of them was Sebastian, gangly and ill-postured, two years older than Olive. Recently arrived in teenagehood, he'd been thrust deep into hormonal ravagement.

Where Sebastian was quiet and slow, Archie gormless and Mandy pretty, Olive was none of these. She had the sudden sharp glance of a child who takes in everything and annoys most adults she came into contact with. And she was fast.

'You've got the devil on your tail, girl,' her uncle William would say, as Olive kicked off her shoes and streaked barefoot across the scree of the driveway. Sprinting to the wide-open spaces she'd do a circuit, then race back to hurl herself over the top of a gate, back to the house and plop herself down on the front steps.

Now, even though they'd only just arrived, Olive ran in a circle around the house, looking for Grace. First to the tree, then down to the dam, but she couldn't see her there either. She set off across the paddock, down the small path made from repeated tramping through the grass and looped back to the front of the house, where she ran up the steps and dropped into a chair. At the end of the verandah her mother was already settled in the seat she liked best, posed like a charming sphinx, insect net folded over her face. Audra didn't look up, only wet a finger and flicked at a page of her magazine.

•

The four children were ranged around the Mixmaster as Rue made a birthday cake. Olive was saying she should have both beaters because it was her special day, and probably the bowl as well. Sebastian and Archie argued their own positions while Mandy kept trying to climb higher on the kitchen stool as the others pulled her down. Once she managed to get to the cushioned top and leaned over the bench, hair swinging forward. Rue shrieked and pulled her daughter's plait away from the beaters. Sebastian and Archie laughed and Rue said she didn't want to go into the details of neurocranial epidermal removal again. The boys danced around shouting, 'SCALP SCALP SCALP!' and slapping their mouths, and it was all Rue could do to keep her voice low, asking them not be so disrespectful to their mother.

'I've just about had enough,' she said, once she'd piled the mixture into the tin and slammed it into the oven. She unplugged the Mixmaster and went and sat in a chair for a moment to despair about how her sons could treat her like that.

'Why don't you use normal words instead of that medical terminology all the time?' Audra was standing in the doorway. 'The children don't understand haemal this and mucosal that. No one's going to get "asphyxiated". You worry about the wrong things entirely. You're always saying you're tired, so save your energy for the things that matter, why don't you?'

Olive stood in the kitchen with chocolate ringing her mouth. She had once heard Rue call Audra 'a flinty piece of work' and that she thought herself capable at everything. 'Except children,' Rue had added in a loud whisper.

Rue was the youngest and most cheerful of the three sisters but could be a bit damp and breathy. She used to be a nurse and had kept the tiny torch from her rounds. It cast a light no wider than her smallest fingernail, and sometimes she used it to check on the children as they slept, making sure they were breathing when babies and in pursuit of worm infestations once they became mobile. But the thing that most seemed to upset Rue was when the children said 'what' instead of 'pardon'. She would lift her chin, inhale deeply, close her eyes and say nothing, and it was the silence that made clear the magnitude of the offence.

The sisters were locked in an ever-moving constellation of shifting alliances. Sometimes it was Thistle and Audra against Rue when she was being 'sensitive' and 'neurotic'. Other times, Thistle was the one left out, with Rue and Audra labelling her 'difficult' and 'wilful'. 'Attention-seeking'. Audra was the only sister who enjoyed consistent partisanship and she passed briskly through her neat world with face and lips set tight.

While the cake baked Rue fossicked in the bin for a while and then started to get the table set. Olive drifted around, ignoring her aunt's instructions to wash her face and unpack her bag.

'If you organise things now you won't have to do it later when you're tired. Just go and look in the mirror. You look like a clown.'

But Olive went to the back door to check once more for Grace. She stood awhile, eyes moving to the sky, the trees, the roofline of the shed with its corrugated metal that had rusted into dark stains. The sun was going down and there was a horizontal piping of pink at what looked like the edge of the world. She wondered how long it would take to walk towards that line.

She went to Mandy's bedroom and quickly unpacked her things. Then she went to find Thistle.

WHERE RUE WAS the kind one and her mother Audra was the quiet one, Thistle was the interesting one. Of the sisters, Olive liked this aunt the most. Thistle was the oldest, big and pretty, and with a snaky laugh that elongated her s's. Sometimes her breath burned and she wore plaits pinned around her head and she'd retained her interdental lisp from childhood. Thistle had always lived at the farm with Rue and William even though she was also a grown-up and didn't much like the night-time so slept with a lamp on. Apart from that there was nothing else that made her bend. She was an assiduous collector of the Tuckfield's Australiana Bird cards (there were one hundred and ninety-two in the series) and every time she dug a card from the packet she lifted it to her nose and proclaimed how much she loved the smell of the tea-leaves.

Thistle adored theatricals. She called her cardigans and slacks her 'skins' and wore them like a uniform. She moved through space to either a silent beat or thunder and chaos, syncopated with her interior state, and never missed the opportunity to remind people that she'd had a career once, as a Kindergarten Teacher Assistant. She emphasised the words with her fingers in the air, not seeing that others shuddered at the thought of defenceless toddlers being 'assisted' by Miss Thistle Nash.

Thistle had never married but she'd had suitors, oh yes-s-s-s, she assured Olive.

Sometimes, Thistle tried to teach the children some German. She had studied it at school, and learned more from little books she ordered from overseas. (She ordered her jigsaw puzzles from overseas too.) And sometimes she hosted theology and philosophy salons in her bedroom, where they read from the scriptures or other texts. Certain afternoons would see a keen Olive and stupefied Archie—mouth-breathing, chewing forlornly on a piece of Stimorol gum, an inferior bribe from his aunt—sipping green cordial and discussing things like 'Is there a God?', 'What is life?', and how good and evil worked.

'It's in all of us,' Thistle would tell them in her special posh explaining voice.

'What?' said Archie.

'Evil?' Olive was excited.

'All of it, in all of us. The capacity for both. Usually it's not either/or. Usually it's both, or everything even.'

'What?' Archie was shaking a finger in one ear.

Thistle talked and Olive interrupted with questions. Olive liked it because her aunt could be easily persuaded away from the usual adult topics. At dinner, the conversation was boring. They talked about the weather, who was sick, who was going to have a baby, who had just had a baby, who had died and what had been wrong with them. Rabbits and sheep (William). The dates for the Nanango Show or something 'of interest' that had been in the newspaper (Rue). It was never of interest to Olive, Rue was wrong about that.

The topics that she most wanted to talk about were: murders, ghosts, whether it was possible to dig a hole to the centre of the earth. Also: aliens, snakes, various types of poisons, poison in darts, poison in fangs, scorpions and their poison, mummies in Egypt, zombies and cannibals. Thistle had talked to her and Sebastian about cannibals, about the *Menschenfresserin*. Dark Teutonic stories of men eating men and sometimes children.

The summer before, Olive and her cousins had talked a lot about how Phil Simmons said Jack Ralton had a tapeworm growing inside him and that part of it had come out of his mouth and the other part out of his bum. They also talked about how Sebastian had heard from someone that the cleaner at the high school found a baby in the girls' toilets. It was only as big as a Freddo Frog and *alive*.

Recent whispers between her and Sebastian had been concerned with whether there really were people who did it with dead bodies and animals, ideas that to Olive were fascinating and revolting at the same time.

For a time, the children had been obsessed with Rue's old nursing book, a compendium of illness and disease with colour plates that displayed pustules, wounds, rashes and infections in exacting purple and nicotine tones. People with scaling skin or hideously enlarged legs, their veins snaking under the flesh like thin sausages. Children with smallpox, chickenpox and measles. Old people with misshapen knees that were far outsized for their stick-thin limbs. Weeping bedsores and bulging necks. Bulging eyes and yellowed faces.

Olive was enthralled by the book well beyond the time her cousins lost interest and she would spend hours with it in absolute wonder, lying on her back in the Green Room, turning the pages, the book propped open on her chest.

For Olive, it wasn't ever dull being with Thistle, as long as her aunt was in one of her good phases. When things got too much for Thistle, though, Rue would try to make her sister lie on the couch so she could hold her feet. If that didn't work, the family would brace for long weepy tirades at the dinner table and classical music played far too loudly. She would move the furniture around in the middle of the night and think it a good idea to go for long walks in her dressing-gown. Once she'd even been brought back to the house at 4 am by Fred Spooner from the golf club. He'd found her walking along the road into town. It had been lucky she wasn't on one of the bends, he told Rue, because she'd been in the middle of the road.

'I could have hit her,' was all he said.

When Olive had been little, before the salons, Thistle would read to her from the Bible. While Olive loved all the stories, her favourite part was the Book of Olive.

'It's to help with her self-esteem,' Thistle explained to Rue, who'd been hovering at the door and heard her announce the day's reading. '*I* know it's Exodus and *you* know it's Exodus, but I want her to feel strong about herself. Girls need extra help in that department, especially Olive.'

'I don't agree,' Rue said. 'That is a child who has plenty of self-esteem or whatever you want to call it.'

But Thistle read the passage to her niece, and after a while Olive would ask for it. Her aunt obliged, adding extra bits 'for context and verisimilitude'.

When Olive saw what a fine baby Moses was, she hid him for three months because bad people wanted to take him away and give him to another woman. But when she could not hide him any longer, she took a basket made of reeds and covered it with tar to make it watertight, like a little boat. She put the baby inside and placed it in the tall grass at the edge of the river and watched it float away. The baby stopped crying as the water rocked him. She was a good girl with brown hair and blue eyes and she stood some distance away, watching to see what would happen.

'The Old Testament is not for children, one wouldn't think,' Rue would say. 'You'll give her bad dreams talking about snakes and floods.' But the stories from the Bible didn't ever give Olive bad dreams. She liked hearing about the serpents, the flames, God and his punishments, and such things never pushed their way into her night-time fancies. Her dreams were usually more dislocated than that. Sometimes there were dreams inside of her dreams: falling or flying, pursuit and persecution—all signs of grandiosity, Rue had said to Audra when Olive had mentioned them. But Thistle confided she'd had the same dreams when she was a girl, that she'd flown and hovered above the earth like an angel.

'Splendid,' Thistle had said when Olive had first told them, but Rue and Audra had looked at each other and Rue had gone to get a piece of paper from the kitchen drawer for Audra to make a note.

•

Olive no longer asked for the story of the baby and the woven basket with mud on it. Just like she'd given up on trying to learn and create new ciphers and codes, including an elaborate tapping version with Sebastian, she had moved on in her reading interests. Now she was preoccupied with *Unexplained: Things You Just Won't Believe*, a book Thistle had received as a free gift when she'd ordered two jigsaw puzzles from America. It was about all the strange things that happen in the world, such as how identical twins can feel each other's pain, how once a woman had her twin inside her and another one had teeth in the back of her head. And the book was right. They were *all* things she couldn't believe. She read about people who'd been buried alive in a coffin and when they were dug up there were scratches on the inside so they started putting in little bells. A man whose fingernails grew so long they curved into his own palms. All of it was absorbing, but what was strangest and most thrilling, what she couldn't seem to stop herself reading about, or even thinking about, were the three pages on spontaneous combustion. People, usually women, who had simply burst into flames for no reason and burned up. There were pictures that showed half-charred legs sticking out at angles, shoes on feet, usually near fireplaces.

Olive learned a new word: *macabre*.

'Why on earth do you want to look at such horrible things?' Rue said and told her not to bring the book to the table. But Olive couldn't help her interest. It was a peculiar, sharp feeling that came over her like a shudder, being drawn and repelled at once. She kept reading the book, careful to keep it out of her aunt's sight.

THE EVENING WAS hot and cicadas were spinning their legs under the dry earth, their cacophony bending the air. For tea, Rue decided on a picnic so William and Bruce carried the barbecue out and set it up under the tree.

The peppercorn hulked in its spot. On the brightest days its lush canopy cast a shadow as big as a house. Once it had been struck by lightning and smoked white for a week before rain had dampened the smoulder.

They carried tartan rugs and folding chairs and plates and a card table for the salads and buttered slices of bread. They filled the wheelbarrow with ice and pushed bottles of beer and lemonade right down into the frozen cold. Olive flopped on the rug and her cousins started to flick each other with fingers dipped in the icy water, until someone dripped down the back of an adult's neck and they were told to cut it out by William.

Bruce and William stood around the rickety barbecue, its tripod of metal legs barely held together with fencing wire. While they waited for the coals to be ready, Rue fussed first about whether they had enough meat and then if it had been out of the fridge for too long. Under the tree Audra sat classic and still. With her glamorous lipstick and an unopened magazine she was a study in serenity, her long white fingers limp like dead birds, graceful in her lap. She stretched out one leg to rotate a slim ankle, then the other. To someone else, she might have looked like she was thinking but she wasn't. She might have looked like she was waiting but she wasn't doing that either.

William clapped his tongs with satisfaction at the barbecue.

'Wool you look at those coals.'

Bruce rocked on his heels and smiled.

William was a sheep man and believed that straight-haired women, like sheep, were badly bred. Sometimes he caressed his wife's dewlap, an expression of affection that caused Rue deep embarrassment and made her twist her thumbs in her apron. When William walked the fences, running his hands along the wires, he would stop for long moments and call out to the animals. No one knew what he might be saying.

If Cleg had been there he would have said something sarcastic like *virile agitur* and settled well away from the action with a glass of white burgundy, but as it was, these brothers had to make do with the sheep puns. Neither of them was able to remember any Latin other than *alibi* (William) and *ovis* (Bruce).

Rue thought Cleg drank too much and that was why something had happened. Olive didn't know about Cleg drinking too much but she was sure that William did. When he had a lot of beer or wine he started 'going on', which was what Rue called it. For a man who didn't talk very much, he really talked a lot then, usually about rabbits.

Olive lay on the picnic rug, looking at the splintered sky through the branches.

'How did the tree get here?' she asked.

'How did any of us get here, girl?' William replied.

'Oh, tell her the story, Bill,' said Rue. 'Tell her about Lenore and the tree.'

William flicked his hanky and blew his nose and told Olive that his grandmother Lenore, the lady in the gloomy painting in the Green Room, had carried the cuttings all the way from Melbourne in little jars of water with hessian tied on top. Then he started to explain how cuttings propagate. Olive stopped listening. William was best at talking about sheep. He knew that the average weight of a newborn lamb is about the same as a human. That a mother sheep sometimes will attack its new baby and have to be stopped from hurting it. While he admitted that goats had a stronger temperament, he could not see any reason for farming them. There was the noise, he said. Just to start with.

Thistle was much better at explaining things. She liked to talk about history and included the interesting details, like what people wore and ate and how dentists worked. But Thistle wasn't there at the picnic under the tree. Thistle was in the house, lying in bed with the blinds closed. For most of the year, Thistle was her normal self but in December she changed. Her phases became altered. Her mood dark.

•

William stood at the barbecue with his tongs in one hand and a rolled newspaper in the other. He kept looking at the sky. Recently Grace had taken to swooping at him. Rue took the newspaper from William.

'I wonder why she goes for you all the time.'

'Thistle says that ravens are the ghosts of dead people,' Olive said. 'But everyone's alive, so it can't be that.' She sat up. 'I wanted to have a raven in the play. I wanted Grace to be in it, but Thistle said no. Grace would be a good actor. I told Thistle that but she still said no.'

Rue started separating the plates on the rug and counting out cutlery.

'Oh well,' she said.

'Do we have to do the play next week?' Archie's voice was pitchy. He had always loved doing the plays.

'Of course,' said Rue. 'What's wrong with you?'

'But why?'

'Because your aunt likes it. It's important to her and she works hard on them.'

Archie groaned. He was on his back, arms and legs angled like brown sticks, drumming a beat on his chest with his fingers.

'Can we go to the dam, Mum?' Sebastian asked.

'Yeah, can we?' Archie was getting to his feet, putting on his thongs.

'But you haven't eaten yet.'

'I had sauce with bread,' Archie said. 'I'm not hungry.'

Rue sighed. 'The food won't be much longer,' she said. She moved the plates and neatened the forks. 'Come here, Mandy, you look flushed.' She put a hand to her daughter's brow. 'Slightly pyretic, I thought so. You can't go. I don't know why you all want to swim there anyway. Horrible place.' Olive looked at her aunt who had stopped talking and was kneeling there with paper serviettes in her hand. Her mouth was open, like a fish.

Rue was a mother who created worries out of thin air like a magician pulled knotted scarves out of a fist. Her knots could be small things, like how the dust got everywhere and made it impossible to keep a clean house. The bigger knots covered everything from broken necks to gashed chests to accidental stranglings by assorted means. Hoods of parkas slipping down to mask a cycling child's eyes, curtain cords, filled and waiting bathtubs. The dam.

The point at which Rue's catastrophising had worsened was marked in the family's communal memory. It was the time when the entire milk bar family, including their dog, was obliterated at the rail crossing while driving home from a picnic.

'Just awful,' Rue had wept at the kitchen table. 'And after such a nice day out.'

40

When younger, the children had barely been able to escape the house without interrogation. They would sneak away to avoid questions about where they were going, for what purpose and with whom. Even now she kept track of them, marking their movements by their far-off voices, the distant dings of bike bells and the thudding of feet as they ran through the house.

'No running inside,' she'd call happily.

The older children stood in a line of three and she waved a hand at them and turned back to the knives. They ran off to the house leaving Mandy behind, whirring with upset on the blanket. Olive went to look for her bathers. It was a good room, with floral curtains that had ruffles. She would like some curtains like that. She went to the end of her bed and looked in her bag, dumping things out onto the floor. She found her damp bather bottoms and quickly put them on before Archie came in. He was always doing it and no matter how much she told him to knock he always forgot. She put on the bather top, struggling her body and arms through it without untying the strings. Then she found a damp t-shirt and held it to her chin before dropping it back on the carpet. She hunted for a dry one, then pulled her shorts back on.

Outside she grabbed a towel from the line, baked rough in the sun. The coloured-plastic fly strips over the back door swung apart as the boys came out and they all ran, with Shaggy roused from the coolish shade barking and making them run faster before stopping at the end of his chain. Olive didn't like swimming in the dam very much. She didn't jump in from the edge, she waded in. A few summers before the dog had grabbed Archie's heel as he jumped in, and his heel had ripped open and blood splattered on the ground in big drops. His father and mother had taken him into town to the hospital, and he'd come back with twelve stitches which he'd shown proudly to Olive and Sebastian. What Olive remembered of that day, though, was how her cousin's mouth had been stained orange and she and Sebastian had been upset there'd been no icy pole for them. Sebastian cried for a long time and had refused to come out of his room. After that, Shaggy was always on the chain.

The dam had been commissioned by Lenore. It was all in the diaries that Thistle had found. Lenore—a natural observer—had recorded the details of early life at Serpentine. She wrote about the trees, the cuttings and the landscape. For the dam, she had envisioned a kind of scenic pond from the old country, with fish and special plants and a little stone seat. She chose a site under a medium-sized swamp box and for several years had tried to foster the growth of submerged water plants: hornwort, ribbon weed, water thyme. It hadn't worked very well, and while the swamp box had once featured a tyre swing, that was gone now.

At the dam, Archie launched himself off the edge with a flattened dive and a cry of 'Omnia extares!', his legs bending back at the knees. Olive bobbed in the shallows with the silty base in between her toes. She watched Archie duck-diving out in the middle. How could he bear to go down so deep? At the pool she could swim almost all the way across with one breath, but here she'd never wanted to go under.

Archie swam over.

'How come your mum always looks sad?' he asked.

Olive looked over at Seb, who was sitting on the bank swiping a stick in the air.

'She calls me *dear* but her voice doesn't mean it and she looks cross even when none of us haven't done anything wrong.'

Olive dipped her head into the dam and her long fringe caught the water. Hair streamed over her face, the ends reaching her chin. She ducked her head again and propelled herself across the surface to the middle, her eyes stinging. She lifted her head, took another breath and went down. She kicked and felt in front with her hands. Eyes jammed shut, everything was silent apart from the beat of blood in her head. She found something to grab, a branch from the felled swamp box and, with her arm stretched, held on and let herself rotate at the shoulder. Her body wanted to rise. Her other arm was spread wide. She relaxed in the deep, let herself tilt like a wet star. Her breath was saved and she held it and held it and pushed her mind forwards. Ending, ending, but still she stayed under just to be in that cool distant place for a while longer.

She saw a white tree filled with meringue-coloured cockatoos and one girl-bird, Grace, sleek on the top branch. Just as she started to hear singing she let go and felt herself turn and rise. She broke the surface—wildly, blindly—and shouted out in surprise. Treading water, she wiped her eyes and looked around. Sebastian was squatting on one side of the dam with Grace next to him. Archie was already out and running across the paddock.

'It's okay, she's here,' Sebastian yelled to his brother. Archie braked and turned with hands on his head. He started to walk back.

Olive climbed out and picked up her towel. She sat down and Sebastian sat next to her on the dirt, hugging his knees.

'Do you know anything about a sister?' Olive sucked at a twist of her hair, scissoring the ends with her front teeth. It tasted like soap and metal. 'Anything?' she asked.

Sebastian's nose was peeling and had a pimple. He scratched in the dirt with a rock.

'Mandy?'

'Not her.'

He threw the rock away. Over the other side, Archie rolled down the slope, dirt and leaves sticking to his body, his eyes shut and mouth open.

Olive picked up her own rock and scratched in the dirt too.

'Well?' she persisted.

'Nope.' He shook his head.

'I went down,' she said. 'It was good.'

Grace was on her knee, shifting her head to look her right in the eye. Olive touched the bird's back where the warm feathers bent a little under her fingers, like fragile spongy ridges. She loved everything about Grace. The way she looked at things with her whole body, how she moved when she saw something, lifting herself taller when she spotted an interesting thing or angling towards a bright glint of treasure, her tail following her movement like the end part of an arrow, a sleek pointer. The way her eyes searched for and found Olive's even if she was high in the sky, even if Olive was in the car looking out the window. Whenever Olive and Grace looked at each other Olive felt it in her heart, a deep tug of love.

'It was really good.'

'What?'

'I liked it, going under.'

'Okay,' Sebastian said. He looked away. They sat as Archie played in the dam, running in and running out, shouting across to them, words that they ignored. They sat until a short while later Rue began to call to them across the paddock, her voice reedy and mosquito-thin.

AT SCHOOL ON Monday everything went wrong. First, Olive got in trouble for throwing a pencil across the room. Bosco Scully kept putting it on her desk. She said it wasn't hers and put it back on his. They moved it back and forth until she flung it. Mrs Barton had stepped outside for a moment and she came back in just as the pencil hit the door frame beside her and fell to the ground at her feet. The teacher asked who threw it and Olive put her hand up. She was sent to the office and the principal was very angry and said she could have taken out the eye of one of his best teachers. Olive wanted to argue with him. She was sure she could explain why Mrs Barton was not an especially good teacher. She was sure too that she could make a convincing argument why something as light as a pencil could probably *not* push out someone's *whole* eyeball, but she kept quiet.

And then just before the bell, they got a new project. The water project. They had to work out how much water their family used in a week and they had to start counting that night.

Olive put her hand up.

'But *how* do we count the water?' She couldn't understand how they could possibly know the number of litres in a flushing toilet or how much went down the sink after her dad did the dishes. How were they meant to measure all of it when the water disappeared? What about hoses in the garden? They had two, one at the front and one at the back. What about those two hoses?

She wondered if Sebastian had done the same project. How had he measured all the water they used at the farm? Rue with her garden? Did he have to count the dam? It was impossible as far as she could see.

'You have to estimate, Olivia. You can work out exactly how many litres in a bucket. And then approximately how many buckets to a full sink for washing the dishes. Or a shower, for having a five-minute shower.' Mrs Barton smiled but it was stiff and mean.

Olive put her hand up again.

'Come and ask me any more questions after class,' Mrs Barton said, and turned back to the board. Once the bell went Olive had tried to pack things into her desk quickly so she could go and tell Mrs Barton her other questions but she was still too slow. The teacher had already left the room.

•

Peter offered to help her with the water project and her father did too, but she said no to them both. Thursday night saw her in dramatic collapse at the tap in the front garden, lying there holding onto the pipe, her clipboard beside her and pencil jammed into the grass. When she looked through slitted eyes at the house she could see the outline of her mother standing in the lounge window, arms crossed. Her mother couldn't help her. She had said she wasn't good at maths.

In the end, Olive made it up. She worked out ten jugs to a bucket, and three buckets to a sink. She guessed thirty for a bath and one hundred for a shower. She didn't care about being right. She wouldn't get a good mark for it but she didn't care anymore, she really didn't. *Not at all* was what she told Peter on the Friday morning, waiting for the bell.

'Talk about the dumbest project ever,' she said.

To make the whole thing even worse, after school she saw Snooky in the hall outside the classroom near the bags, telling Mrs Barton that she'd really liked doing the water project and that she hoped they had projects like that at high school next year.

Olive wrenched her bag off its hook and walked to the bike shed where she waited for Peter.

'You know you're soaking in it!' he said as he approached.

'Snooky is such a suck,' Olive said. Snooky always wanted the teachers to like her. She gave them cards and little presents at the end of each year. Olive supposed she would do the same this year too. 'She said she *liked* the project. Let's go to the silo.'

Peter put his bag across his front.

'Alright. I'll dink you to your place to get your bike?'

She climbed onto his pack rack and shoved her school bag in the gap between her chest and Peter's back.

'You can hold on to me if you want.'

Balancing her toes on the cog set, knees set wide, she said it was okay and gripped the metal rack behind her. They rode on the footpaths and sprinklers tossed wet arcs of water over fences, loops of spray that caught their bare legs and pattered across their chests, their foreheads, their arms. Peter shouted *hey!* each time, but Olive just perched behind him, upright and grim.

At her place, she left her bag and got her bike and they were off again. Pedalling down the side streets she was in front. The air cooled her skin as they flew under the plane trees. She avoided the bubbled mounds in the bitumen, all the places where the physics of heat and rupture had created fissures in the road, the spots of molten tar that had pushed up, their crusts glinting in the sun. She knew every depression and every bump. The spots where she had to swerve to the right or left, rise up off the seat, bend down under a low-hanging branch. Behind her was the hum of Peter's wheels, the rhythmic tick of the saddlebags buckled onto his pack rack. A couple of summers before he'd had a bunch of spoke clackers from cereal packets, plastic clips that made so much noise as he rode that she said he had to take them off. They were too loud and made people look. Olive liked to stream past humans, dogs and parked cars in a way that felt like invisibility, delivered into a kind of trancelike state of ecstasy where everything she did was swift, high and complete.

They cut through the housing estate, a wasteland of rubble and smooth new bitumen, courts curved and broad in contrast to the gridline streets of Stratford proper. Then they rode away from Shady Villas! and headed in the direction of the outskirts of town. They passed the memorial pines and the English-style shrubs and emerged on the old highway where the gums grew right up to the road, large bushy blocks that abutted twisted barbs of wire fencing. Here were the beginning scraggles of blackberry bushes that grew on the verges, sprawling thickets with berries still green in their cups.

About halfway to the silo she started to get dots across her eyes and a hollow ache in her head. She held up a hand and they pulled off the road under some trees where she lay down in the dirt with her arms spread wide. She wondered if she was getting sick. She never got headaches or dizzy but lately it had happened a few times.

Peter sat upright, hands holding his knees, his watch arm carefully on the outside of the other.

'What's so good about that watch anyway?' Olive said, shading her eyes.

'I told you, the war.'

'It's really old. It'll probably break soon.'

'Not if I'm careful.'

Nearby, a flock of galahs landed and began to circle in a cluster, turning as they shrieked. Peter stretched out his arm, looking at the watch.

'I also told you, it was my grandfather's.'

Olive rolled over and got to her hands and knees.

'You've got bits of stuff in your hair,' Peter pointed.

Olive got on her bike.

'Let's go,' she said.

•

The heat had a noise to it, a faint pulsing sound. They stood at the base of the silo. It was a three-cell structure, conjoined biscuit-coloured edifices that rose into the air where they loomed against the hard sky. The sun was sitting directly behind the main carapace and created an outline of the latticework, a conglomeration of metal staircases and walkways affixed to it. Down the shaft of the tower the words of the company were written in faded green letters: THE NEPEN GRAIN CO. Nearby at the back of the station were the buildings, abandoned since the 1970s. An old ganger's hut, a farmer's shed, a large corrugated-iron goods store and a fuel depot. Beyond the silo was a place called Soldier's Paddock, a block of rutted land dotted with mines made by an ex-soldier who went mad looking for gold after the war. Two generations of children had been told by their parents never to go inside the fence, an imperative ignored by most.

Ganger's was a squalid single-room shack with a broken window, jammed door and no working light. Inside were a small cot and empty beer bottles that lined the walls which were covered with abrupt statements about rooting and screwing.

Olive dumped her bike and walked over to the cement pipe that had been left behind after roadworks. She climbed inside. When the pipes had first arrived three years before they'd played in and around them, Sebastian trying to get a complicated spaceship game going and Archie saying he couldn't get on top and wanting Peter to give him a boost. But all Olive wanted to do was lie inside and spread herself against the smooth wide curve of the walls. She loved being alone in the warm stone tomb, listening to the liquid rumbles of voices outside, the pings of their shouts. And when she wasn't inside one of the pipes she wanted to drape herself on the outside, lay her cheek against it in a hug.

'You wanna go up?' Peter's face was at the opening.

She made him go first and they climbed, wending a vertical path through the cloister of metal that scaffolded the sides. At the top, they lay down on their stomachs and looked over the edge at the flattened landscape scored by railway tracks, roads and pathways. Trains used to bring the grain that filled the towers and she could remember how the wheat dust flew in the air, specks of yellow illuminated by daylight.

The trains had almost completely stopped now.

'Nothing is real down there,' she said to Peter. 'Our life is here.'

'I guess. You've got little dots of sweat on your nose.'

She wiped an arm across her face.

'We could burst into flames it's so hot.' She flopped back.

'Yeah, spontaneously.'

There was a hairy caterpillar moving along one of the metal bars and Peter put a finger out to touch it.

'Don't, you'll get itchy.'

'I know.' He kept his finger extended, holding it just above the hairs.

She watched him. 'I said don't.'

'I wasn't.' He moved his finger away.

A train was coming. Olive watched as it slowed and trundled past the ganger's hut and the group of trees that stood by the crossing.

She looked at her legs, at the hairs. She hadn't even noticed them until Archie had said something. A grasshopper landed on her knee and she flicked it off.

'Why's there so many crickets?'

Peter said he didn't know.

'Maybe the plague is coming, like in the Bible.'

'Maybe.' He told her how his mother had a story about a mouse plague.

'When?'

'I don't know, but it was a long time ago.'

'Which year was it?'

'I said I don't know? But before my mum was born. It was her grandmother maybe. God, why do you always have to know every little thing?'

The caterpillar was almost at the ladder and she stretched her finger out to it.

'All over the floors in the houses, small grey ones. They caught millions and millions in about two days.'

'Your great-great-great-great grandma?'

'Not just her. And they were eating all the wheat, the mice were, and my mum said that it was horrible—that's what her mum told to her. That they had to sleep somewhere else, not in their beds.'

'Where? In their cars? On a table?'

'I don't know, maybe it was.'

'Maybe on a table. Like the mother who put her children to sleep on the table in the kitchen because there was a snake inside? I saw it in a movie at school.'

'I remember. That was a good movie.'

Olive thought about mice chewing at the wheat, jaws running like machines. What if that many grasshoppers were coming right now, flying towards them in a cloud that would cover the sun?

'It's so hot,' she said.

'My dad told me that there was another kangaroo head at the station—out the back on the roof of the police car. It had a cigarette in its mouth.' Peter lifted his shoulders and laughed in his special ghost voice, a laugh he'd been practising.

'Who do you think it is?' she said, and Peter stopped the laugh. 'It's probably Gary Sands,' she said. 'Sebastian's scared, but don't tell him I told you so.'

'I won't.'

'Maybe it's Jethro.'

'Maybe.'

'It's really hot.'

The caterpillar was coming back. She put her finger out and touched it then pulled her hand away.

'You know the girl he used to go out with? Gary?' she said. 'The one with the straight hair that goes in a V down her back? I think he did something to her even though she was only fourteen, that's what I think.'

'Cindy?'

'I think so.'

'The really pretty one?'

'Yeah. She's got the bathers with the palm trees on them?'

They were silent.

'So?'

'So do you know anything about that?' She closed her eyes. 'Like does it hurt? They say that it hurts the girl.'

'Who even knows.'

'Are you ever going to do that?'

'Nope.'

'Never?'

He sat up. He looked over the edge again. 'Stop talking about it.'

'God, I'm just asking.'

'The feelings—' It took him a very long time to find the words. 'It's very mixed.'

'Do you want to kiss?' She edged herself upright. 'Just a little bit to see?'

She thought he was going to look over the edge forever but he slowly turned and leaned forwards, closing his eyes. She kept her eyes open and watched his face as it came closer. When their mouths touched his was soft and he kept his lips closed but it didn't feel like anything, just that someone was too close to her, which he was. He was breathing through his nose, pushed up against her face. She pulled back and they both wiped their mouths.

'I used to think the man does wee inside the woman,' she said.

'Me too.' Peter pulled his shoe off and shook dirt out of it.

'Which is not right.'

'Yeah.'

From a distance came the sound of motorbikes, a group of them going past on the highway.

'Bikies,' Peter said, lifting his hands to imaginary handlebars in the air.

'You know bikies do things to girls when they have their, you know, their blood?'

'Like what kind of things?'

'Kissing? Down there?' She flapped a hand at her school dress. 'They train dogs to do things to women too when they blow a whistle; I think the bikies blow the whistle. Someone told me about it.'

'That's so off.'

'And some people do it with dead bodies.'

'The bikies?'

'Probably.'

'That's really so off.'

'Yeah. And some people eat humans, but I don't know if that's bikies, maybe that's just people from another country. My aunt told me about that one.'

'Thistle?'

'Yeah.'

He made a face.

'Humans are disgusting,' Peter said.

A grasshopper walked on his arm for a while then flew off.

Olive got onto her hands and knees and started to move to the ladder.

'I have to go.'

'Yeah, your mum'll be waiting.'

She edged her feet to the rungs. There were slices of shadow in the space formed by the cage around the ladder. The cage was to stop people from falling, to help them going up and down.

'Can you come for a swim?' he said once they got to the bottom. She shook her head.

'We're going to the farm again, for the plays. It's my aunt's birthday.'

'But it was your birthday last week.'

'I know.'

'Which one? Thistle?'

She nodded and Peter made a face again.

'What types of plays? Can I come and see?'

'I don't know, boring Greek ones. She says she likes it to be free but really she just wants to be bossy.'

'What do you mean?'

'With the plays. She won't let us say any of our own words. She won't let Grace be in it and she won't even say why.'

Peter shook his head. He didn't understand. Sometimes she had to be very patient with Peter.

'So you can't come for a swim?' Peter asked again.

'No. But listen.' The mention of the pool brought it to the front of her mind again.

'What?'

She wanted to ask him about what Luke had said at the pool. Luke had said everybody knew.

'Do you know anything about a sister?'

She followed Peter to the bikes where they lay on their sides near the hut.

'Do you?'

Peter leaned down and hooked a little finger around a spoke and gently pulled. Then did it to another, and another.

'Pete?'

He shook his head, still leaning down to the wheel.

She slung her leg across her bike and stomped on the pedals and lurched from side to side to get up speed. Through the hot air she flew, leaving him behind. As she passed the trees that lined the space between the buildings and the road, she caught sight of something out of the corner of her eye—a shadow. Once out on the road she realised that it was her own shape thrown across the tarmac, bobbing up and down as they made their way back to town.

IN THE THINNING dusk and with hair damp against their heads after their baths, Olive, Sebastian and Archie went to the back garden in shortie pyjamas, their thongs *snap-snapping* down the flagstones. Each of them took a swing on the clothesline as they passed and then paused in a hushed line at the shed door, looked around once, before they started to go inside. There was a rush of feathers and Grace slammed into Olive's chest and dropped to the ground. Olive stopped and the bird flew up to her shoulder.

'No, not now.' She pushed the bird off and slipped into the shed after her cousins.

When Archie had been sent looking for props for Thistle's upcoming play he'd found something he wanted to show them. It was a magazine with rude pictures in it, pictures where you could see the *hair*. They looked through drawers and cupboards, on shelves and in boxes. They saw old tins of paint and gardening equipment, boxes of weedkiller and rat poison, but they couldn't find the magazine.

'Look at this,' Olive said, lifting the box of poison from inside a white cane baby basket. 'For when he gets too annoying.' They both looked at Archie but he was at the back of the shed rummaging. Then Olive saw a flat box high on a shelf and pointed at it.

'What's that?'

She got up on a chair and brought it down. It was tied with string, with lots of knots and while Sebastian wanted to cut it open with his pocket knife, she insisted on untying each one.

'Otherwise they'll know we've looked,' she said. 'Spies put a hair across the doorway, to see if someone's gone in. That's why you have to leave things *exactly* the same way you find them. Nine knots.' Sebastian snapped his knife shut. Finally, she got the last one untied and took off the lid. There were papers in it and some photos. They looked through them.

The pictures were of holidays and birthdays. There was a Christmas photo with a small doubtful Olive looking at the photographer and holding out a toy telephone. Deeper in the pile was one of a baby in Olive's father's arms. It had red hair and was dressed in a yellow frock. She could see her father's ears underneath his short hair and the hand that wasn't holding the strange baby was at his side, stiff like a soldier's arm. She looked at the next picture, another one with the same baby, being held by Aunty Thistle. Then the redheaded baby was in Audra's arms with a small Olive standing at her side.

'Oh,' she said.

Sebastian reached over and tried to get them from her, saying to put them back. Archie came up behind and stood there, breathing.

'Who's that kid?' He extended a finger towards the pictures.

Olive moved the box away.

'Hey, that's you.'

He tried to snatch the photo.

'*Pffft*, I wanna see. *Fleeeeece?*'

'Stop using my joke. Make up your own, Archibaldman.'

Archie blinked at his brother, halted by the low blow.

'There isn't any left, you've taken them all.'

'I said go away.' Sebastian turned back to the photos.

'Wait, I don't get it. That isn't Thistle's baby,' Archie said. 'She's a sprinster.'

'That's my joke,' Olive said, holding the pictures to her chest. 'And they don't have to be married, they just need the sexing.' She slipped the photos onto her lap and put the lid back on the box. 'I don't think anyone would sex Thistle though.'

She waited for Sebastian to say something but he didn't. Archie moved away. She wrapped the string around. 'Nine knots,' she said.

Sebastian got up on the chair and she passed the box up to him. Archie came up behind again.

'Lookit this.' He was waving a mousetrap on the end of his finger.

'Put it down,' said Seb. Archie moved away.

'HEY, LOOK AT THIS!' Archie shouted from the old shelving at the back.

'I said SHUT UP.' Sebastian was at the door now, about to leave.

'I know about those,' Olive said, looking at the board Archie held. In old-fashioned writing there were letters and numbers printed on the wooden surface, and whole words such as 'YES' 'NO' and 'GOOD BYE'

'What is it?' Archie said.

Olive held out her hand to take the wooden slider. 'It's a Ouija board. You use it to talk to dead people, like in a séance. Thistle told me about them. I think she used to have one when she was younger.'

'Did she talk to dead people?'

Olive said she didn't know.

'We should try it,' Archie said.

'If you do you'll get possessed,' Sebastian said. 'Like the girl in that show. With the doll she burned in the oven.'

'I'm taking it,' Archie said. 'I'm gonna use it to talk to some dead people, probably tonight.'

'No you're not,' said Sebastian.

'I am.'

'Not.'

Olive left the shed and walked back to the house. In the bedroom, she took the photos out. One was the picture of the red-haired baby with her father. She put it to the side. The second one she had seen before. This was an important photo. At home, she'd stood in front of the mantelpiece, trying to figure out its significance. It sat right in the middle of her mother's collectibles, in a silver frame. In the line of displayed items above the fireplace there were a small vase with raised coloured bumps, a royal-looking ceramic Scottie dog, a fan from somewhere overseas, maybe China, and a smooth glass box with a gold keyhole. Olive was not allowed to touch any of the things.

Sitting on the floor, Olive studied the photograph. There was her young dad with his arm around her mother, around her *waist*. He was laughing so hard that it looked as if he was going to explode. What had made him laugh like that? And here was a person Olive had never seen in real life. The young woman in the black-and-white photo had the same pretty hair as her mother. It was done up in a bun at the back of her head. She had the same features as Audra. Her eyebrows, her chin. Her left hand was raised to clutch her father's fingers on her shoulder. You could see her new wedding ring. It was a plain silver band and it shone white and bright. She had a frothy marshmallow veil on her hair and her face was tipped up towards Bruce, smiling. Olive had never seen her mother like this. Her teeth were very even and her eyes were so shiny they seemed wet.

As she studied the photograph there was a noise in the hallway. She stretched her legs against the door just as it opened hard against her feet. Mandy Milk complained on the other side. She said there was a wolf coming to get her and she wanted to come in. That it wasn't fair, it was her room. Why was she always getting shut out? But Olive didn't say anything, just stayed on the carpet, her knees locked and feet held firm, until her cousin gave up and went away.

THE FAMILY WERE at the table eating dessert when Archie drew in a breath.

'Did you ever have a baby, Aunty Thistle?'

Olive's neck tightened and Sebastian inhaled a crumb and coughed.

Archie took a casual sip of milk. He moved leisurely—authoritatively. Thistle was lifting her spoon as if she hadn't heard what Archie had said and Rue was in the middle of a smile, rubbing at the tablecloth.

'Beetroot—it's just so risky,' she was saying. She stopped rubbing and looked up. 'What?'

'We saw some pictures of one.' Archie took another drink of milk.

Sebastian tried to kick him but missed, sliding down in his chair. He hit his chin on the edge of the table. Olive looked to see what her mother was doing.

'Were you in the shed? You know you shouldn't be out there.' Rue didn't often get angry.

'They were helping me. Looking for realia,' Thistle said.

'Well, it was a kid but it had red hair,' Archie said. 'Maybe it was a girl but more like a boy, if you ask me. Aunty Thistle was holding him and he had a yellow top on. It was pretty short hair, but at the sides—'

Audra got up and went out. Bruce folded his napkin, put it beside his plate and followed her. William was chewing even though it seemed like he didn't have any food left in his mouth.

Olive turned to the window. She wished she could go outside.

'No,' said Thistle. 'Not mine, that one.'

Sebastian made a noise and it sounded like his mother, an expression of deep, low-seated tiredness. He swung his head to the side and scowled at Olive and she shook her head back at him. It wasn't *her* fault. They both glared at Archie.

A tap-tapping at the window made them turn and William started to complain about the noise.

'Well, it's her dinner time too,' said Olive.

'It'll be pecking the eyes out of lambs in no time,' William said. It was what he always said.

Olive told him that she wouldn't and she tipped her chin at Archie who ran out to shoo Grace away from the window. Olive shouted after him to give her some meat and Mandy joined him and their voices filtered back to the family.

'Me,' Mandy was saying. 'Me.'

'A pet crow has no place on a farm.' William wiped his mouth with his serviette, rolled it and put his ring on it. 'They're just trouble.'

Olive looked at Thistle, who had drawn herself up in her chair.

'Harbingers,' Thistle said. 'They bring truth to those who need it. Warnings even.'

William pushed his chair back. He left the room too.

•

It had been back in September, when the trial was on in Darwin for the baby taken from the tent. It was cold and windy and had been raining overnight. The grass was slippery and littered with sticks that had fallen and they heard her before they saw her, a tiny balled creature with no sign of pin feathers. Olive picked it up and carried it inside, careful of the bird's neck and conscious of the staccato beat of its chest against her fingers. How it sat, cold as a rock in her palm. It was opening its mouth, a small rose-pink cave.

'It's hungry,' she said.

Archie ran beside her, and she wanted to tell him to be quiet but she couldn't even breathe because this tiny thing she held in her hands was so precious. Sebastian went ahead to hold open the door and call to his mother that they had a baby bird and they needed a box.

'And it might be dying!' he shouted.

'We need something soft for a bed.' Olive was whispering. The bird was in her hands and it was looking at her. Blue eyes.

'I've got an old t-shirt,' said Archie. 'It's too small.'

Crystal blue. Unblinking.

'You never grow out of anything,' Sebastian said.

'What?'

'You're a shrimp.'

'WHO SAID?' Archie hadn't grown much since he was seven, though this had nothing to do with the blocked nose and the hearing, everyone had agreed. The doctor in the city had no answers but Archie said he didn't care because he wanted to be a jockey, like Grandad Fletcher.

'Shhh,' said Rue, coming into the kitchen. 'You'll wake the whole house.' She went to the laundry. 'I'll get some rags and there's a shoebox in the hall cupboard, I think. Down the bottom.'

'What's a good name?' Archie said, pulling the stool over.

'Better not 'cause it'll probably die,' said Sebastian. Rue came back in, sorting through a plastic bag. 'Right, Mum? It'll probably die?'

'He's so beautiful,' Olive said. The bird's neck was skinny and its eyes were shutting now, the lids like small blackish peas.

'Not really,' said Sebastian.

Thistle came in and began to make a cup of tea.

'That is a raven, children, an Australian raven, the cleverest bird of all. I had one when I was a girl and he brought me messages. He sat on my shoulder. What a lovely deep voice he had.'

Rue was wiping down the bench with the Wettex.

'She didn't have a crow, children.'

'It's not my fault if you don't remember. He and his friends lined the roof, sat in the trees in the back garden and spoke to me all the day long. Besides, not a crow. A raven is to a crow as a wolf is to a dog.'

Rue kept rubbing at the laminex.

'What did you feed him?' Olive asked. 'What was his name? Did he stay with you for a long time?'

'I fed him chopped-up mice and other bits of meat. Cat food. The cat had died but there was still food in the pantry, wasn't there, Ruey? Oatmeal. Hardboiled-egg yolks. Ground-up cow hearts. Peas. Not bread. Never bread.'

'Where did you get the mice from?'

'From traps. We had them behind the fridge and they snapped in the night and I collected them in the morning.'

'It was revolting,' Rue said over her shoulder. 'Snipping them up with shears and once even my craft scissors.'

'I knew you remembered.' Thistle put two spoons of sugar in her tea, stirred and sipped. She leaned forwards to the sugar bowl and tipped in one spoon more. 'My raven was called Claudius.'

They got the box and Thistle sexed the bird and Olive fought to name her. Rue made comments about mites and germs and said the bird really needed to stay outside, that she didn't want it in the kitchen. Olive argued that it was just a baby and had no mother and Sebastian pushed for it to be on the stove top, just for a while so that it didn't die. If it went in the laundry or outside into the wind it would definitely die, he said. He was almost crying. Audra came in and made it clear that the bird would not be coming home with them under any circumstances so Olive should not even think to ask. It was as if she knew how Olive's mind worked because it was true, Olive *had* already started to fantasise about the bird sleeping in a white basket at the end of her bed and then, once bigger, riding around on her shoulder.

Thistle helped with a list of names and sulked only slightly when her suggestion of Azaria was rejected. She offered alternatives: Grace, Mercy, Joy. She told the children that the bird would grow to be their friend. That she would want to stay close to them, like baby lambs when they imprint. Ravens, she said, were loyal, smart and excellent problem solvers.

'She will bring you treasures and make you laugh—but only for about four months, and then she will go away.'

'What kinds of problems?' Archie wasn't very good at maths.

Olive wiped a finger across the baby raven.

'She's going to leave?'

Grace rotated her head to Olive.

'Of course. A caged corvid will dement.'

'But she's not in a cage.'

'She is but you can't see it. She'll drift off around January, I imagine.' Thistle went to the fridge.

'No.' Olive's chin jutted.

'Consider it a summer romance,' Thistle had said, even though it was still spring. 'She can't stay here forever, Olive. She'll think she's a girl.'

'She can be a raven *and* a girl.'

Olive ran to her bed and lay face down. For someone who didn't cry it was a shock, this almost-weeping that had tried to take over her whole body. Sebastian opened the door and she screamed at him to go away. She could hear him and Archie outside whispering and she screamed once more until the hallway became quiet. All she could hear then were the faint sounds of William's voice out in the paddocks and the grind of the oven door opening and closing in the kitchen. Olive became the coldest she'd ever been when she let herself think that Grace might leave. She decided it was impossible and pushed all thoughts of it away.

.

Later, in the hallway, Sebastian grabbed Archie around the neck and told him he didn't get it, that you sometimes just needed to shut up and that he probably needed to do it more than most other people. Archie wriggled out from under his brother's arm and ran down the hall, swinging his legs going 'aaaahhhhh' and saying he was Frankenstein while Olive leaned against the wall and wondered if she could ask for another piece of strudel.

THE VERANDAH AT Serpentine was like the deck of a ship. Out there the air was soft and the scent of Rue's roses mixed with the sweet chemical tang of insect repellent. Mosquito coils burned along the wide window ledges as Archie went around touching the ash even though his mother told him not to. Mandy had been taken to bed saying she was scared to go to sleep, that it wasn't fair, but Rue was impervious to childish terror.

'Not much about life is fair, my girl,' she said and walked her inside.

Thistle was in the corner where the light from the weak bulb barely reached and the shadows made her features shift from aunty to ghoul and back again. It was the place she liked to sit so that she could make her sideline comments.

William had his back to the rest of them, his hands on the railing as he stood looking out across the land. He talked about the excellent dark-sky sites he'd known as a child and how the moon was pulling away from the earth a bit more each year. Olive didn't like to think of the moon leaving like that. It made her sad. Then William mentioned something called sprites, said that he'd seen some once, when he was a boy. Olive asked if they were like fireflies. She was desperate to see a firefly. Thistle started to reply but Sebastian cut across her.

'Not like that, dummy,' he said to Olive. 'Like lightning but different. You never listen properly.'

Thistle clapped her hands.

'I was going to contribute,' she said. 'Sprites can also be spirits, or ghosts. If they hear you say something, like a wish, they make the opposite happen. That's why we say "break a leg" in the theatre.'

'Well, that's not what I'm talking about now,' William said and turned back to the dimming sky. Rue came back out and stood next to him and he reached for her under-chin.

Olive sat on the rattan couch on the verandah with everything made strange about her. It often happened at the end of the day that she realised she wasn't in the world. She could see that all else was as usual but that somehow she wasn't. The same trees lined the drive. The sprinkler tetched in lazy circles near Rue's garden. But things turned and were made solemn by the departed sun and the growing shadows, the quietness of the adults' voices and the children's pleas against bed. They were too tired to do their teeth. They were thirsty and wanted another glass of milk. They wanted to read, just for a little while. Anything to elongate the uneasy trans- ition between day and night and forestall the inevitable submission to sleep.

The areas around the front of the house deepened as the navy garden transformed into an enchanted place, one where even the shadows made shadows. Olive didn't go into the garden when it was full night, no matter how much she might hope to see the outline of an owl against the sky.

Rue started to talk about the big fires, when they'd all had to stand in the dam. The wind had been hot and impossible and sparks had plumed hard, straight up into the night sky. Thistle had refused to leave, saying if the house was to burn it was best she went with it. Only William had been able to make her walk to the dam. As they waited, with the water up to their necks and wet towels on their heads, Bruce and William made puns to keep everyone's spirits up.

'Enjoying the dip?' they'd said.

Later, they found the stock had burned and were lying on their backs like charred pincushions, legs sticking up in the air. There'd been no jokes then as they got the ute and began to drag the bodies into a pile to burn them once more.

'Did we help?' Archie asked his mother.

'It was before you were born, before Olive too, but we had a small Sebastian with us.'

'How little was he?' Even more than stories about disasters Archie liked hearing about a time when his brother was small.

'Too young to stand on his own so we had to hold him in the water.'

Archie smiled. 'Was he scared?'

'I wasn't scared,' said Olive.

Sebastian pushed her leg with his foot. 'You weren't even there.'

'I was.' She crossed her arms. She remembered it exactly as Rue said.

'Of course we were frightened. The sound of the fire was like a roaring monster,' Rue said.

'But why did you go in the dam?' Archie said. 'I would drive away in the car.'

'Fires are too fast for cars.'

'*Pffft*, you can't even drive,' Sebastian said to his brother.

'But I still would. If there was a fire I could do it, I bet I could.'

Rue had forgotten what she was saying but Thistle's prompt came from the corner.

'It was like hell. God burned the moon orange that night and it was that boy who started it.'

'Not now, dear,' said Rue.

'What boy?' Olive said.

'The children should know how it changed and what a bad colour that can be. They should know how to play with the talking board too, how to keep safe,' Thistle said. 'Is someone going to make another pot?'

Moths were around the bulb above.

'Which talking board?'

'Our old one.'

'Yours, not "ours",' said Rue. 'Mum got rid of it, I thought. Are you saying *they* have it?'

Thistle hooked a finger at Archie who stepped forward as if pulled by a string from his chest. Archie was a bit scared of Thistle, especially after she'd told him about the boy who'd been swallowed by the sand dune in America.

'We found it,' he said. 'In the shed.'

'I told you not to go out there—just before I told you, didn't I?'

'It was the same time. We're gonna use it to talk to some spirits.'

'You most certainly are not,' said Rue. 'Go and get it now, please.'

Archie went thudding inside and came back carrying the ouija board. Rue took it from him, along with the heart-shaped planchette. 'You won't be playing with this and I'm taking you to the barber next week.'

Archie collapsed in a moan. 'But it's my strength.'

'This is your doing,' Rue said over her shoulder to Thistle.

'Come here, boy,' said Thistle. 'Shhh, it grows back, you know that.'

Rue went inside with the board.

Archie wrapped an arm around Thistle's neck. 'Tell me about the boy again, Aunty Thistle. The boy who was underground.'

In the story, there'd been tunnels—sandy pits—that the boy from Maryland had fallen into. The first time they heard it Olive had been asking about the Devil's Triangle and Thistle had been the only one who really knew anything about it. She told them of planes pulled into the ocean, instruments spinning. Ships that disappeared, sucked down to where the giant squids lived.

'I think I'd just like to stay on land,' Olive had said, and that's when Thistle had told them that the land could be just as dangerous as the sea. That it can move when it shouldn't and swallow children up. Then she'd told them about the Maryland boy.

Olive hated the story. Her aunt's descriptions of the sand, making it sound as if it flowed like liquid, consuming rocks and leaves like a hungry river coming to rest around trees whose roots formed caverns under the ground. Thistle's announcement that nature had no sensitivity, formed no attachments in the way humans did, were concepts that she only half grasped. That people were weak and emotion ruinous. She wondered if her aunt was right. That it might be better to be a plant instead of a girl.

On the verandah, Olive tried to push the image of a shifting body of sand away because she didn't want her own bad dream to come, the recurring one she'd had as a younger child. She'd tried to tell Sebastian once about the wall of sand that filled all her scope and throbbed forwards and backwards to the sound of a drum.

He had been unimpressed. 'That's it? That's not a nightmare, not if it's just sand. Nightmares have monsters, or bad guys with missing fingers.'

'But it has the sound, too, which is actually the worst bit.'

Sebastian had been unconvinced and gone and locked himself in the bathroom.

In her corner, Thistle kissed Archie's head and told him to go and play.

He stepped away from her and looked down into the hydrangeas and agapanthus. The thought of being in the garden on his own at that time made him go and sit near his father.

Things fell quiet and Rue started to say again it was time for bed. She began to collect the teacups but before she could take them inside they saw that a car was making its way up the drive, beam-lights slightly rotated so they scissored through the darkness. Archie jumped down the steps to run towards the slow-moving vehicle.

'Oh,' said Rue and put the teacups down. 'It's Cleg.'

CLEGWORTH LOVELOCK WAS the third brother and the sisters were unified in their distaste for him. Cleg was the oldest and had taken the name but left the farm. The city had beckoned. Melbourne: *mater urbium*. Nothing was dull or predictable in the city, Cleg said, and besides, there were jazz clubs.

'Show me a jazz club in Stratters.'

For Cleg it was his lack of love for the country, not his penchant for claret, which had ended his own small family. It wasn't that he'd driven on Boxing Day night, rather it was his haste to get back to civilisation. Rue had begged him not to get in the car but William had shushed her and called her 'woman' and waved his brother and pregnant wife off down the driveway. Rue never said anything like 'I told you so' to either William or her brother-in-law.

Cleg had applied himself to his work and post-prandials, adding female company to the mix after a suitable mourning period. He was a lawyer and kept a nine iron under a tartan blanket across the back seat of his car—in case he needed to fat shot some bloke's head, he said. His richer clients subsidised his poorer ones, and William was always telling him if he didn't catch up on his invoicing he'd go bankrupt.

'Everyone has the right to representation,' Cleg would say. 'It's the fair thing. More important than the money.'

Cleg's car was a beast, skewiff as it shambled up the driveway, drawing into the ring of illumination thrown from the front of the house. He'd become a nervous driver after the accident, but it didn't stop him from crawling around the countryside, well under the speed limit, dragging a small caravan behind him.

'Still looks like a hobo,' Rue muttered as Cleg walked up to the verandah.

'Nothing's changed with the death trap, I see,' William said to his brother.

Cleg put his tongue in the corner of his mouth and jabbed a finger at the car. 'All the other drivers, truckies included, keep a wide berth, Blondie. No one wants to tangle with that beauty.'

The children were happy to see him, mostly because it meant they could stay up later, but also because there'd be driving lessons. Archie still had to sit on Cleg's lap and just steer but Olive had graduated to proper driving with the gears. Sebastian had become unenthusiastic, saying he already knew how to do it and that it wasn't such a big deal.

'It's got yellow bits on it, and green too,' said Archie, looking over the railing at the Holden, its panels held in place with masses of fluorescent tape. It had been the Mercedes Cleg had crashed, no insurance. 'And I can see one door that's different, maybe grey.' Archie went and stood next to his uncle. 'It looks funny.'

'Looks aren't everything, little man,' said Cleg. 'Just check out your dad and Brucie.'

'You have a very deep voice.'

'Old *basso profundo*, that's me. Not like my brothers. That's mid-range over there . . .' He raised his glass at Bruce. 'And this one here we used to call "wheezy", but he grew out of that.' He slapped William's chest with the back of his hand, then reached for Archie. 'Come here, you look like you need a horse bite.'

William asked Cleg about business and Cleg said he had a new case, a group had contacted him the month before, asking for help.

'Please tell me it's not more fruiterers,' Rue said.

'They're women this time—a regional group I suppose you could say.'

'Not women's libbers?' Rue was standing with her arms crossed.

'They're mothers. The organiser is from the city. She started the group, but there are historical connections to regional hospitals, like Bendigo, and Melbourne ones too.'

Thistle looked up. 'Bendigo?'

Rue said she would make another pot.

'What is the group?' Thistle said.

'Ah.' Cleg looked like someone who had just remembered it was a person's birthday. Olive was waiting for him to say he was sorry he'd forgotten her birthday. It had only been a week ago but she saw no sign of a present. Rue said she wasn't ever to ask.

'Say it.' Thistle's voice had dropped.

'They're women who've lost their babies.'

'Lost, you say.' Thistle was folding and refolding her fingers, pale white bones moving in the corner.

'What?' said Archie. 'I don't get it.'

'Taken away from them without their mothers' permission right after they were born,' Cleg said.

Olive sat up. This sounded interesting.

'Cleg, please,' said Rue.

'I thought you were making another pot,' Thistle said.

'It needs to be talked about more—which is half the problem in the first place, if you think about it,' Cleg said.

'Agreed,' Thistle said.

'Some people aren't meant to be mothers,' Rue said.

'But what happened to the babies?' Olive wanted to know.

'It was probably witches,' said Archie.

'Doctors and nurses. Social workers, not witches,' Cleg said.

'That's a matter of opinion,' Thistle said.

'Why?' Olive wanted to know.

'Because they were evil,' said Thistle.

'No, why to Cleg.'

'Because they weren't married at the time. Most of them were only girls.'

'Like me?'

'No, not as young as you.'

'Anyway,' said Rue. She looked at William then kept on, her words clipped. 'These women, they're not really mothers, not if their babies were taken. Not that I'm saying it was a good thing, but I do wonder why haven't they forgotten by now, moved on?'

Cleg cleared his throat but Thistle interrupted.

'The babies would be wondering what happened,' she said. 'They'd be looking for the mothers.'

'If they know,' Rue said. 'Better they don't, if you ask me.'

'No one is. And what do you mean "if they know"? Of course they know, they have to. Especially, if they are over eighteen—and it should be sixteen, even—but certainly by twenty-one.'

Rue shushed her.

'Don't pat me. And what do you mean they're not really mothers? Of course they're mothers, that bit doesn't ever change.'

'They should keep it to themselves,' Audra said. She'd come out for a last menthol. 'It's a ridiculous act of "look at me". Why tell the world? Publicising their anguish, if you ask me. Careless, unthinking revenge.'

'Nobody is, I said. Who is asking any of you?' Thistle had risen to her feet and was standing in the corner.

'So,' said Cleg. 'Don't look at me like that,' he said to Rue, lifting a hand in Thistle's direction. 'As for you, madam . . .' He turned to Olive. 'Care to earn some pocket money?'

'Yes,' said Olive. She liked money a lot and had eighty dollars saved already. She was going to buy walkie-talkies and a hand-held microphone for her tape recorder and hopefully have some left over for ice creams.

'Well, we'll see,' said Rue. 'Time for bed, children.'

'You look like Santa,' Archie said to Cleg.

'It's Father Christmas,' Rue said. 'We don't say Santa, only the Catholics say Santa.' She started to gather the teacups again.

Cleg went to park the caravan out the back and Olive watched from the window. She saw William had moved the ute so it faced the tree with the rabbit spots on, to light the scene as Cleg circled it like an old dog getting ready to sleep. It took him forever to get the van in place because he'd had beer.

In the bathroom, Olive rinsed her mouth and sucked a squeeze of toothpaste off her finger. She got into bed. Mandy was breathing lightly and there was a sweet yoghurt smell in the air. Olive climbed under the sheet and put her arms inside. She rocked to one side, then the other.

She couldn't sleep on her front anymore so she tried spreading flat on her back, arms wide. She thought about the play the next day and whispered, 'Bloody hell'. Rue said it was important that they all try to help Thistle be happy.

'But what about me?' Olive said under her breath.

She reached her hand to the window ledge where she had her things, her collection of gifts from Grace. Moving her fingers across them she listed them in her head. The twist of orange plastic from a drink bottle lid. The half-bead (blue and green mixed). The scrap of wire with a soldered end. The eyelet (from a shoe, Thistle thought). The pink scrap of ribbon. There were more at home, lined up with her wishbones on the ledge in her bedroom. She was collecting the things, all the treasures that Grace gave her. They were important in a way she couldn't have explained. 'Junk,' Sebastian said it was. 'Rubbish,' said Rue. But Thistle had understood and tried to keep them for her when Olive wasn't there.

Mandy groaned in her sleep and Olive went through her wishes: to get a pony two hands taller than Snooky's friend Megan's, to find a baby owl and to be magic. She kicked at the sheet, threw her hands over her head so that her wrists were crossed. She thought about what Luke Sands had said at the diving pool and made herself think about it until, without knowing it, she fell to the true dark.

THE
VERANDAH
PLAYS

THE SUMMER PLAYS as Thistle called them had transformed over time. They'd been running for as long as Olive could remember. At first they'd been simple animal pageants, and Olive's favourite had seen her dressed as Peter Rabbit with socks on her hands for paws. She had stood a long time in front of the mirror, loving herself. Cardboard cut-outs, a painted moon and stars that one child or another might move across the stage, and once, a free-standing tree around which the actors played with the plinking sound of the record player coming through the open window of the front room.

One year, real objects had been introduced. A picnic basket, an umbrella, a tennis racquet. There'd been a graduation to short poems—one year it was 'Hist!'—but with acting. They'd had a Chekhov run, which had been deemed satisfactory, but then came the summer, three years before, when things had changed. Thistle had been in a high state of crisis. She had prepared and delivered reimagined, lengthy and scattered monologues that were supposedly from *A Streetcar Named Desire* but to Olive sounded made up. The children were reduced to props themselves, including Sebastian, who was placed centre-stage to stand—startled, skinny—in a white singlet: a trembling Stanley to Thistle's sybaritic Blanche.

Last year, Thistle and Olive had clashed over artistic differences. Olive saw the plays as an opportunity to make it all up and do whatever they liked. It was freedom. While Thistle agreed that freedom was important in creative endeavour, she insisted there was greater liberty in telling truth. The whole purpose, Thistle had said, was to hold up a mirror to humanity.

'She says she likes to be free but really she wants to be bossy,' Olive said to Sebastian afterwards. 'She's a real hypocrite.'

Olive resisted, launching a counter-production of her own. She recruited Sebastian and Archie to be her co-stars. She'd approached some of the adults to play parts (thinking she could take a turn and arrange *them* on stage, have them standing or sitting and give them no lines but keep them like extras in a film), but each one declined saying they'd rather watch than be in it, which she knew was a lie one thousand per cent.

The Haunted House had been a flop. The actors had lost track of what they were meant to be doing and the adults had become restless and started talking in the middle of it. There was no real story Thistle pointed out, and dramatic turns that fell flat and showed lack of preparation and thought. You couldn't just let things happen onstage, she said. Everything had to be worked out, which was why there were scripts. Olive had stalked offstage but not before seeing the satisfied look on Thistle's face.

That day they were doing Shakespeare. The afternoon had become sluggish as the air quietened after lunch, and the actors were fatigued even before taking their marks.

Thistle came out wearing trousers and a belt and a man's shirt. She was holding a pile of white fabric for the ghost and she gestured to her niece and told her it was the call.

'You're lucky.' Thistle was putting on her bright face because of the play but her voice was flat. 'I wish I were a girl again.'

Olive didn't think she was lucky and was going to say so, but Thistle made a circle, arms raised.

'Oh my porch, my porch, oh my new porch . . .'

Thistle had typed out the reworked scripts using purple carbon paper to make several copies. She had simplified the language, she told them in the pre-performance meeting. Made some adjustments because it was important, of *utmost importance*, for this production more than any other year, that the audience be able to understand. The words needed to be clear, both in meaning and enunciation. Archie had complained because his script copy was the faintest and he couldn't read it properly so he was in the corner of the verandah going over it with pencil, asking how to pronounce 'Lareties' and squinting and shaking his head at the pages.

'It would be better if we had a real skull,' said Thistle, looking at the rock she'd found in Rue's garden. 'One with the tongue still in it.'

'What about the one in your room?' Olive got up to go and get it.

'That's a sheep's head, not a man's.' Thistle tapped her nails on her arms. 'No, this will have to do. It looks like a face, don't you think?' She started fussing with the fabrics.

Archie came up to them with the umbrella.

'So I have to stab you? With this poison sword?'

Thistle nodded.

'But gently, of course.'

'Why isn't Sebastian the man?' Archie was pointing to the script pages, where Thistle had written the parts. 'Why are you the man that I kill?'

'Because it's the lead role,' said Thistle. She put her hands on Archie's shoulders. 'It's the main part, so of course it has to be me, even though it's not *exactly* my story.'

'But why didn't you choose a play that has a girl as the main? Are there even any?'

'Because girl parts aren't as exciting as man parts,' Olive said.

Thistle went to the end of the verandah. She called for Rue, who came out with clothes pegs.

'Boil me some eggs!' said Thistle loudly in Rue's face.

Rue told her sister not to be so ridiculous and to help pin up the material. They stretched it along the railings, bunching it in poufy masses at the end. Olive didn't understand what white material had to do with the play but her aunt said they were clouds, that they represented the shifts in the emotional climate.

'That looks like a camel, doesn't it?'

'I suppose so,' said Rue, not even looking.

'Oh no. I see it now. A weasel.'

'Whatever you say, dear.' Rue went inside.

'Go and put your costume on,' Thistle said to Olive. 'I'm going to warm up with something else.' She began to orate, her language clipped and precise:

Look, do you see them
Sitting by the house
The younger ones, like
Shapes seen in dreams?'

'Where's Seb?' Olive said to Archie as she left the verandah. 'He's such an idiot.'

Archie's face brightened at the rare moment of alliance.

'Yeah,' he said. 'What an idiot.'

Archie was dispatched to find a goblet and he walked inside confused. Olive went in too and got the shirt she had to wear. It was from when they did *Peter Pan* and it was green. She hated it, hated the whole thing. She wished she could sneak out the back, grab Seb's bike and go find Peter, go to the silo. Even running into the Sands brothers down by the railway would be better than this. Having to stand like a suck on the verandah, with the adults gathered, men drinking beer, their laughter getting louder, her mother smoking, her aunt Rue wanting to complain about having to make another birthday cake, or something else about dinner, or the garden.

Olive stood up and took off her shorts and t-shirt. She found a singlet and put it on, not liking how the fabric wasn't properly flat across her chest anymore. She put her jeans on and the shirt, put on her runners and went down the hall back to the verandah.

'Oh no,' Thistle said. She put out her hands to adjust Olive's shirt. 'Tuck it in. Don't you have a waistcoat? And proper shoes—what about your school ones?'

'They're at home.'

Archie arrived with a metal vase.

'I've got this.'

'Pardon me?' Thistle was turning the vase over in her hands.

'My school shoes are at home.'

'Oh.'

Thistle became distracted with whether this was the best possible prop. Whether Denmark in those days would have had that type of metal, with that particular type of handle. Olive and Archie's eyes met and they pressed their lips together in mutual entrapment.

'I suppose it'll have to do,' Thistle decided, and put it inside the window where she could reach it later. 'This is for the poison scene. I think it will be fine.'

•

The family moved out onto the verandah and the door clapped with each exit, rhythmic and loud. The men preferred to stand at the back even though Thistle had placed chairs for them around the proscenium of the back door.

'Why won't you sit down?' Thistle said to the three brothers, poking her head through the back door. 'I just don't understand it.'

Mandy was complaining about being hot.

'I don't know what you want from us,' Rue said, sitting down. 'You want us to watch but you don't want us to come through the door.'

Thistle had circulated a communication to the audience (by way of lavender-scented notepaper) about approaching the stage from the backyard, wanting the audience to walk around from the back door. They could then simply walk up the front steps and find their labelled seats. *The Trap* would be commencing at 3 pm.

'Why am I at the front?' Rue said. 'Is there a reason for putting me here?'

'You never want to know about the harder things,' Thistle said.

'What is that supposed to mean?'

'Some of us can't just bake or prune things away.'

Rue twisted in her seat with exasperation.

'Oh really, Thistle. Do you want a cake or not?'

Thistle went inside and Rue turned around to Audra with her hands raised in the air.

Olive waited in the front room and looked through the window where the record player was. Her job was to start the third song once Thistle gave her a sign from the doorway. In that room were a small table which had been moved under the window, a desk and some bookcases. The desk was interesting, it had a top that rolled: little strips of wood that joined in a curving wave that you could pull up—or down—using two brass handles. Olive was not allowed to touch the desk but she knew that inside it were some secret cubby holes, drawers and sliding parts. And inside one of the cubby holes was a key. An old-fashioned key made of metal with an end that opened into a circle. Olive had always wondered what that key was for. She had snuck it out to try to find an opening that it would fit into, inserting it into various locks around the place, but so far she hadn't worked it out.

In the doorway, Thistle held a finger up. The air flattened and then her aunt dropped her hand. Olive lowered the needle onto the third track. She didn't know what it was called, this music. All she knew was that it was like clouds, a billowing of pulsing white energy that built from one thing into something else. It was the perfect piece of music, Thistle said, and it matched the first of the scenes they were about to perform. This was music that described an interior life, Thistle said, but to Olive it just sounded like strong round sounds.

'No, it's about feelings, not simple entertainment. Feelings about death and feelings about revenge, though I'm calling it a comedy. People are more comfortable with comedies, and it highlights the tragedy when you have both together. It's about love, too.'

Olive had wanted to ask what type of love it was. Was it for playing or a favourite food? Heidi had lost her love, which was the love for her grandfather and his mountain home. She'd thought to ask her aunt if it was that kind of love but then realised it was probably about loving a *man* which was the most boring type of love there was.

Olive had heard her mother say to Rue that Thistle and her plays were 'provocative' and 'ridiculous'. It had been mean to say that out loud and it was mean for her to say that about her own sister too.

The music continued and they all went to their positions. Olive stood at her spot and felt sweaty inside her armpits. They read their parts, the lines that Thistle had insisted they recite word for word. One time, in the middle, Sebastian was speaking too quietly and William told him to speak up.

'I can't say it properly. Bio-logical ip- imp-erative?'

Thistle nodded. She turned to the audience and broke character.

'Quick exposition. Greyfriars Bobby was not a successful dog. The one on the tuckerbox, also not. They did not fulfil their biological imperative, which was to move on and breed. These dogs that lie mourning where their masters fell—not successful dogs.' She nodded and went back into character and things proceeded.

Olive had lost her place several times and kept looking up to see Archie, smiling in a superior way, pointing at his rewritten two pages.

Everything went alright until towards the end when Thistle was doing her solo talk. Olive had stopped listening because it was long and dull, about the killing and stealing of love. Thistle had stopped reading her words and was ad-libbing, which made her aunt a double hypocrite. Olive looked at Sebastian and he glared back as if it was her fault, but it wasn't. Nothing was ever her fault but she was always getting blamed. She didn't tell their aunt to go on and on about putting poison into an ear. She couldn't help it if she, Olive, was the prince and not Sebastian, that he was in a minor role this year. It was all mixed up but at least he didn't have to play a girl part.

'She moved like quicksilver upon that man,' Thistle said. 'Turned him to spurn. She will be guilty, look, see! Did she say "hate" where I told "love"?'

Rue got up and went inside and Thistle's head stayed fixed towards the empty chair. Then Archie stabbed Thistle in the stomach with the poison umbrella and she slid to the floor with hand to brow to say a few final words as she died. That was when Archie's rectum emitted a high, tuba-like squeal. The children fell down laughing. Even Sebastian sat down on a chair with a smile.

'That boy's flatus,' Audra said. 'I just don't know. Is it diet? Dairy?' She breathed out smoke and answered herself. 'It's offensive is what it is.'

'What, may I ask, is the problem?' Thistle, resurrected, was getting to her feet and standing over Audra.

'Nothing. Do go on.'

'When the last days come, people will appear who will mock you.'

'Oh stop that. Continue the play.'

'I can't. That's it. I've died!'

'I'm sure you can try again.'

'Rue has to be here for this bit.' Thistle went inside and came back out, steering her sister by the arm. Olive picked her nose.

Thistle sat Rue down again and looked at the line of men at the back, where they leaned against the railing. She returned to her mark, tipped her head back and shut her eyes to gather herself. The children all moved back and found their spots as Thistle lowered herself to the rug. She lifted her arms over her head and looked at Olive to do the flowers.

'Come the recorders,' Sebastian said, and Archie stepped forwards and started playing 'God Save the Queen'. Olive reached into the window where the record player spun with a gentle crackle, the music finished. She took out the bag that was filled with rose petals. As instructed, she sprinkled them slowly over Thistle, who lay dead. At the sight of the flowers Rue began to shout. Her roses! What had they done to her roses? But before anyone could say anything, Archie broke wind once more and Olive folded forwards with a quick sharp bray. Rue went inside again and Thistle stumped in after her. The men carried the furniture back to the kitchen and it was Audra who had to go to Thistle with a cool face washer.

The play was over for another year.

RUE AND THISTLE argued in the hallway. Olive had never heard Rue's voice like that, a piccolo sound, high and constant. It made her think of a carnival ride, the music that was played as the carriages spun higher and higher. She went and opened the door, made a narrow crack to watch.

'How could you?' Rue was saying over and over. 'My flowers. The show.'

'I don't care about your flowers, no one does.'

'Audra does, she cares.'

'She doesn't. She just says that. My question to you stands: what did you say?'

'I don't know what you're talking about.'

'What did you say that day? I was sick. I gave you the message. Did you say the word at all?'

'You're being ridiculous. What word?'

'Did you mention *love*?'

Rue's face was awful.

'You didn't. Oh, villainy, HO!'

'I have to get the dinner on.' Rue went to the kitchen.

Half an hour later, Olive walked down the hallway and stood outside Thistle's room. She could hear muffled sobs. She opened the door and peered in. Thistle was lying prone in the middle of the mess. Her mother was there, helping Thistle, and it was a strange thing to see.

'I want to die,' Thistle was saying. 'Again, nothing. All this time.'

'There, there, dear,' Audra said.

'I won't. Not there, not dear.'

Audra got up and went to the record player.

'What about some nice music?'

'I can't, it's the violins. They sting me.' Thistle's voice was a hideous croak.

'Shhh . . .' began Audra, looking at the door and seeing Olive. 'Dear—'

'No, I'm not your dear. I'll get one of the guns, William will give me one, he'd be happy to, he's always hated me.'

Olive stepped back and knocked an empty mug to the skirting board.

'Who's there?' Thistle's voice was muffled. 'Is it him?'

'It's no one.' Audra waved Olive back. 'Do you want me to rub your feet with some cream?'

'No, I do not.'

Olive closed the door. She wanted to go outside, get higher than the trees, scramble to the top of everything. She would climb the ladder at the silo, up and up, until she was above the world where she could sit calm and fresh in the hay-coloured wind.

•

At dinner that night Cleg drank a lot of wine and kept waving Rue away as she tried to put food on his plate. He pushed his glass forwards for Bruce or William to fill. Thistle called Cleg a wretched log and a thrown clog and he told her to keep her dirty anagrams to herself.

'You impossibly dreadful man.' Thistle held her napkin to her face and Cleg combed his beard with his fingers. He caught Olive's eye and winked.

'She's just putting it on,' he said. 'It's a performance.'

He turned to Thistle. 'You may not be the lithest anymore, oh sister-in-law, and she tilts.' Cleg said this last bit to Archie, who was sitting next to him. 'Let's hit the list, let this, eh stilt?'

'What?' said Archie. 'I don't get it.'

'Stop it, you two,' said Rue. 'Please.'

'Certainly, Ash Rune.'

There was a tapping at one of the windows and Olive jumped up but it wasn't anything. She sat down and cut up some of her sausage and held a tiny bit to her lips. She saw her aunt's look and slipped it in and chewed.

'What's a anagaram?' Archie said. 'What does that mean?'

'Ah,' said Cleg. '"Meaning".'

'It was never you,' Thistle murmured. 'It just wasn't, wasn't just, nothing just, nothing was.' Then she announced she was going to the dam but in the end sat stiff in her chair, looking at her plate.

Archie lifted a finger. 'Sheepish, you look sheepish,' he said to William.

'Twenty and one,' Thistle said. 'Ten and eight and one and one and one.'

'Why is she saying numbers?' Mandy said.

Olive felt the pull of the trees. How would it be to float out of the window, up over the roof and away from the earth? To be far from the hard emotions that ran underneath the dinner noises?

'Did you all know each other when you were kids?' she asked.

Rue folded her serviette and put it beside her plate. She tucked the edges under the rim but before she could reply Thistle dropped her cutlery and said she wasn't feeling well.

'But you haven't finished, dear,' said Rue.

'I've had quite enough, dear.'

Olive was a *quid nunc*. The lines were too complicated and she'd known not to ask. She was as bad as Archie, blurting things out like that.

'Would you like me to bring it in to you on a tray?' Rue asked her sister.

'No, I would not. Please don't bother yourself.'

Thistle went to her room.

'Well,' said Rue, her eyes moving. 'We all knew each other, of course, since school, but the first time we properly talked, I suppose you could say, as older people, as teenagers, not children, well, it was at ice-skating in the city.'

'It bloody was not,' William said. 'Ice-skating.' He made a blow-ing-out noise.

'It doesn't matter,' said Olive.

William kept talking. 'It was the show. The Nash sisters. Of course, people joked about them being a singing group or something, didn't they, Brucie? Country and Western? They were something, what a bunch of giggling gerties.'

'I *can* sing.' Thistle's voice came from the doorway. 'And Audra and I were never gigglers—that was Rue if you remember.'

'That's right, love,' said William, closing his eyes. 'You can and you weren't.'

'Don't tell me you don't remember?' Thistle glared at William from the doorway then walked down the hall to the verandah.

'Well, you tell the story if you want to,' Rue said. 'And please don't swear.'

'Oh no,' William said. 'You'd be interrupting every minute anyway.'

'Alright.' She leaned forwards. 'You can put in anything I forget.'

'Were you teenagers?' Archie asked. 'Did you know them before?'

'Well, yes, of course. We'd seen them in town, around the place. At school,' said Rue. 'But our . . . our—'

'Our mother didn't like us mixing,' said Audra.

'So yes. At Nanango,' Rue said. 'Audra had agreed to come with me to see the cakes . . .' Rue's hand moved to her throat. 'I was just little, about ten or twelve. I couldn't go by myself, so Audra took me.'

'It was Thistle,' William said.

Cleg leaned back in his chair. He rubbed his hands together and said something about circus maximus.

'Was it?' Rue said to her husband. 'What a good memory you have for some things. Wedding anniversaries, well, they're not the same I expect. The baked items had been wonderful the year before and I begged her to take me. After the cakes and the dogs, we decided to eat lunch in the stadium. I think the horses were on. Our mother had let us go but we had to come straight home.'

'What did you eat at the show?' said Mandy.

'Sorry, dear?' Rue's voice was loud.

'What did you have for the lunch? Was it hot dogs and chips?'

'In those days you took your lunch, you didn't buy food other than maybe a sweet but never a waffle. We probably had something like hard-boiled eggs, with some salt and pepper in a twist of wax paper, buttered bread. Maybe an apple each.'

'Was it a toffee apple?'

'No.'

'Chips?'

'No, no chips. Tea in a thermos, that was always nice, I liked the little cups we had. They stacked inside of each other, see?'

Mandy was disappointed. 'Not a waffle? Why not a waffle?'

'Because of the cream, of course. It needs to be fresh and it never is at those places. Anyway,' Rue went on. 'These two boys started talking to us. Your father,' she told Mandy and her sons, who weren't listening anyway. They were looking under the tablecloth and whispering. 'And yours, Olive. Two brothers.'

'Who is the brothers?' said Mandy. She was holding a sausage that she'd dipped into tomato sauce and there was sauce all over her peas as well. Mandy was in a 'sauce phase', as Rue called it. 'You?' Mandy said, pointing at Sebastian with the sausage. 'You're a brother?'

'My dad and your dad are,' said Olive. 'You already know that.'

Mandy licked sauce off her wrist and wiped her eyebrow with her sausage.

'William is my dad,' Mandy said, putting her other hand on the sauce bottle and looking around the table. She spat up half-masticated food onto her plate and started crying.

Rue felt her daughter's forehead. 'Anyway, it was the first time we'd spoken to them properly. Before it had been children calling out things, you know, running around and chasing each other, that sort of thing. Not any conversation like a grown-up would have.'

'Stand-offish you were—or you two, anyway,' said William.

'Well, if that's what you call being dignified so be it. People talk.'

Rue cared a lot about what other people thought and it seemed to Olive that the less close the people were, the more important their opinions seemed to be. When she had asked who the people were, Rue couldn't even say. So why did she care so much about them?

'Then what happened?'

'Well, we tried not to talk to them. Our mother had told us not to fraternise with any show people. Gadabouts, she called them. "Worse than circus people."'

'He's a clown, alright,' William said, jerking a thumb at his brother, but Bruce didn't look up from his plate. He kept chewing

his food, bones sliding mechanically at the base of his cheeks, eyes
on his plate. Cleg was laughing, watching Bruce.

'What was the show?' Mandy was looking at her father. 'Was it
puppets?'

'A ram,' said William. 'We got first for it. We were there with
our father.'

'Dad's haircut was funny,' Rue told the children. Her voice had
become very high and she was speaking fast. 'The front bit would
flop over his eyes, like Elvis. He got up on the bench in the stadium,
he was tall even then, as a boy who was fifteen or sixteen. He stood
over us, telling us about sheep and rabbits, and I was determined
to ignore them because that's what our mother had told us, but
Thistle—oh . . .' Rue looked at William. 'You're right, I remember
now, it *was* Thistle. They talked us into meeting them at the milk
bar the next week, for a milkshake. Well, William did. Bruce was
the quieter one, not much to say back then either. William said to
bring Audra if she wanted to come too.'

Audra was pressing peas onto her fork.

'Dad had a milkshake?' Mandy said. 'Was it a chocolate one?'

'I did not, little girl,' William said. 'Neither did Bruce. We never
went in for that muck, but the girls did—sweet tooths they had.'

'But why was it Aunty Thistle who went?' Archie looked around
at the adults. 'Why didn't you go?' He was looking at Audra. 'For
your husband?'

'Who was at the milk bar?' Mandy said.

'Oh, well, it was me and—me and Thistle and . . .' said Rue,
getting up. 'I was a young girl, really, watching my older sisters. . .'

William pushed his plate away and Audra picked up her menthols.
'I need a break before pudding.' She trailed long fingers across the
table.

Olive glanced at her mother's plate. The usual moderate amount, barely touched.

'Lots of scrapings,' Rue said. 'Olive, why didn't you finish yours? Did you take too much?' She looked at Mandy's plate. 'Licked clean. She'd eat the plate if she could, look.'

Mandy sat, her wet face tight with shame.

Bruce's ears were red as he carefully continued to make his knife and fork do their work, but after a couple more chews, William tossed his knife onto his plate and left the table. Olive pushed her food around and Mandy asked if she was going to eat her mashed potato. She said no and scraped it off onto her cousin's empty plate.

'What about yer other sausage?' Mandy said. She hooked a sly finger over Olive's sausage and transferred it to her own plate.

Rue rubbed at a new spot on the tablecloth. Did every one of them have a mark?

William came back in with another bottle of wine. Olive knew the odd atmosphere that came over the adults on nights like these. They loosened, all of them, their faces got red and their talk accelerated and became louder. All except her mother, who stayed exactly the same. Cool, assured and untouched.

•

Olive looked over at Mandy's bed and saw that her cousin's eyes were open, watching her.

'Go to sleep,' she said. 'Close your eyes.'

'I don't like it when they're angry.'

'But it's not at you. Go to sleep.'

It was another hot night, the air heavy and still. Olive lay flat on her back and tried to sleep but it seemed the more she tried the harder it was, as if her straining for the thing she wanted most pushed it further away. Mandy huffed and turned, complaining that her pillow was too hot and her neck was hurting as well. Olive ignored her. She listened to the sound of furniture being moved down the hallway and the voices of the grown-ups out on the verandah, their gentle murmurings in the distance making it sound as if they had moved back towards something approximating harmony.

SUNDAY MORNING AND the sun rose on the bleached Mallee landscape and lit the distressed greens and greys. The magpies carolled before they left their trees to feed and the farmhouse began to stir. Grace was at the back door knocking on the glass. She had been under Rue's sprinkler and as she sat on Olive's lap, her feathers looked like they'd been sewn with dozens of tiny diamonds. Drops of water, sitting in perfectly round jewels.

When Olive held Grace's tail feathers in her hand, there was a soft sharpness to the edge against her palm, the interleaving feathers cross-hatched as they narrowed from the body to the tail. With her face right down close, looking on an angle, she could see that the feathers were not solid black at all. There were secret colours hidden, all types of purples and greens, and like petrol in a puddle they were iridescent, oily and beautiful.

There were no mice in the traps so Olive soaked dog food and sat on the back step and hand-fed the bird as she walked up and down her leg. Then Grace sat awhile on Olive's shoulder, pushing at her ear with her beak. A bird so shiny could never be a ghost or a harbinger like Thistle said.

Nearby were some ravens, bigger than Grace, their feathers slick and wet-looking. Their noise was a gathering of *ah-ah-aaaaahs*.

'Over there, Grace. Your friends.'

Grace lifted her body, her head rotating.

Sebastian came out yawning.

'It might be her family,' Olive said.

'She'll go with them soon.'

Olive considered this. She ran her fingers meditatively along the frilly under-feathers of Grace's chest, the ruffle on her throat. Her wings all tucked and neat, her feathers layered in a pattern. The breeze stirred her petticoats and made them lift.

The touch of her was always surprising. How warm and alive she was. Like the snake Olive had held at the zoo on the school trip two years before. The muscular twisting length of it warm in her hands, not cold as she had expected. She'd stood there, the reptile laid out all along the span of her arm, its tail braceleting one of her wrists. As she looked at the class her eyes found Snooky Sands, who was watching, scared. Olive had smiled. Snooky was frightened of snakes.

She picked up Grace and put the bird on her lap.

'No, she's with us now,' she said to Sebastian. 'She can't go away.'

She closed two fingers around one of the bird's twiggy legs and made a wish.

•

Olive and Sebastian sat in the kitchen and ate their cereal. The toy had come out in Olive's bowl and Sebastian seemed mad about it. It was a small green alien with big ears, one in the series he was collecting. She didn't want it but refused to hand it over to him. He seemed to think just because he said he was collecting them that he should have it. She thought he was too old for it and said so. He said she always got the wishbone, which wasn't fair, so why couldn't she just let him have it. Before that they'd been talking about how to get the blue-tongue lizard out from under the house. They had agreed bacon would be best but then the alien had emerged from the cornflakes and stopped everything. Now Sebastian was in a bad mood they probably wouldn't even try with the lizard.

Thistle was at the table as well, having her first cup of tea and her triangles of marmalade toast. She didn't make her s-s-s-s-s-s laugh because she was never happy around her birthday which Olive couldn't understand. Surely it was the best time of year for a person. But Thistle wasn't happy. She was bossy and wanted to lecture all the time.

'Mind the lizard doesn't snap at your fingers, Olive,' Thistle said in her deep voice. 'He'll leave them ragged and bleeding and take the tips back to his den for supper. Best to leave the bacon in front. He'll smell it. Their sense of smell is the best of all the reptile fellows.' She lifted her napkin to her lips. 'They like snails. Maybe your aunt Rue has some. To spare.'

Olive had just taken a mouthful of milk and she made sure she swallowed it before looking at Sebastian. Out of the corner of her eye she knew he was looking at her wanting to make her laugh. That meant the alien was forgotten.

'Yes, in her garden, she crushes them when the pellets don't work,' Thistle said, finishing her toast.

Olive heard Archie's footsteps coming up the front verandah steps and she and Sebastian pushed back their chairs in one move and ran out the back door.

They squatted around the side, watching for the lizard. They could hear Archie's voice in the distance moving away from the back of the house. Olive snuck inside to get some bacon and when she came back they put it on a brick near the hole. They squatted again, their hands greasy.

'She doesn't care about my fingers,' Sebastian said.

Olive didn't reply. In the dirt, where the weatherboards met the ground, was the hole, half hidden behind a small shrub. She lay down on her stomach and stretched her hand into the burrow.

'What are you doing?'

Her cheek rested on the earth and she pushed her arm in further. The ground was rich with the sharp stink of ants and her shoulder began to ache. She pushed a bit deeper and her fingers closed on something. She pulled it out and showed what she had to Sebastian. A narrow bone, delicate in the bright morning light. She placed it on the ground beside her and reached in again.

'What's it even from?'

Slowly, one by one, she pulled out four more pieces of bone. They were shapes, parts of a skeleton. She liked bones. Once she had been on her own digging down the back garden near the small wooden crosses and had found some bones that Sebastian said were probably from one of their cats or dogs. He'd been upset but she'd sat turning them over and over in her hands.

'How would you like it if I dug up someone you cared about?' he'd said.

She'd said she probably wouldn't care as much because she wasn't a sook like he was.

Beside the house she counted the fragments and tried to fit them together. There was a tiny skull, too. She couldn't tell if they were from one animal or many.

'Aren't they interesting?' she said, looking up at him. He was shaking his head. She offered him one to have but he said no, he didn't want to touch them.

'Are they rabbit?'

'Who knows?' He stood up.

'Wait.' She lay down again. 'There's something else.'

This time she brought out a packet of pills. There was no box, just the silver-backed sheet and the white tablets in their bubble pouches.

'Might be useful.' She got up and put them in her pocket.

'You're such a weirdo.'

Olive told him he was the weirdo. The weirdest weirdo.

'Let's go,' she said. 'The lizard's not coming out.'

They left the bacon on a brick and agreed they'd go back later to check. Ants were already walking over the meat. 'Extra vitamins,' Olive said over her shoulder.

FOR THISTLE AND Audra, it was almost time to leave for church, the only interest they seemed to share. They drove in on most Sundays, at Easter and at Christmas, the air in the car stained with a perverse martyrdom. When Thistle sang in God's house it soothed her whereas Audra was made deranged by it because Thistle had a particular style. She would lean into the harder bits of the hymns and at the places where the other voices usually faded away she would get louder. She said it was the only time she could breathe properly. When Rue and Audra heard her say that it made them seethe, but Thistle didn't care.

The church was an old red-brick building that squatted on the road on the other side of Stratford. The attached hall had pressed tin walls and scarlet-lined theatre seats with floors that had once been famed for being so polished they'd been known as the fastest in all of Victoria. 'Kerosene and sawdust,' it had been reported in the local paper, and in the old days, in the newly married days, Audra and Rue and their husbands would go to the dances, sometimes taking Thistle with them.

Audra waited for Thistle in the sunroom, rubbing the ends of her fingers together in small circles. She was always ready well ahead of time and would not have considered her sister might delay on purpose. Rue never came with them. She was out in the garden, having got up early, unable to lie in. She had to see if she could do anything with the roses. There was no chance for the Nanango Show but maybe she could salvage something for the house. She walked down the rows of nubbed bushes and tried not to cry. Kneeling in the garden bed she noticed a fresh hole, partly filled in. Pushing some dirt out of the way she saw there was something shiny in it. She knelt down, reached in and pulled out several packets of pills. She sat back on her heels and wiped her top lip, looking at the house.

·

Audra drove and Thistle began to open her side window, to let some of the quiet out. Silence had always disturbed her, ever since she was a little thing, just a blob of hot meat lying on a thin rug on the floor with legs walking all around her. As she grew older, once she became a jazzy twist of girl, she'd been left alone with noiselessness all around her.

'Can you please leave it closed?' Audra said 'Because of the dust?'

Thistle closed the window and stretched a finger towards the radio.

'Thistle, really, it's quite a nice drive.'

She pretended to forget, forget, but remembered more than they would guess. A sound in the distance, the front door opening and slamming, perhaps the wind but more likely rage. Along the windowsill, a fly buzzing, fat and laden with age, its time ending. Another fly in the window. It lifts, a furry zeppelin batting against the glass, sad in its attempts to reach the outdoors.

One hour, two hours since, and years later, a girl sat in a house that was overstuffed in the way of cushions, couches and table lamps. The soft carpet underfoot denied the atmosphere, tried to stifle it, but could not win. Could not win. A profile, a finger against the backdrop of white, a set, the four walls converted to scrims, hard plaster become transparent enough to show a view of this inside world but at the same time with an opacity that removed sharp profiles and rubbed them into vagueness. What category of horror, the whitened masks and vampire fangs and undead rising decomposed from dusty graves?

There were kinder set pieces flat on the wall, gentler to young eyes. They didn't shout or exhale with impatience. They didn't meow and scratch and bite. They whispered, these paintings, and this was a good thing for a young girl whose mind was dishevelled but not yet lost.

They arrived and failed to find a park in the shade and Audra said *Sheba* under her breath. By the time they got inside the church and sat down they were fanning themselves with their hands. The minister gave his sermon on the typical themes and they sang the usual hymns, Audra in her self-conscious falsetto and Thistle's deep voice echoing in the space, sounding a moment longer when the other voices paused. Even as a child she had sung long and hard in church despite what her mother did afterwards. It was a terrible thing, the sight of Gladys Nash counting to ten as she walked down the long hallway, head tipped to the ceiling, numbers booming as she pulled off her Sunday gloves. But still, in church the next week, Thistle sang her loudest.

'Why do you do it?' Audra had asked her one Sunday evening. They were two girls sitting rigid in front of lamb loin chops, peas and thin mashed potato, their mother about to join them from the kitchen.

'You wouldn't understand.' Thistle held her arm gingerly. She never told the sisters that she did it for them. That she was suffering for the littler children.

At the front of the church the minister read from Isaiah.

'"Come now, let us settle the matter," says the Lord. "Though your sins are like scarlet, they shall be as white as snow; though they are red as crimson, they shall be like wool."'

Thistle shook her head. Red and white, white and red. Forgiveness comes next, probably the Ephesians. Why bother with it all? You wait, you wonder, you are patient, but in the end it all comes to nothing.

"'Get rid of all bitterness, rage and anger, brawling and slander, along with every form of malice. Be kind and compassionate to one another, forgiving each other, just as in Christ God forgave you.'"

Thistle stared at the minister. She tried, yes she did.

"'Happy are you when people insult you and persecute you and tell all kinds of evil lies against you because you are my followers. Be happy and glad, for a great reward is kept for you in heaven.'"

A snort through her nose, she couldn't stop it.

"'You have heard that it was said, *An eye for an eye, and a tooth for a tooth*. But now I tell you: do not take revenge on someone who wrongs you. If anyone slaps you on the right cheek, let him slap your left cheek too.'"

Thistle lifted her head and blinked and the collection plate went around and it was over. Audra shook the minister's hand in the doorway on the way out then stopped to talk to Mavis Sands. Thistle went ahead to the car. She didn't want to talk to Mavis Sands. She hated Mavis Sands. Mavis Sands was a *quid nunc*.

Thistle waited in the shade for her sister. Slander, forgiveness, no. Revenge and cheeks. *You have heard that it was said,* as if it was a mistake, or misreported. But that was the old God, in the original book. These New Testamenters. Twisting it right under people's noses. Changing the message.

The vinyl car seats were hot, so Audra pulled out the striped beach towels from the back so they could sit without their thighs burning through their frocks. Audra drove home, her fingers splayed on the wheel as if she had just applied nail polish and Thistle faced the yellow scenery breathing so heavily through her nose that it whistled. She thought about babies and birthdays. About sisters. How the gardener came home when she, Thistle, was almost five.

She remembers everything from that day. How her mother called out 'Can you bring her in?' to her father and walked ahead to the house, opening the clasp on her handbag and getting out her set of keys. Thistle had stood by the car watching her father and the baby they told her was to be called 'Rue'. Inside the car it was starting to make cat noises and her father smiled and opened his hands.

'What the heck do we do now?' he said. He carried the basket into the house.

The baby had a red face and there was a dent in her forehead and a small scab with dried blood. She was wearing all pale pink clothes because she was another girl, wrapped tightly in a blanket, like a grub with no arms or legs, which was maybe why her mother was angry. Coming home from the hospital Thistle had sat in the back with the new baby and her job had been to hold the white wicker basket so it didn't slide off the seat. She had held on to it tight.

Her dad picked up the crying Rue. He held her to his chest, knees bent as if the baby weighed a lot. The blanket was beginning to fall open and her father's glasses were slipping down his nose.

'Here, you have a hold. Open your arms, that's it.'

He put the baby on Thistle and she looked at the legs that were kicking and something squished inside her and it felt like it might be her heart. Her father watched them both, jingling coins in his pocket with his happy face. Thistle tried to cover the baby's legs with the blanket but it wouldn't stay in place. Then she heard the toilet flush and her father came forwards to pick the baby up.

'Maybe she's hungry?' Thistle said to her father.

'No.' Her mother came in. She'd put more lipstick on. 'She's been feeding off me endlessly for the last week. I swear that child would eat me if she could. I'm starting her on formula today and I don't know why I let anyone suggest I feed her myself. They said it would help with weight loss but it's such a hideous sensation. The others had bottles.'

Gladys dropped her slender figure in a chair.

'Dennis, what are you doing? Wrap her properly.'

He went to the couch and laid the baby down.

'Pass me the Ronson, will you?' Gladys opened her cigarette case and pulled one out. Thistle got up and passed the heavy silver lighter. When her mother bent her head to the flame Thistle saw the part at the centre of her head and it was like a knife slash.

'Give her to me.' Gladys waved and breathed out smoke at the same time.

Thistle stepped away and her dad handed the baby across. The blanket had fallen to the floor and baby Rue's legs were hanging free. Thistle worried that the ash would get on the baby's head— she already had a sore and no hair—but Gladys rested the cigarette in the ashtray on the little side table and rewrapped the baby. She had her up against her shoulder in seconds and her hand slapped the baby's back, which didn't seem to hurt rather made Rue a little bit quieter.

'Well, what do you think?' her father said. 'Three little girls now.'

'What's that sore on her head?'

Dennis was quiet but Gladys said she'd got stuck and they'd had to pull her out with tongs. Thistle wanted to ask stuck where.

'It will heal,' said Dennis.

The middle sister Audra came back from the neighbour's house and they had sausages and bread with butter for tea, and sometime after that her father went away and it was forever but Thistle stayed in that house for as long as she could, until her mother was lying strapped in a hospital bed, her beakish nose lifted to the ceiling and arms ribboned with scratches. Her life was leaking out and it was a joyous thing to stand over her and see her on her way. Clap her to the abyss with love from the double-skinned daughter.

Going to church and singing always made Thistle remember her mother but the readings about forgiveness were the only ones she refused to amen. She sat in the car and looked out the window, her fingers curling in her lap.

OLIVE AND SEBASTIAN circled the house a few times, steering clear of Shaggy on the end of his chain. They checked the bacon but there was still no sign of the lizard. Olive worked hard at keeping occupied, rehearsing her various movements and skills. How to walk along the line of rocks that edged the driveway without over-balancing. How to climb the peppercorn using only her strongest arm and then doing it again using her other arm. How high she could jump and how low she could do the limbo, using a stick they found by the shed. Sebastian said 'not really' almost all the times she asked whether he wanted to join in. They got apples and went to the pines along the drive and climbed one to keep a lookout for Archie. They took turns with the binoculars, watching for cars on the road in the distance, and observed William doing something around the shed, Rue at the side of the house, running the hose out of the bathroom window to the hydrangeas.

'Let's go down and check for yabber bubbles,' Olive said and Sebastian agreed to that so they climbed to the ground just as Audra and Thistle drove past. They bobbed behind the tree. Car doors slammed and Audra walked to the house, not waiting for her sister, who followed behind with her head set at a funny angle.

'She's mad about something,' Olive said, and wiped her fingers across the tops of the grasses that lined the base of the tree. There was a ripeness in the air that matched the thick line of clouds across the horizon.

'Forget it, you're not a psychic,' Sebastian said and karate-chopped the grass.

Olive stood and watched her mother and aunt go into the house, her fingers moving across the grass. It had a pretty name, Thistle had told her: *danthonia*. She had been calling it wheat grass but her aunt told her it wasn't wheat, just like the white butterflies in summer weren't really butterflies but a type of moth. The only moths Olive knew were dust-brown and thick-winged, but these white butterflies were so small and pretty she'd insisted they had to be butterflies. Thistle corrected her—*cabbage moths*, she said—but Olive ignored her. They definitely were butterflies, she said, and Thistle had given in with her hands in the air, saying, 'I can only try to teach you something, I can't force you to listen.'

•

Later in the afternoon Thistle set up at the card table on the verandah. She looked over at Olive, who was sitting at the end of the couch picking at her toes.

'Olya. Come.'

Olive didn't like the name but went and sat beside her aunt who started to sort out the straight-edged pieces of the puzzle into two piles of grouped colours: white and blue. She picked up the lid and studied the scene. It was a mountain covered in snow with a sky background and small wispy clouds.

'It's the Matterhorn,' Thistle said. She was organising the darker pieces now—browns and blacks—all the straight-edged pieces that would form the bottom of the picture.

'In the Alps, along the line between Switzerland and Italy. People say they are two countries that could not be more unalike. One that professes neutrality and the other a nation of corrupt war-joiners.

But I'll let you in on a secret. At least one is open about it. Don't be a denier, Olive.'

Olive promised that she wouldn't even though she didn't really understand what her aunt was saying.

'Good. Now. Speaking of wars, how is your Lovelorn Lieutenant?' Thistle turned over some puzzle pieces.

'What?'

'That Peter.'

'He's not my—what was it?'

'Will you marry him one day?'

'I'm never going to get married.'

'Very good. One shouldn't marry and not just because it's dull.'

Thistle quickly started putting pieces together to make a section of the bottom frame, the foundation upon which all else would be built. She was a fundamentalist when it came to her religion and her jigsaws. She believed in an angry punishing God and pooh-poohed all that soft Jesus poppycock. The book said that people were small gods filled with the power of the Almighty and able to enact their own lives, dispense wisdom and justice. What people loved in others, they loved in themselves. What they feared and hated too. It was the simplest of truths but sometimes she wondered if she were the only woman on earth who could see it. She held up the box cover, studying the scene.

'How come you're not married?'

'My bird and I, we disagreed.'

Olive reached out a finger to the pile of blue.

'Bird is avis,' she murmured.

'Clegworth is a fool with that Latin nonsense, you children shouldn't listen to him. That gesture he does with his tongue, it's so déclassé.'

'But didn't you want any kids?'

Thistle leaned to the side, brought her mouth close to Olive's ear. 'They tried to come but could never break through. In the end, they were just gas and air.'

'Gas?'

'There was one stone baby but mostly they were gas. It might have been the mother wound that did it.'

'What?'

Just then, Rue came out of the house, her white golf shoes pliant on the wood. They were ugly shoes with their removable top tassel and basket weave sides.

'Audra and I are going for a game with Mavis.' She snapped the press studs on her gloves. 'What are you two doing?'

'I'm helping Aunty Thistle.'

'Clear as day, Rue, what we're doing. And I'm telling Olive about the stone baby.'

On the verandah, Rue hesitated. Her fingers worked at her belt. She was uncertain, standing there in her cream culottes, her slim-fit collared t-shirt in orchid. Rue asked her niece if she wanted to come to the club. She could sit inside and have a Sprite and Mr Spooner would be happy to keep an eye on her. She could read a book.

Before Olive could say yes, that she did want to go, Thistle said she needed help because she was at a difficult part.

'And you know how the beginning makes me nervous, how the anxiety stings.'

Rue stood still. 'Don't fill her head with your mumbo-jumbo, Thistle. Please.' The last word was soft and unexpected to all of them.

'Oh, I shan't.' Thistle flipped over some puzzle pieces.

Rue went back inside, her legs pushing at the fabric of her culottes, kicking the pleats. To Olive, even her legs seemed cross. Thistle looked at the closed door for a long while and then they both went back to the puzzle.

•

Audra was waiting in the sunroom but Rue unsnapped her gloves and took them off.

'What is it?' Audra said through the door.

'Nothing. I remembered I have to do these few dishes. I'll be quick.'

Audra sat down to wait.

Rue did the dishes and set them to dry in the rack. She went to get her bag and Audra walked ahead to the car. Rue was always late, often forgetting things, and the longer it took her sister to appear, the more maddening it was for Rue. Finally, the door opened and Rue got in the car, apologising. They didn't speak, other than Rue asking herself and confirming that the hose was off. She started to say that she must remember to give the roses a good soak tomorrow morning before the heat set in, that the show was soon and she needed some perfect stems to enter, but she caught herself and stopped before she said it. She held it as long as she could then let it go. 'I thought I had a chance for the blue ribbon this year. Thistle can be so cruel and unthinking sometimes.'

'Mmm, yairs,' Audra said, and turned her head left.

•

Thistle considered the closed door through which her sister had passed. Where was the gratitude due her? All that she had done and it was a lot.

'No,' she said, turning a puzzle piece over and fingering the arc of the tab, moving her little finger into the slot. 'I've always thought of these parts as slots and bubbles but did you know some people call these parts male and female? Makes sense, I think.' She connected it to another piece. 'But no. No. The mother wound is not on the outside of your body. It's mostly inside where you can't really see it at all.'

'Like my—' Olive was embarrassed '—hole?'

'No, that's just where they put the stuffing in at the factory.'

Thistle went back to the puzzle. She formed a section of sky across the top stretch, getting all the straight edges done, completing the frame and leaving the interior ready to be filled in. This was a girl deserving of protection. And yet. 'It's not the beginning that's the hardest part, no that was a jolly fib to make that sister leave us.' Thistle picked up another piece and scanned. 'Come on,' she said. 'You're here to help.'

Olive picked up a piece. Thistle was the person to ask when something was bothering her. She was the only one who explained what was wrong with the beetle. Olive had found the creature one day—electric and green—and carried it in her hands to her aunt and asked for a matchbox. They'd put it in and she'd listened for the rest of the day to the scratching noise coming from inside. Whenever she slid the box open, the beetle had been moving, its legs rowing against the cardboard, but by the next morning when she peeked, it had gone still.

'It is dead,' Thistle had confirmed. 'Everything dies and once that happens it's forever.'

But the beetle didn't look dead so Olive kept it in the matchbox to show people so they could see how polished its nacreous casing was, how bright and beautiful. That even though it was dead it was still important. That time Thistle had been the only one to answer her questions but eventually she had to go to a special doctor because she was asking too much about the things they didn't want her to. She couldn't remember anything really about those visits other than that the doctor had eyes that made him look sleepy.

Olive turned a puzzle piece around in her fingers.

'Do you know if there was ever a baby in my family?'

Thistle worked on the frame, head bent over.

'One that died?'

'Who told you that?'

'Nobody, just someone.'

Thistle looked out to the garden. In her hand, she held a piece of mountain.

'Well, Olive, I'm not going to lie to you, as you know. I have always thought that it is better to know when you are being lied to. It's important that we turn and face the mendicants, and show them that we know. Has your mother told you anything?'

'Not really.'

'No surprises there. Unlike my sisters and their fool-men husbands I believe in truth being heard. I said as much in the play.'

Olive tried to remember what Thistle had said in the play and couldn't.

'Did the baby have red hair?'

Thistle bent to her puzzle pieces. She searched for another piece to put along the edge. She did the side and the bottom part of the frame, hands working fast. It was natural the child would be confused but this was the moment, the moment. This girl was not of her, not from her, but thefted still.

'You had a sister. She died when she was a baby.'

The car was coming along the side of the house. Olive kept her face on her aunt but her side sight registered the car, moving slowly. Rue always inched off the property in case a child darted out from around a corner. She said she would never forgive herself if she was responsible for the death or injury of one of the children. Sometimes the boys would run beside the vehicle, tapping on the window and laughing, which made their mother flap her hands at them, her mouth forming a silent yawp behind the glass. Then the boys would laugh and tap even more.

Thistle sat, her hand hovering over a piece. She picked up a long hair that had blown onto the jigsaw puzzle. Holding it in her fingers, she showed it to Olive.

'Do you know how thin the line is between heaven and hell? See how fine it is, how we are so close to both.'

The hair floated until Thistle let go of the strand and the air took it away. She looked at Olive. Good on her, the sturdy rabbit, trying to control her face, her physiognomy crumpled, the fresh trust of a minute ago vanished. She had to know about it sooner or later and if Thistle left it to her sister, to either of them, this moment may never come and the girl would grow up blighted and ignorant. She did not want another girl in the family to grow up like that. Certainly not this one, her understudy, a girl only now beginning to step out of the hallucinatory world of middle childhood.

'I don't get it,' Olive said.

The station wagon was moving into the distance, the back of it aflame with the reflected sun. It had passed the ant-bacon, the side of the house, the beginning of the verandah rail, the front garden beds, the first of Lenore's pines straight in their row. It had passed all of those known things, the places where she could have run after and caught it to knock on the door yelling that she wanted to go with them, that she did want to sit at the club and have a Sprite and read her book. She did not want to hear any of these things on the verandah but it was too late now because she had asked the question and it was a mistake.

'Yes. Red hair. You had a baby sister and her name was Aster and she drowned. They should have talked about it, I told them not to complain to me about it later, when you became an angry teenager, possibly going "off the rails". But you've come to me, you have, and that's a good thing.' Thistle's voice was singsong and Olive's ribs sucked inwards. 'We need to do the sky now.'

'Aster?'

'That's right. Sweet but what a noise-maker—howled constantly. Water soothed her, but you can't keep a child in the bath all the day long.'

Olive helped her aunt put more pieces of blue into the frame. There was one piece she was sure fitted but she tried it every possible way and in the end it wasn't right. She put it back on the pile.

'How did she get in the water and drown?'

'Someone put her in but it wasn't their fault. Do you understand what I'm saying, Olya?'

'Not really.'

'I'm saying they didn't mean to. It was an accident.'

Olive saw the dryness of her aunt's skin, the dandruff along her sketchy hairline. They all knew about Thistle's little bald patch and how in the middle of the thinning hair was a raised red spot like an especially non-delicious raspberry.

She wanted to go inside the house but couldn't move.

'I think the person meant to hurt Astra.'

'Sometimes it can be painful and it can embarrass us if we are thinking one thing, because to be wrong is very hard. Do you understand?'

'No,' Olive said, even though she probably did.

'An example is you thinking you were in the dam during the big fire.'

'But I was.'

'We only had Sebastian, you weren't born until the next year. You need to learn about oscillation, Olive. It's an important part of growing up.' Thistle placed another jigsaw piece. 'Disaster is like a grey smoke cat and wherever it settles, that's the spot for trouble. The doctor gave Audra medicine and told her not to have another baby for at least a year. There were plenty of baths but no more babies for her, for her. One tried to come but she lost it in the lavatory in a clump of jelly.'

Olive looked at her aunt.

'All those headaches and complaints. Such an Olga.' Thistle was slowing, her eyes looked sleepy now. She would have a nap soon. 'A queer woman, she always found things a struggle, wanted to sleep too much. Gave thee life and bid thee feed, but after you were born do you think we could get that woman out of bed? Odd behaviour, even then. So-called migraines.' Thistle hummed. 'Stepping on snails after rain when she was little.'

'The Sands brothers have smoke around them,' Olive said. 'They hurt animals and sometimes people.'

'Most of that is just braggadocio. Talking about a girl's body parts as if they are somehow separate to a person who might have feelings. The girl ceases to matter, just holes.' Thistle's voice trailed away. 'People don't like it when a girl is strong and while we think it's men who try to control us it's the mothers mostly.'

There were ants on the railing. A linear stream of movement and purpose. Insects, sisters, nieces. On one level, they were all the same.

'There's nothing so powerless as a girl child and what are women but former little girls grown up? Which is why we have to enact and reach. You are crossing over shortly, better to be equipped.'

'I have to go to the toilet now.'

'Alright, dear, you go ahead.'

Olive went inside but in the hallway, she stopped. There were two things in her head. One was the word SISTER repeating in a scroll like on the movies. The other was an awareness, something that was the width of a single red hair.

OLIVE WAS IN the peppercorn but her mind was higher still, wedged in the crook of a limb at the top. She hung on, ignoring the bird that walked from her knee to branch and back again. She was trying to remember. She'd always been the one with the good memory. At parties, playing the memory game, it was Olive who recalled everything on the tray once the tea towel was put back over the spoon, the clothes peg, the safety pin, the salt shaker, the playing card, the newspaper, the nail scissors, the toothpick, the packet of jelly, the golf ball, the lipstick, the shower cap and the tea strainer. She was so good at it the other kids said it wasn't fair, that she shouldn't be allowed to join in. That she had cheated. But she never cheated. She didn't need to because she was a girl of magnificent brain. She could remember what she got for Christmas the year before. She could remember too that they had been mad about anything to do with tennis balls back then and rode the streets of Stratford looking for a good brick wall to play against. The year before that she got a bee sting on Boxing Day and Rue had scraped it out with a knife and put a wet, blue bag on it. And the year before *that* she'd been recovering from chicken pox at Easter time, and Rue kept telling her off for scratching her itchy scalp as she sat in front of the television. But before that, she couldn't remember anything of what Thistle had talked about.

'Go away,' she said to Grace. 'Leave me alone.'

'*Kark*,' said Grace.

She wrapped herself around the branch. Sebastian pulled at small berries and started to line them up in strands, arranging the pile of peppercorns in the crook of the branch.

'I asked Thistle. About the baby.'

It was as if he hadn't heard her. He seemed happy for once, probably because Christmas was coming. He wanted a model plane and some sort of science toy that he would do real experiments with, using real chemicals. He'd told Olive he thought he had a good chance of receiving both.

Olive stood up, balancing on the branch, arms aloft.

'Seb?'

'What?' He raked his head up.

'Did you hear what I said?'

'Leave me alone.' He went back to the peppercorns.

Olive swung out, over the ground. If she let go and dropped, her legs would splinter and break. Part of her wanted to do it.

'Do you want to get the bikes?'

He shook his head.

'Go to the dam?'

'Nup.'

'We could look at the guns?'

'You hate guns.'

'*No* I don't.'

'Yeah, you do.' He stopped throwing the leaves. 'Remember? When we went rabbit shooting? Remember that? You're such a hypocrite.'

'I am not.'

She held on to the trunk of the tree. It was true. There'd been the night William had taken them spotlight shooting. She'd known that rabbits would get shot but she hadn't known how she would feel about it.

They'd dressed in their warmest clothes because it was August. A short drive with the three children squeezed along the seat and they'd arrived at a place where William said there would be lots of rabbits. He turned off the headlights and they got out. He told them in a low voice to keep quiet. He'd left the inside cab light on so they could see the guns. William handed one across to Sebastian and took one out for himself. The guns were long and black in the night. William reached into the back for the box of bullets.

'What about me?' said Olive.

William started to object.

'Why can't I have one?' she said. 'I'm not going to just *watch*.'

'Alright then,' said William. He plopped the long thing across her outstretched arms. 'Not loaded yet. None of them are loaded but you hold them like they *are*. Got it?'

'Roger,' said Sebastian, saluting and snapping his heels, then sidestepping the cuffing that shot out.

'Don't be a smart-arse, Seb,' said his father. 'Smart-arse and guns don't mix. I'm bloody serious.'

'Sorry, Dad. Sorry.'

William said that Archie would aim the spotlight and the three of them would do the shooting. They all had to be careful to stay in line with the car, just in front and not to the side, and no one was to change their angle. They had to stay inside the dark zone and let the light be out in front. That's where the rabbits would be. When he counted to three Archie would turn on the spot and they would get as many as they could. He told Olive and Sebastian to aim for the ones closest and he would go for the ones at the back. They had to be quick because while the rabbits would stay still for a bit, staring at the light, eventually they would run. Olive listened. She nodded. She could work out what to do. She had shot at cans.

She was used to the motion of the gun and the sound. She wasn't an idiot.

She saw William was lifting a hand and he said the numbers. Archie flicked on the lights and she turned back. In front and to the sides of the ute were what seemed like hundreds of rabbits. Big ones and small ones. Some were sitting upright like in Beatrix Potter, their bobbled black eyes on the sides of their heads. Others were hunched as if shocked into a state of coldness and these were mostly the babies. Olive did not expect babies.

'I'm not shooting babies,' she shouted.

'They grow up, girl, into big bastard bunnies,' William called from behind them. 'We have to kill them as well.'

Sebastian shot three rabbits by the time Olive said she wanted to go back. William made Archie turn the lights off and then came over to her.

'You didn't even load my gun,' she said.

He took it and put it in the back of the ute. Sebastian was kicking dirt with his shoes.

She turned to William. 'Do the mothers ever try and protect them?'

'What?'

She said it again.

'Look. I'll stay here with Archibald. Unload, son.'

'*Dad,*' Sebastian moaned.

'*Unload* I said, and put your gun in the back. *Now.*'

Sebastian did as he was told.

'You go back with her.' William cracked one of the guns open. 'Off you go.'

Sebastian and Olive walked to the house. Above them the moon sat behind thick clouds. Sebastian hadn't said a word to her all the way home.

Olive sat down again in the tree.

'Maybe when Dad gets back, we could get him to show us the guns. Maybe,' Sebastian said.

'Where are they?'

'He's gone with your dad and Cleg into town. Probably to get more beer, knowing them.' Sebastian made a scoffing noise. He hated his father drinking.

'Not the fathers, stupid—the guns.'

'Don't call me stupid.' His fingers worked at the peppercorns. 'He keeps them locked in a cupboard in the shed.'

'Know where the keys are?'

He said that he did and twisted another sprig.

'Let's have a look ourselves, we'll be careful.' She began to climb down, dropped the last little way and landed in a crouch, knees bent and fingers spread on the grass.

'Like a cat,' she said to herself.

'No, Ol,' Sebastian shouted. 'He said never to.'

'What about the ute? I know where those keys are.'

She was already running to the house. By the time he caught up, Archie was there too, hollering about how he could never find them and why were they always hiding from him. Olive was coming back out the door and held the keys up to them. Sebastian followed.

'I'm driving,' he said, meeting her at the car. He gripped the steering wheel through the open window.

'No, you already know how but I need more practice.' She was at the window, her hair swinging over her eyebrows as she tapped her finger on the open window. 'I'm doing it.'

He opened the driver's door and tried to push in beside her but she pushed too, edging her bottom onto the seat. There was a scramble as he reached for the wheel again but she managed to get her feet up into his stomach and shove him back out of the car. He sprang back.

'You don't know how to do the gears,' he said, grabbing the wheel again. 'Not properly.'

'I do know. God.'

She peeled his fingers off and he saw the white lines of spittle on her lips and that her skin was shiny and splotched with purple. He let go and said 'flock' under his breath, then went around to the passenger side and got in. She slid forwards on the seat.

'Just don't kill us,' Sebastian said. He clicked his seatbelt and crossed his arms.

'I'm almost as good as you.'

'I don't think so.'

There was a sound at the back and it was Archie climbing into the tray, tapping on the glass window behind them. He had dirt under one ear and down the side of his neck. His tongue worked one of his lateral incisors, making it ratchet back and forth in its gummy bed.

'Let's go before Mandy comes,' he shouted, and twisted to look back at the house. 'What a pain, right?'

There was a face at the window. It was Mandy, holding a puppet.

'I'm tellin' on youse.'

'Nick off.' Sebastian leaned across Olive. 'If you tell, a dingo'll get you. And don't say *youse* or I'll tell Mum.'

Mandy retreated to the clothesline to watch.

Olive had a little trouble getting the key in the right way and then held her breath while she turned the ignition. The car lurched forwards.

'You gotta put it in neutral!' Sebastian shouted, triumphant. 'Don't you know anything? Jeez.'

'Shut up, let me think,' said Olive. She moved right to the edge of the bench seat and pushed in the clutch, then moved the gears a bit. 'You're putting me off.'

After several tries to get the car moving, and stalling three times, and with Sebastian becoming increasingly pleased, Olive let go of the wheel and leaned back.

Sebastian reached over, and they tussled over the gearstick. She pumped the accelerator and started the car then slowly tried to let the clutch out. The car stalled once more. She pumped the accelerator again, batting Sebastian's hand away.

'You're gonna flood it. You don't even know what you're doing.'

She got the car going and it started to move, then jerked forwards, the heavy heads of the long grass slapping the metal doors. She could hear Archie laughing in the back, and then she thought of her mother's sadness and her foot went down and it was like she went into a trance. Sebastian yelled, telling her to turn, and she got confused and pushed the accelerator by mistake and the car increased speed. She panicked and pushed down harder and she turned the wheel to steer away from the fence that was coming at them in a rush. Too late she realised she hadn't put her seatbelt on. She took her feet off the pedals and let go of the wheel and the car slowed down in the long grass and juddered into a stall. Archie was bouncing up and down and clapping, his feet thumping on the base of the tray.

'Fruit, Ol. You almost crashed.' Sebastian got out of the car.

'I didn't, nowhere near. You put me off.' She walked back to the house, tasting blood. She would never make that mistake again. She turned and looked around. Sebastian was reversing the car in a half-circle to get it back to where it had been.

At the door, Mandy was sucking her thumb and Olive pushed past her, reminding her that everyone hated dibber-dobbers.

When Sebastian came in a few minutes later she was sitting in the kitchen. He went to the fridge to get the milk.

'You were pretty scared.'

'What's w-wrong with you?' He swung around.

'Hey, S-Seb. You gonna s-start that again?'

He ran over and pushed her and she pushed back and then they were on the kitchen floor, pulling each other's hair. She tried to bite his leg but he managed to lock her head in place with his knees, gripping her ears so tightly they stung. If an adult had come in and called them animals, Olive wouldn't have been surprised, in fact she was expecting it to happen soon. But no adult did appear, there was only Mandy, standing at the doorway with her fingers at her mouth, and Archie was there too, saying, 'Go, Ollie.' Eventually, the two of them fell apart, exhausted, Sebastian gulping while she lay on her back, put her hands behind her head and smiled hard at the ceiling.

MANDY TOLD OF course. William roared at Sebastian and sent him to his room until dinner but Audra waited, and Olive waited too, and now was the moment as they sat side by side on the verandah, in the late afternoon.

Her mother began. She talked about responsibility and respect, about taking care with physical safety, especially if others were involved. Olive watched Rue in the garden.

'Mum,' she said, as soon as her mother had finished, 'why didn't you have another baby?'

Audra half turned her head. There were subtle lines on her face, her skin shaded by the fly-netting on her hat and faint colours that rested there—lilacs and mauves. 'Why is it just me?'

'It's quite rude to ask that.'

In the front garden Rue was bending and straightening with her hands on her hips, shaking her head. Olive felt a separation from her body as if she was a puppet in Mandy's homemade theatre. There was a hand up the back of her clothes, moving her arms and making her talk. Maybe it was rude but she wanted to know.

Audra brushed away an invisible fly. Olive ran her finger along the edge of the couch cushion and the seam went under her nail. Her mother took a long time to speak.

'No other babies came.' She kept looking at her magazine.

She'll say something about God now, Olive thought.

'It's God who decides when a baby is born, and when they come they need to be taken care of. It's a lot of work to keep them safe, but—' and here Olive felt her mother look at her '—if they don't stay safe, sometimes it's nobody's fault. Accidents and the like.'

She thought about what her mother was revealing to her. There it was. *God* didn't think it was safe to send another baby to her family. Her mother was giving her a message about what happened to her sister, a kind of code. 'Babies need a lot of care,' her mother was saying, but Olive didn't hear her properly. All she knew was that the stream of water coming out of Rue's metal can was as clear as what her mother was saying. She saw the row of bushes her aunt had just clipped, how straight they were. Clear and straight.

Audra went back to her magazine and Olive saw the skin inside her mother's ear, pink and clean.

'Mum?'

Audra raised her hand to the bridge of her nose and rested it there. It was the smallest movement but it said a lot.

Olive got up. 'I'm going inside now for the punishment.'

'Good girl.'

She was careful not to let the screen door slam behind her. She walked past the kitchen, down the hall and into the bedroom. There was the hum of the washing machine spinning the clothes and Mandy crying outside and, behind all of that, the faint sound of heavy furniture being dragged across wooden floors.

IT HAD ALWAYS been Rue she'd run to when William threw a dead lamb into the incinerator behind the shed, or she skinned her knee so badly the blood dripped down her shin. She would climb dry-eyed onto her aunt's lap to have her back scratched for a quick minute. It was a furtive thing they'd shared, this offering and receipt of comfort.

Olive knew Rue would put an arm around her if she sidled up and leaned into her hip with a sly question about a sister but her aunt wasn't one to talk to about things other than suncream and biscuits. Thistle was the one who explained how ants breathed, how birds made babies and how butter came from milk. Thistle could say how old stars were but Olive knew Thistle had told her all she would.

She had thought happiness was to be found at the farm. All the weeks and years as if she'd lived there, grazing it with her finger-tips, able to forget herself and her mother's dark glow. When they'd been little, William and Rue had let their children come in their room on Sunday mornings to bounce and snuggle on the bed, and Olive would be welcomed along with her cousins, even though Sebastian would give her a bit of a look. He didn't like sharing his parents, which she understood because she had her own. It wasn't as if she was an orphan or anything melodramatic like that.

'Why are you always here, anyway?' Sebastian had shouted at her once. They'd been walking along the driveway, dragging their feet to make dust clouds on their way to the dam. He had made a net from a pole, some wire and a pair of his mother's old stockings, and she had told him he wouldn't catch any yabbies with such a stupid-looking net. He told her to rack off and she pushed him so he tripped and fell across the line of stones that edged the driveway. She didn't know what to say. She didn't know why she was always there, why sometimes she was there even when her parents weren't. She was brought and taken and had no say about any of it.

'Get your things, Olive, we're leaving,' or, 'You'll be here a few days, I don't know how long exactly,' her mother would say.

'Why don't we ever stay at your house?' Archie bleated one time.

'Are you my sister?' Mandy had asked another.

She floated between the two houses and each set of parents as if they were essentially interchangeable and it had always been so.

•

After her punishment, she went to find Rue in the rose garden. Rue stood with the hose in hand watering the nubbed stems, all the colour stripped from her plants. She had been there for a while as there were puddles all around on the ground. Olive positioned herself in front of her aunt.

'I want you to tell me,' Olive said. 'About the baby.'

Rue put a hand to her throat.

'Can you say what happened to her?'

'Go and turn the hose off for me.'

Olive did and by the time she got back Rue was moving on the other side of the bushes.

'Can you tell me?'

Through the gap Rue waved her secateurs and said it was not her story to tell. That there was nothing *to* tell. She fumbled for a moment at her belt, tucking in the sharp blades. She pulled on her gardening gloves and said she wasn't able to get into the *specifics* of it.

'But do you know?' Olive said. 'Do you know what happened?'

Rue shook her head as if testing for coins in a money box, checking the weight of what was in there.

'Your mother always tries to do the right thing. So much so it could be capitalised, the importance she puts on it. Sending RSVPs in that formal third-person style. Taking fruit to visit someone in hospital.'

Rue walked down the row, reaching out a hand to her decimated bushes as she went. She bent and coldly took hold of the base of one of the bushes. She started to tug. It didn't move so she pushed and pulled it in the garden bed until it levered its way free. She lifted it, shook the wet dirt from the roots, lifted it over her head and tossed it to the side with a grunt. Rue was stronger than she looked.

'Our mother was tough on the three of us but hardest of all on Thistle.' Rue moved to the next bush and started to do the same.

'What are you doing?'

'What?' Rue turned. '*What?*'

Olive took a step back.

'Nothing. But why was she so mean to Thistle?'

'What are you talking about?'

Rue took her secateurs and started snipping at leaves and slender twigs, her hands blurred. She stopped, tucked the clippers away again and grabbed another bush. She rocked it back and forth and pulled. It lifted out of the mud.

'I want to know.' Olive's hands were sweaty. 'I want you to tell me what happened to my sister.'

'I really don't think we should be talking about this.' Rue kept her back to Olive as she worked.

'Did Thistle ever come to our place? To help when Mum had me or Aster?'

'Oh.' Rue stopped. 'Thistle doesn't "help". Listen to me. I think you should go back into the house, or go and play with the others.'

'But—'

'No buts. Enough. I've had it, with all of you. Just go and find something to do.'

Rue held herself for a moment before she whirled and started kicking at a rosebush, her rubber-soled lace-ups hefty against the trunk. She grabbed her secateurs again and took all the leaves off a bush and there was a noise that she was making, a kind of shrill buzzing sound.

Olive stopped at the corner of the house and looked back. Rue was wiping at her eyes with the backs of her wrists. She glanced up, saw Olive watching and waved her away.

At the back door, Grace flew down to deposit a small yellow piece of plastic at Olive's feet. Olive bent and picked it up. She put it in her pocket and went into the house.

OLIVE WAS LYING on the floor in the Green Room. It was on the shady side of the house and the walls were myrtle-green with old-fashioned wood panelling like they had at the town hall.

She'd been there for over twenty minutes, looking at one of Lenore's diaries. Lenore was the woman from the big painting, the lady with the lace collar and wide jaw. The writing in the diaries was hard to read and no matter how Olive squinted, it seemed only Thistle could interpret the old-fashioned letters that flourished into words on the small beige pages. Thistle had told Olive about Lenore and her husband Edgar, that the Lovelock family had been in Stratford since even before the 1900s. It was hard country, Thistle said. A wide and sandy land that produced quiet men and tough women.

'And we are those tough women,' she said often, when they were reading or doing a puzzle together. 'It's important you remember that.'

It was a place where the olden-day people had somehow managed to scratch out a start with some sheep, or wheat, and where you inherited a stretch of soil, some trees, perhaps a ramshackle house.

Edgar had been sent from England by his family moderately equipped, Thistle said, with funds and a pioneering spirit, both of which were destined to deteriorate over the next two generations. He had arrived in Stratford with his new bride, intent on making a living out of the shelly soil. Just off the bullock dray, though, he'd stood in shock while Lenore marched into their newly built house and shed several layers of weighty Victorian costumery. She reappeared in a pair of her husband's trousers, rolling up her sleeves and suggesting they get to work. She directed him to a shovel saying, 'Come on, Edgar.' She had him dig holes for the moss-wrapped cuttings she'd transported in jars all the way from the city. Some of them were stubby finger-lengths from a Scots pine, and they took well enough to the loamy ground along the driveway to be dropping globate fruit decades later. Another was the peppercorn (*Schinus molle*) whose surface roots would provide sanctuary for the small Olive in decades time.

As she lay on the carpet, Olive's mind kept going to the thing that was in her head, like a tongue returning to a cracked tooth. There was a mystery here, maybe one with clues. She'd decided she was going to work it out, like a detective.

Her mother had said they were going home soon and not to disappear so she hadn't, but they were still there because Rue had decided to get the Christmas decorations out. She said it was time to do the tree and wanted the children to help her.

Her aunts came into the Green Room. Rue—calmed—was carrying a box.

'The decorations.'

She went out again as Thistle settled on the couch, then came back in with a long box and put it on the floor.

'The tree. Are you going to help me? What's wrong with you today?'

Olive said she didn't know. Rue started to open the box.

'Good Lord, what rings under your eyes.'

'I don't feel good.'

'Well,' said Thistle. 'You don't feel *well*. Here, girl.' She held out some tea-packet bird cards, a small fan of three. Olive got up on her hands and knees and went over to get them. Scanning them, she saw there was no King Bird of Paradise (11), Magpie Goose (41) or Eastern Whipbird (64). She lifted them to her nose.

'Doubles?'

Thistle nodded and Olive nodded too and put them in her pocket.

'What's this word say?' She held out the diary to her aunt, her finger marking the place.

'That says "liminal". And do you *ever* wash your hands? Give it here.'

Olive handed the diary over and crawled back to her position on the floor.

'What does it mean?'

'In between. In the middle. One thing was the climate, you see.' Thistle opened the book. 'The extremes. The other, though, was the vegetation. While some of the lichen crusts and winter mosses were familiar, Lenore missed the furze and whinstone of her home country.'

Rue sighed.

'The Mallee flora discombobulated the young Lenore and Edgar,' Thistle said. '*Eddie* she writes here.' Trees that shed their bark through the year, the stark, hostile landscapes with their eerie inter-dune swales and odd heathlands. The hoary frost hollows, Thistle interpreted, reminded Lenore of home, but only when viewed from the periphery. 'She has quite the turn of phrase.' If she turned to study them directly, they were as foreign and bizarre as she imagined another planet might be. It was a landscape both unsettling and hostile, as if border to an infinite void.

'*A distant place where everything is inverse,*' Lenore wrote, and Thistle read aloud now. Rue was opening the boxes. '*The air is constantly awash with particulate matter. Shadows stretch and retract during the day when the sun is at its height but it is at nightfall, when the blinding heat of the day can be subsumed by a dank coldness, that a person feels,*' Thistle read, '*she might be living in two entirely disparate places at the one time and it has a state of liminality that persisted for longer than it might have had we gone to settle elsewhere in the world. There is no gloaming here. I feel I'm constantly walking widdershins.'*

'What a word,' said Thistle, squinting at the tiny writing then closing the diary. '*Widdershins.*'

'Where was she born again?' Olive asked. 'Which island was it?'

'The Shetland Islands,' Thistle said and drew a finger between herself and her niece on the floor. 'Lenore was like you and myself. Quite a spiritualist. A woman of independent inclinations.'

But it wasn't the isolation or oddness of the countryside, or the meaning of smoke in the sky, that most threatened to undo Lenore, Thistle went on. Nor had it been the cycles of war and drought that followed, conditions that made it hard to succeed on the land. No, for Lenore, it was her trouble holding a pregnancy.

'Lots of *stillbirths,*' Thistle said, mouthing the last word, but only because Rue had straightened with hands on hips. Thistle wasn't coy and did not believe in censorship, but her sister could be loud in her objections and boring with her talk of protecting children's sensibilities. 'Yes, she was a tough bird. She would deliver on her own and hand them across—*dead*—to her husband in a wrap of fabric with an apology. Girls I knew just birthed into dirt holes and covered them up, which was not the same as losing them. That was hiding them.' Thistle paused. 'All Lovelock children have battled the cervix to be born and struggled to grow in their own mixed type of soil. Patchy fertilisation up here, you know. "What canna be changed mun be accepted."'

Thistle could be a bit dramatic and Olive lost interest whenever her aunt began to mix her own fairytale narratives in with the diary stories.

Rue straightened with a piece of Christmas tree in her hands.

'Is it the top or the bottom?' she said. 'I really should label it.'

'That's what you say every year,' said Thistle. 'Doesn't she?'

Olive nodded. It was true. It was what Rue said every year.

'Are there lots of ponies on the island?' Olive asked.

'I beg your pardon?' Thistle said. 'Lots of ponies where?'

Olive sat up.

'Was your mum kind?'

Rue went to sit next to Thistle, pressing her fingers into her sister's arm like a cat's paw, nesting and pushing. Outside, the boys shouted in the distance. Rue's fingers moved up and down.

'Why do you ask?'

'Did she give you hugs?'

'Oh. Ours was definitely not a hugger.' Thistle crossed her arms. 'She did not care for my theatrics. We were told it was best for a person to keep their problems to themselves. Reputation. The people and so on. She didn't like my infernal singing either. She called me Babylon.'

Rue laughed and said that wasn't true.

'My plays, my plays, she did not like my plays.'

Olive flipped onto her side. Her stomach was hurting.

'Do you remember?' Thistle said. 'The time Grandfather died and Mother caught us in his room?'

'Were you looking at his things?' Olive liked to look at her dad's toiletries. His razor, his shaving brush sitting squat and upright, the ivory-backed hairbrushes that had no handles and fitted together like twins. His stick deodorant that smelled of him instead of the other way around.

'No, we were looking at him,' Thistle said. 'He was on the bed, in his pyjamas.'

'While he was dead?' Olive thought of her own grandfather, lying in a box. She hadn't seen him dead, hadn't been allowed to go to the funeral because Rue didn't believe children should be present.

'It wasn't only me,' Thistle said. 'My sisters were there as well but they wouldn't even touch him. They were up against the wall, those scaredy-cat sisters in their flower frocks. I remember how soft his eyelids were. Mother came in as I was looking down his pants.' She clapped her hands and they made a boom. 'The sound of the elastic, as it snapped. I can still hear it. Just like that.' She clapped her hands again.

'I think—' Rue began.

'Let me guess. A nice cup of tea and a biscuit.'

Olive listened from the floor. She imagined a mother grabbing three girl children, pulling them out of the room in a clump of skinny legs and floral-print dresses with bows at the back. Rue smiling confusedly, her mother calm with a bobby pin in her hair and Thistle grim and with scabs on her knees.

'It was all such a long time ago, please try to forget, dear. And I *am* going to boil the kettle. We'll do the tree later.'

'I do forget, I'm forgetting all the time but it comes back and when it comes there's no stopping, you don't understand. What it's like. A train.' Thistle's fists moved to bunch on her thighs.

Archie ran in and announced there were some big birds sitting in a tree along the driveway, that they looked like Grace. He ran out.

'That boy is stunted,' Thistle said. 'Am I the only one to notice these things?'

'Can you read the ballad again?' Olive liked it when her aunt read aloud.

Thistle flicked through the diary. 'Is it in this one? Oh yes. Here it is.'

'With the accent?'

'Naturally. *As I was walking all alane*
I heard twa corbies making a mane;

The tane unto the ither say,
"Whar sall we gang and dine the-day?"
"In ahint yon auld fail dyke,
I wot there lies a new slain knight;
And nane do ken that he lies there,
But his hawk, his hound an his lady fair."
"His hound is tae the huntin gane,
His hawk tae fetch the wild-fowl hame,
His lady's tain anither mate,
So we may mak oor dinner swate."
"Ye'll sit on his white hause-bane,
And I'll pike oot his bonny blue een;
Wi ae lock o his gowden hair
We'll theek oor nest whan it grows bare."
"Mony a one for him makes mane,
But nane sall ken whar he is gane;
Oer his white banes, when they are bare,
The wind sall blaw for evermair.'

Olive stretched on the floor after the words ended. She loved the poem. She loved the way you got most of the meaning, how it didn't really matter that she didn't understand all of it exactly. She loved the sounds of the words and she loved the spaces around the sounds, spaces that had meanings of their own. It was a better poem, she and Thistle always agreed, than the other one, the one with the three birds. It wasn't realistic, but apart from that, there was no way they could see that *lacke* and *back* could ever rhyme. But this poem had beauty in it, in the words, even if you didn't understand them.

Olive got to her feet and went to the trees.

•

Archie stood down the driveway under the pines with his head tipped back. The birds were ravens but bigger than Grace, a group of them lined up along a branch, crouched black and thoughtful, their beaks curved into what Thistle said was Roman-style. Olive stood beneath the tree, and in her mind sent each one a message about Grace. She wanted them to leave Grace alone. Not take her away. Now Grace was flying down to the end of the driveway to meet them when they came back from going out on their bikes. How happy it made Olive to see the bird waiting on top of the letterbox with a piece of bright green wool in her beak, or a coloured glass bead from Mandy's broken bracelet, or a twig-tool.

Olive had tried to sleep with Grace at the farm. She'd waited until Mandy was still then gone to the window where Grace waited, eyes glossy behind the glass. She lifted the sash as quietly as she could, neck twisted towards her cousin, checking the rising and falling of her chest, making the gap larger until the bird stepped in and made her small noise. The first time Olive had heard the noise Grace made it had been unexpected and surprising. It sounded like the hard, single knock of a knuckle on a door and seemed to be produced from deep within the bird, from the centre of her. Now whenever she heard it she thought of it as Grace saying 'Hi' in raven. That night, as Mandy slept, Olive took Grace into her bed and got her under the sheet with the torch. Grace was lying down beside her, on her back in the funniest way, feet up in the air and wriggling from side to side to scratch her back when Mandy woke up saying she was thirsty.

'What are you doing?' she said.

'Nothing. Go back to sleep.'

Olive waited but Mandy got up and lifted the sheet anyway.

'I'm telling Mum.' And she had and Olive told her she hated her.

Another time she had smuggled Grace home from Serpentine in a box. She told her mother there were flowers in there, she'd collected them in the garden and was going to press them into books. Her mother hadn't found out for several hours and it had been a blissful time, together in her own room, showing Grace all her things. Grace had sat on her windowsill and gently moved the wishbones with her beak. Then she had looked out into the McCullers backyard for a while. She walked across her blanket and rested her head on the pillow. Olive had brought a shallow dish of water and put it under her bed, along with some newspaper that she hoped Grace would do her messes on. She made a small nest under there too with one of her old windcheaters, preferring though that the bird would sleep with her, maybe she would, she really hoped so. Grace could lie on her pillow, beside her head, and they could look each other in the eyes until they fell asleep. In the morning, she would continue to teach Grace the words she'd been learning: *Hello. Love. I* and *You.*

Thistle had told her: Grace is a wild animal and she is choosing to be with you. Even though she is free and can go where she likes, she is choosing you. So Olive had decided she wanted to give Grace something back. She had decided to give her words.

She'd crept downstairs to get some minced meat from the fridge, reshaping the ball in the white paper packet so that her mother wouldn't realise any was missing. And she played soft music on her clock radio to cover the sounds of them chatting. But it was the music that made Grace become louder and louder. She sang and made her cawing and even though Olive switched off the radio and tried to shush Grace, Audra came. She just opened the door without knocking and found them on the bed, Grace lying on her back in the crook of Olive's arm wrapped in a tea towel, relaxed as a baby after a feed. Olive was brushing her feathers with a toothbrush. In that moment, before the door opened, Olive had never been happier, but the door did open and Audra raised her hands in the air and said for Olive to come on, put the bird in the box, they were taking her back to the farm.

And so, even though it was half past nine at night, Audra drove Olive and Grace back to Serpentine. Olive begged all the way for Grace to stay just one night but her mother stayed very cold. It would have been easy for her mother to say yes. It wouldn't have been hard at all. She had begged and begged but still her mother had said no.

For the first time that night, with the cool beak against her cheek and the little murmur Grace made in her throat when she was stroked on the head, like a gentle cough, Olive had let herself imagine what it might have been like not to be the only kid at her house. Grace was everything she wanted in a companion. Constant. Fleet. Smart. Funny.

Olive and Archie went back to the house, the ravens behind them making their chorus of *ark ark aaaarrrrrks*, the wavering tail end of the call dropping away behind them as they ran. Archie was begging her to play a game of Around the World. She said no, said no again, then finally she said yes and they played.

Around the World goes like this: The house is a boat going to America and everything else is ocean and the goal of it all is circumnavigation of the house. You have to keep your feet off the ground. If you step down you drown and there is no coming back to life (until you play again, and it has to be another day, it can't be the same day, no one was quite sure why).

After fifteen minutes of playing, Olive was at the side of the house with one foot precarious on the garden tap and trying not to step on the block of hand soap wedged there. Her front foot stretched across the weatherboards as it sought purchase on a jutting piece of board where the wooden slats joined unevenly. 'The joining of the house,' they called it—the centre line—but Rue called it a mistake. 'It was meant to be less obvious than that,' she said. 'The builders didn't match it properly. It was supposed to be exactly in the middle but it's slightly off.'

Olive hovered in virtual splits and Rue appeared to run the bathwater out of the window to the garden. She saw Olive clinging to the sill and her exclamation of surprise made Olive drop to the ground.

'You seem to be feeling better.' Rue bent to the hose end on the ground. 'Oh, look what you've done. I wish you'd keep your feet away from the soap, you've made it dirty, see? I've got the tree up and we'll do the decorations in a minute. Isn't anyone going to help?'

Olive said she didn't know.

'Well, never mind,' said Rue. 'You'll be going home after dinner, it's school tomorrow, and only two more weeks until Christmas. Isn't that nice?'

Olive said yes and walked around to the back of the house.

AT DINNER MANDY said she was counting the sleeps and Archie said she couldn't count that high. Mandy said she was going to start school next year and Sebastian said not to expect too much. Olive thought of the dam and how still it had been below. How it was strange that the places and people that were meant to make you feel comfortable could become altered in no time at all.

Rue started to clear the plates, walking from table to kitchen and back again. She told Olive she had to finish her dinner before they could leave because her parents were tired and just wanted to get home. Olive wondered why they didn't leave earlier, why they came in the first place. Why it was that the words adults said so often didn't match what they did.

Once she'd eaten all her dinner she was allowed to leave the table and go and put her things in her bag. She got in the back of the car and waited for her parents to finish their goodbyes. She wondered if this was how Lenore and Edgar had felt, far away from their home in such a strange place with everything turned upside down. In the back of the car she looked at her hands. The nails were bitten and the skin around her thumbs pulled.

In her own bed the thoughts came, her mind turning and holding and turning again. When she slept, it was not for long. During the night, she woke to find herself standing outside the house, the doormat scratchy under her bare feet, the moon coming up over the next-door neighbour's roof. Behind her the door was wide open. She stood there awhile looking into the front yard, at the fence and the moon, at the seam of light above the silver ash tree. Then she took herself back to bed, walking on her tiptoes through the house.

AT HOME, THE house filled with commonplace tension. The air was sucked out as a tide pulls back from the beach and Olive was left as a solitary crab scuttering on the sand. She woke up on the Monday for the second last week of school. In the quiescent house she made her lunch as usual. Vegemite sandwiches, sultanas in a twist of paper, an apple, two bear biscuits and a crooked slab of cheese with the silver foil still on it. From the back of the class she concentrated on what Mrs Barton said as well as she could but the activities were stupid. Making paper lanterns, eggshell mosaics and Christmas cards to give to classmates.

On the Tuesday, she sat on the edge of the playground, fiddling with small stones and bits of tanbark and thought about centaurs and what it would be like to be half girl, half horse. She also thought about what it would be like to be a boy, but mostly she kept coming back to what dead felt like. When Peter came up to her she told him to go away.

On the Wednesday, something bad happened. She'd leaned on the shoulder of the pretty sports teacher at lunchtime, like the other kids had been doing. Snooky Sands was there as well, on the other side of the teacher, who was short and young, and she had put her arm on a shoulder and it had been okay. The teacher had smiled at Snooky Sands and was signing autograph books because the year was finishing. When a shoulder was free, Olive took a turn to lean and the teacher got cross at her.

'Don't do that,' she said, shrugging Olive off.

Olive felt her face go red but she stood in the group of children surrounding the teacher until the bell went. She walked back into class with the rest of them.

In the afternoons, she went home and wandered the house or garden, reciting Latin under her breath. She sat against the fence listening to the neighbours talking next door. She squatted near the incinerator and hummed and picked at the flaking rust, noticing how the sun filtered through the top of the high bush next door to throw splotches of creamy light on her bare feet. She missed the sound of her cousins' voices, the way they layered on top of each other. How Archie's runners made small piffing sounds as he crept around underneath the trees, peering upwards, looking for her, his eyes not catching her form as she moved behind the trunk. She thought of the sheep and how they turned their heads when she went near. She decided once and for all that she really believed she might be psychic and all she had to do was work out how to prove it.

Every evening she waited for her father to come home from work. She hovered around the front door, checking again and again whether he was home yet, her head poking out of doorways, looking around corners, opening and closing doors with a listening period in between.

'Olive!' her mother would say if she was downstairs, exasperated to see her face again at the doorway. 'What are you doing?'

'Seeing if Dad's home.'

'Go and find something to do.'

Olive withdrew and kept out of sight, listening but finding out nothing. There was an occasional phone call with her mother on the phone to Rue saying, 'Yairs, mmm,' but she never said anything useful.

'Let your father get in the door,' Audra would say, once he arrived. Olive's need made her hateful and hot.

'I think we're having chops for tea,' she said when her father got home on Wednesday. 'And mashed potato,' she added. She stood in front of him, stepping from foot to foot.

She and her mother were two black planets and he was the only one who made the sky a little brighter.

•

Up to and including that previous Sunday, when she had found herself with her world shifted Olive had been a smudge, with dirty nails and a wilful heart. In the past, whenever she'd started to feel the family atmosphere get too close to her skin she had gone to the trees, but at home she stayed on the ground.

There were thoughts inside thoughts and she was remembering. Once she had been high in the peppercorn at the farm and seen something. They were at the end of a long and fractious game of hide-and-seek. From her eyrie she could see Mandy's red-and-white frock moving across the grass in the thin dusk. She stayed quiet, pinned against the diminishing sky. She was waiting to see Sebastian or Archie, thinking she might drop some spit when she realised someone was coming. It wasn't one of the boys though. What she saw was a man and a woman and they leaned against her tree on the side away from the house. She strained to see who it was but it was dim and there were too many tendrils of leaves and strings of red peppercorns in the way. She couldn't let go to use her binoculars because she would fall, but as she tried to see, she knew the people were kissing, and, oh, was it Thistle? Cleg? She couldn't tell, but the woman started to make noises, wet lippy sighs. The two people didn't talk, just stood very close to each other and then the man touched the woman's clothes a little bit and Olive didn't want to know any more so she leaned back, wrapped her arms around the trunk and waited until she was sure they had gone.

•

Yellow shampoo smell. Red hair in water, spreading like seaweed and copper and blood. Had it happened in a bath? Her mother's body floating in the bath water. Flicking her fingers dry and reaching for a cigarette, balancing a small cut-glass ashtray on the side or in the soap tray, placed on a wet face washer so it wouldn't slip. An ashtray that said PERTH or NOOSA. Her mother liked baths and would lie for ages with the door locked, the only sounds that Olive could hear as she pressed her ear to the wood the watery swooshing sound of her mother as she lifted and dropped her hands, the faint plink of water from the tap. She could imagine steam clouding the mirror, the lines of wetness rolling downwards. Maybe it had happened in a bath.

A proper memory arrived then, like mail through a slot. A little girl, her, leaning on the back of an armchair. She is looking through the window into the garden and beyond, out to the street. Over there is the letterbox and there is the bush with the small berries she mustn't put in her mouth. There is the tree that drops the prickly conkers and there is the crack that runs across the whole paving stone, the crack you have to step over as you walk holding the big hand. Sometimes the big hand belongs to her father but when it's her mother's she doesn't want to hold it because it's too tight and hurts.

But now she was hovering out of reach, practising something new. If she held herself, with her breathing the only moving part of her body, she knew she could work it out about her sister. She sat in the middle of the lounge room floor or down by the fence in the backyard and let her mind click along the connections. Sometimes her mother would step into her bedroom and ask who she was talking to.

'No one,' Olive would say and turn back to the window.

•

On the Thursday, after school, she took the things to the woodshed and sat under the wall where her father's wool samples were stored. She had found an old wooden fruit box and used it to make a display. A stolen candle, some drawings she'd done, two pretty pebbles and the photo of her dad with the baby in the yellow dress. She sat in the dust, speaking soft words and drawing circles on the floor with her fingers. She thought it was a safe time, that her mother would be asleep, so when Audra stepped around the doorway Olive jumped and made a fuffing noise.

Her mother stood with the brightness of the day behind, her body white-edged and, at the centre of it dark and amorphous, her features pushed into each other. Audra stepped inside.

'What have you got there? Who told you?'

'No one.'

'I can't believe she dared, and you should not be playing with matches.'

'It's not playing.'

On the wall opposite there was a spider, curled inside a home it had made from a leaf. Its legs poked out in a fan of sharp needles.

'This—' Audra waved her hand at the box and its iconography '—is too much.'

'But I miss her.' She had let herself begin to imagine what it might have been not to be alone.

'You didn't even know her.'

Olive wrapped her arms around her head and brought her knees up.

'What did she say?'

'She told me I had a sister who died.'

'Did she say anything else?'

Olive shook her head.

'Has Sebastian said anything?'

Olive shook her head again.

'Alright.' Her mother stepped forwards. 'All you need to know is it was a terrible, terrible thing.'

'Can you tell me what happened to her?'

Her mother didn't answer.

'Can you?'

'No,' Audra said after a few moments. She walked to the shrine. 'I can't. But I want you to stop.' Audra pointed. 'All of this.' She gathered the relics up in her arms and took them away.

The back door of the house slammed. A sparrow flew in. It looked at her, twitching and dumb. It hopped once and again. It came forward a little, then to the side. She thought if she stayed still for long enough the bird might come right up to her, even hop onto her foot and up her leg and onto her lap, up her arm to her shoulder, where it could stay. The sparrow flew out of the shed.

This was the reason no one had told her anything.

It was because they didn't know.

•

Later, when she was in the lounge, watching the path for her father, her mother came in. She wondered if a person could ever die of nothing. She thought of the book, of the spontaneous combustion and the charred bodies on floorboards and hearths where they'd spilled out of armchairs. Old brickwork, discoloured chimneys, thin rugs. Audra asked if she had anything to say and she shook her head. She wasn't going to say sorry.

'Can I have the photo back?'

Audra said that she had thrown it away but it was a lie, one thousand per cent. The falsehood sat small and wormlike in the air, in front of both of their faces. Olive made her eyes go hard. It was easy to do.

'We talked about it once with you but you didn't seem to remember and we didn't want to make you sad. It might have been a mistake but that's what we did.' Audra paused. 'Do you remember going to the special doctor?'

'No.'

Her mother wasn't even looking at her, she was at the doorway doing something with the knob. Olive looked at the things on the mantelpiece. The Scottie dog, the little glass box that looked like a coffin for a fairy. The wedding picture, her father laughing, his eyes wide. Her mother's mouth, how it showed her happiness was real. She decided she did have something more to say. She told her mother that she'd seen her father kissing Thistle at the farm. Her mother said to go and read a book, to please just find something to do. Olive said alright and went and did that and her mother stayed in there for a long time, even when her father got home. Olive ate her dinner and lay on top of her bed, eyes closed in concentration. They didn't know but she would. She would find out what happened to her sister and then she would know. And she would tell them and they would look at her with wonder. A girl of magnificent brain.

THE PLAN

PEOPLE WERE TALKING about Christmas and pudding and decorations but for Olive there was only one thing and it had nothing to do with the time of year. It was a short song, one with seven notes, and it came at her hard. Like a message, a question, urgent and rushing: *What happened to my sister?*

She had realised she needed to become a better spy, a more cold-blooded one. She would wait and be patient, in a tree or on the ground, behind the embroidered curtain in the Green Room. She would ride the streets with her binoculars hanging around her neck. She would find the answer somehow. She would try to trick people into giving away everything that they knew, and then she would put it all together. The song was in her head almost all the time now, repetitive and insistent.

What happened to Aster?

•

Peter lived two streets away and on Saturday they were in his back garden, working their way through a pile of plums. They talked about the bits of dead animals that were being found around town. A kangaroo head in the bin outside the newsagent and a sheep head at the oval. Dead snakes, too, hanging from trees and fences, their lank forms sinister and threatening. Peter's father had said whoever was doing it 'had problems'.

'He asked me if I knew who it was. I told him it was probably the Sandses,' Peter said, chewing a plum pip and spitting it at the garage wall. 'I wish I had a brother, maybe two, but not like them, more like Seb and Arch. To play with. Five more each,' Peter said.

'Brothers aren't that great, besides, your mother's too old now I think, no offence,' Olive said.

She got up and climbed the tree, stepping off it onto the garage roof. She started to throw tennis balls and a couple of footballs down to the grass.

She stood, positioned her fanned fingers, one across the top of the other so they were made cheliform. She held them up to him. 'Can you do this?'

'What is it?'

'Flippers.'

Peter shook his head and went back to the plums. 'Five more each,' he called. 'What about you? Didn't you want a brother or a or a—' He stopped.

She shook her head. 'I know why my mum didn't have more and why I'm never having one when I grow up.'

'Because they hurt when they come out?' He spat another pip. 'Mum said it did hurt a bit with me.'

'No, it's mainly 'cause they can die.'

Peter blew into his cheeks and said he guessed that was true.

She climbed down.

'You're really never having one?' His hair hung across his eyes.

'Nope. But listen. I have to tell you something. It's about a séance and we're going to have one soon. We found a ouija board, Thistle calls it a talking board. In the shed. I haven't worked out where to do it yet—somewhere spooky, though. I've decided I'm going to find out what happened.'

'What are you even talking about? Find out about what?'

'I did have a baby sister but she died.'

'Woooah.'

She was satisfied with how long his mouth stayed open.

'She drowned. I think in a bath, I'm not sure yet. I'm going to start my investigations, which is why we need to have the séance.'

He looked at her.

'What do you mean?'

'What I mean is I'm going to find out what happened to her.'

His lips made another shape.

'But the grown-ups would know. If you ask them they'll tell you.'

'I did ask my mum and she said she doesn't know. And I asked Sebastian. He doesn't know anything about it either. But Thistle told me. Thistle said it was true.'

Peter looked down at his hands.

'But Thistle told you the weird fairytales. She lied about that.'

Olive had to agree. Thistle had changed those stories. She remembered when she'd consulted with Peter and he had told her the proper endings.

'And what happened to Goldilocks?' Peter had said, wide-eyed.

'The bears ate her. Didn't they in yours?'

'No way. She broke the chair and ate the porridge and went to sleep in the bed. All that's the same. But when the bears came home they were all friends and that was the end. Even though they'd been angry at first.'

He had another thought.

'What about Hansel and Gretel?'

'Both eaten.'

'Snow White.'

'Dead, not eaten. Not sure why. I think parts were eaten. Her heart maybe?'

'It was her heart the queen wanted, but the huntsman cut it out of a deer in the woods anyway. *She* doesn't die. What about the dwarves then?'

'*Dwarves?*' Olive looked blank. They both sat there, thinking for a moment.

'It's the *Menschenfresserin* version I guess,' said Olive.

'Menschen-what?' asked Peter.

'*Menschenfresserin,*' said Olive. 'Cannibals. You don't know about it?'

Peter had said of course he knew about cannibals but not that word. He didn't think his parents knew it either. When Olive had gone back to Thistle and asked about the endings, her aunt had confirmed she had changed the stories.

'I adjusted them, yes, to their more natural conclusions,' Thistle had said. 'It would be a fairly unsuccessful family of bears other-wise, wouldn't it?'

In the backyard, Olive took a last plum.

'So Mum doesn't know,' she said to Peter. 'Don't you get it? You never listen to me. They *don't* know otherwise they would tell me. They would tell me everything.'

To Olive it was an irrefutable piece of logic. There were two things adults didn't like admitting: one, that they didn't know something, and two, that they were wrong. Mr Coppin at school was a perfect example of this—he would even make up answers and Olive had caught him out by checking something he'd said in a book at home. Then she'd gone to school and told him that he'd been wrong. She got into trouble but it had been worth it.

They lay on the grass, Olive propped up on her side.

'A cave would be the best place for one, like at the beach I went to that time.'

Peter was glad there were no caves around Stratford and said so.

'I don't know if those séances really work,' he added, and relaxed a little.

'Yeah they do, I saw one on telly. It worked really well. And Thistle told me how to do it. They don't know who they're dealing with.'

Peter knew who they were dealing with, that she would never let go of a thing until she was satisfied. Sometimes she would try really hard to let something go. He'd seen her walk into another room, get a book, lie down on the floor. Pour herself a drink of milk, sit in front of a television show. Physically keeping it from spilling out of her. But it was no use. Soon she'd be back in front of him, pushing her face right into his, saying, *You have to tell me.* He'd decided early on that it was best to offer up everything straight away to avoid the attack that followed, a barrage which could continue over days. He'd seen movies on telly with torturing, people with water dripping onto their faces or tied onto wooden machines that slowly pulled them apart. Or trapped in one of those mummy cases that closed on the person and there were spikes on the inside. He knew how those people felt. He knew about giving in because you just didn't have the strength to keep her out because you got too tired. She was a girl who *never* gave up.

Once she had sat in front of him, determined to find out what Snooky Sands had said about her the week she was away from school, when she got her tonsils out. She had her notebook open, ready. Had Snooky asked about her? What had her face been like when the teacher had explained the reason for her—Olive's—absence? Whose idea had it been to make the class card, had it been Snooky's or the teacher's? Who had she played with at play-time? At lunchtime? What had they done and in which part of the yard? Did she let anyone hold her swap cards to flick through themselves or did she hold them up one by one, not letting any of the other girls touch them?

And it had been the same the time she'd found out he didn't want anyone to know his middle name. He hadn't cracked for almost a whole week, and they'd both been miserable until he'd finally told her that if she promised to never ever tell a single person, he'd say what it was. She assured him she would never tell, not anyone, not ever.

'Promise. I'm really serious about it, 'cause if you break it, I won't be friends with you anymore.'

'I promise, I do.' She saluted.

'Don't laugh, but it's Dewey.'

And she hadn't laughed. She had nodded and her face stayed the same, and it was why he trusted her one thousand per cent. Every other person at his other school in the other town, child or adult, had made him feel bad about his name but Olive had proved she was a person you could trust.

Peter's mother appeared at the back door and said it was time for him to come in for tea. She asked if Olive would like to stay but she said no thanks, that she had to go home. She stood up, binoculars around her neck.

'Are you going to watch *The Ghost and Mr Chicken* tonight?'

Peter said he wasn't sure.

'But you missed *Trilogy of Terror.*'

Peter shook his head. He *had* watched *Trilogy of Terror* because she'd said it was really good. He had begged and begged his parents to be allowed to stay up to watch it, but it had been so frightening he'd had nightmares. When Olive asked if he liked it he said he'd forgotten about it and just gone to bed.

Olive watched a lot of TV even during the day, always with the volume down because of her mother. If she kept it low enough she could watch for hours sitting close to the big set, finger ready to shoot out at the first sound of the tread on the stairs. Sometimes she crept down and watched when her parents had gone to bed.

Peter's mother called again from the house and Olive picked up her bike. She told him she wanted him to make a pinkie shake, to promise to help her.

'What with?'

'Just the thing.'

'That's not fair if I don't know what it is.'

She waited with her pinkie extended and tapped her foot until he linked fingers. Their hands went up and down three times, then snapped apart and they both clicked.

'I really am going to solve the mystery and find out what happened, just you watch.'

'What are you talking about?'

'I told you. My sister? I'm going to find out what happened to her.'

'You don't seem very sad about her,' Peter said.

She flicked at her bell.

'And I don't think it will work.'

'Why?'

'If the adults don't know then you won't be able to find out.'

'Why not?'

'Because you're just a kid.'

She was affronted.

'A cave would be best but we don't have one,' she said. 'But there's Dead Girl's,' she said. 'The tunnel. It could be good but we need to go first and check—we can do it tomorrow.'

Peter was shaking his head. 'People don't go in there, Ol. Not ever.'

'Exactly.' Her smile was all wrong and she started to push her bike away, shouting over her shoulder at him, 'See you tomorrow!'

Peter stood, looking at his still-bent finger.

'Not there,' he said.

His mother came to the back door again.

'What's wrong with you?' she said. 'You look like you've seen a ghost.'

'It's nothing. Just Olive.'

His mother rolled her eyes and said to hurry. Peter got up and pulled one more plum off the tree and went inside. Maybe she'd been joking and he wouldn't have to do it. Maybe she'd take Sebastian instead.

OLIVE WALKED HOME along the streets, pushing her bike. The footpaths were wavy in the heat and small flashes of light bounced from the lenses of her binoculars. There was a bird in a tree up ahead so she stopped and let the bike fall against her hip. It took a while for her to find it again through the binoculars but she did and it was a dotterel with a yellow patch. Common, nothing special. She was keen to see a whipbird or a treecreeper, even though they weren't around much anymore. Thistle had seen some when she was younger.

She let go of the binoculars and walked on. She was almost at Violet Rise. She thought about Peter's mum. Mrs Stonehouse was a mother who made good things, like pork casseroles with chunks of pineapple, curried sausages, even homemade pizza. They had a crate of Loys soft drink delivered every Friday, and chocolate biscuits in the cupboard all the time not just for special. Peter's mother often asked Olive if she'd like to stay but she would say no thank you, that her mother wanted her to eat at home. She had stayed once for dinner and Peter's dad had talked about his work, telling funny stories about flat tyres and lost wallets, and Peter's mum kept reaching across to grasp his dad's arm. She did that a lot. Olive preferred to be at her own dinner table with her father chewing in his soundless way and her mother pretending to eat and none of them talking.

She pushed her bike. She knew exactly how many steps were between Peter's place and hers so she reduced her foot swing and took little lady steps to make the time stretch out.

JETHRO SANDS WAS driving his brothers to the shops for ice creams but they had to stand outside the milk bar, on the footpath, he said. No eating in the car. He'd only said yes because they'd nagged, saying it was too hot to walk all that way, that their bike chains were off and they couldn't fix them. Gary was the worst. He was a kid who never stopped pushing, so Jethro had said okay just to shut him up, and they all piled into his car, everybody arguing and shouting except John. Jethro had thought about changing his mind but then his mother ran out with her purse and she was so happy that he was taking his brothers down the street she'd given him the money for the ice creams.

As he pulled out of their street Luke was in the back yelling something about his t-shirt getting all stretched and Mark was trying to rile Luke even more, singing right into his earhole, a single note until his breath finished, while John sat looking out the window. Gary swung around from the front, his fist connecting with Luke's ear. Jethro pulled the car over.

'Stop it—you're going to make me crash, you dickheads.'

He waited until they were quiet and turned back out and they were almost at the intersection of Kellda Street and Violet Rise when Luke started shouting again, something about a girl, saying to stop the car, to pull over, pull over.

'It's her, that's the one, the one I told you about.' Luke was leaning forwards, his arms over the seat back, talking to Gary.

'I know her,' Gary said. 'She thinks she's really good.'

'She's a weirdo,' Mark said from the back seat. 'Check the binoculars.'

Jethro watched the girl as she walked along, pushing a bike. It was Olive Lovelock.

'She's friends with that big kid, the copper's son,' said Luke. 'They think they're so good. She's the one who pushed me in the diving pool.' Luke tapped a knuckle against his teeth. 'Snooky says they used to be friends but then she stopped playing with Snook. Yeah, she just dropped her—what a little bitch.'

Luke's speech seemed to activate Gary and he turned to the window. Gary was like one of those dogs that smelled something weak and locked their jaws and wouldn't let go.

'Don't worry about it,' Jethro said.

'Nah.' Gary straightened from his slouch. He lifted his hand and held out his mangled finger so that everyone could see it. 'Anyone who disrespects a brother or even a sister needs to be careful, I reckon. Otherwise it's gonna be trouble.'

Jethro tossed his butt out the window.

'She thinks she's so good,' Gary said as he watched Olive Lovelock walk down the street.

Jethro flicked the indicator. They went to the shops and got the ice creams, but even as Gary chucked his wrapper on the bonnet of a nearby parked car he was saying, 'That Olive Lovelock.' And driving back home, with Luke still sitting forwards, his arms over to the front, nodding in the rear-view mirror, Gary kept saying, 'Yeah, that Olive Lovelock.'

ON HER BED, arms crossed over her chest, Olive lay trying to be dead. This was how they slept in the pyramids with black crayon on their eyes. They had a pet cat in there too and some gold. She wondered how her sister had been buried and guessed it must have been in a coffin but a very, very small one.

She had written down everything Thistle had told her about séances. One: ouija boards were also called spirit boards and talking boards, and they had been used since the olden days to make contact with dead people. Two: you had to really be careful because the spirits weren't always friendly. Three: you could only ask a question once and the words might come through in the wrong order, which was why it was a good idea to have someone writing the letters down. Also, some spirits couldn't spell or make proper sentences, usually the young ones or the babies. Which made sense, Thistle had said, and Olive had nodded, realising it really did make sense.

Thistle had also said that if spirits asked you to do unusual things, something with your body and especially your private parts, you had to stop and put the board away. Olive had asked what sort of unusual things and her aunt hadn't answered, and it was the only time Olive could remember that Thistle had refused to answer a direct question, even though she made it seem as if she hadn't heard.

She turned the page in her notebook. Four: it was important to never play alone. Five: don't use the board if you are ill because then they can get in more easily.

'Get in where?' Olive had asked. 'Into the house?'

'No,' Thistle said. 'Into you.'

Olive had looked up and Thistle continued, telling her that it was children who got possessed by the spirits most easily and when it happened they started acting in odd ways. Strange things could happen, like the feeling of being watched, or of doors opening and closing on their own, or hearing footsteps in a house where everyone was asleep. Oh, and hair being pulled and fingers pricked, being held down in bed with no one there. Scratches. Those sorts of things, Thistle had stated matter-of-factly, as if discussing a list of to do items before bed. Empty bladder, wash hands and face, brush teeth. When she'd said it, Olive had been overcome with a very exact, crawling sensation on the back of her neck, the same that they talked about in horror stories. She would have to make sure she didn't get taken over by any spirits.

She closed the notebook. She was right. They had to do a séance. It was the only way. Luckily she had Peter to help her. He couldn't ever say no to her. She was his best friend and, even though she didn't like to admit it to herself, he was hers.

IT WAS SUNDAY morning and they were at Dead Girl's. The entrance was on the side of the main road out of town, near the back of the scout hall. The opening was barred with a fence but there was a gap at the side that they could squeeze through. Some kids said it was for escaping during the war, some said it was for cutting up the bodies of bad children so they could be carried out in bags and buried far away. Whatever its origins, for a long time teenagers had gone in there with petrol bombs to scare away bats, kiss and smoke cigarettes. There were also persistent stories of painted figures on the walls that no one could describe. Another thing most people agreed on was that a long time ago a girl had gone mad in there. She hadn't said anything for days afterwards but they found her with scratches all over her body and she had to go to hospital.

Dead Girl's was one place in Stratford that Olive had never been tempted to go, until now. Without hesitation she pushed through the gap beside the fence and told Peter to come on. They were in a tunnel that was quite high overhead and about as wide as a car. The surface was gritty underfoot and it was dark and cool. They walked to where it began to slope downwards and Olive switched on her torch.

'That girl didn't talk for weeks afterwards,' Peter said. It was like she wasn't even there anymore, they said—in her body, I mean.'

'We don't even know if that's true or not, plus why do they call it Dead Girl's if she didn't die?'

They went in a way before Olive turned to see where they'd come from. The light from the entrance had lessened to the point where it was almost as dim behind as it was in front, beyond the reach of the torch. They kept going. Periodically she shone the torch on the walls on either side, to see if there were any drawings, but there'd been nothing so far. Peter was right behind, almost stepping on her heels.

'I'm going to switch it off, just for a second,' she said.

'No, wait—'

The surroundings clicked to black. In front, she couldn't see a thing, nor to the side, both sides, or the back. She heard Peter breathing and switched the torch on again.

'If we go a bit further we'll be under the road.'

'Don't turn it off again, Ol. Don't.'

'It's mine, so I can do what I want. Besides, you forgot yours.'

They continued and the ground became rubbled, the loose rock making it harder to progress. Then she thought about what would happen if she twisted her ankle, and the idea of being stuck there and not able to get out gave her a hot squirty feeling. Peter would have to get help and her battery would finish and she'd be left to go mad like the girl with the scratches. She realised in that exact moment that she was scared of the tunnel because Thistle always said darkness was where evil lived, that it was light that cleaned a person's soul, not water and soap. Thistle said evil people had no sunshine in them, that even their mothers wouldn't love them because they were all bad.

'One thousand per cent?' Olive had asked.

'Yes, more than that,' said her aunt. 'Like a killer who does it for fun. He hurts people because he enjoys it and doesn't feel sorry for them or guilty afterwards. He's happy he did it. He loves it.'

'Like Gary,' Olive said in the tunnel and shone the light on the wall. She stopped walking and Peter knocked into the back of her.

'What?'

'Look,' she said.

A series of figures were daubed on the cement walls, their naked torsos white, arms lifted, hands extended as if to grasp, fingers ending in claws. Small ones—children—and big ones too, with red on their faces where their eyes should be. Some tall and thin, others shorter. Chests with three red dots in a line, or a slash. Hunched shoulders, wound-like mouths and pointed ears. Jagged shark teeth in weirdly extended jaws, some with horns coming out of their heads, others with bloody stains coming from their eyeholes and noses.

These were faces caught in the moment of unimaginable agony, reflections of more terrible acts than Olive could even imagine. Things that were beyond the realm of childhood, that even grown-ups would struggle to name. Wretched and frozen in the middle of their pain-suffering, laid out in a line along the wall. And on the other side, more of the same.

'Does a person's soul leave the body when someone dies or does it stay there?' Olive asked.

'Don't talk about that stuff,' said Peter. 'Just don't.'

As they looked at the pictures on the walls there came a sound, a booming that built to a pounding that reverberated in waves down the tunnel. Olive stepped back and put her hands over her ears and the torch moved in her hand, shattering the darkness all around them, illuminating the bricks of the roof above. She and Peter screamed a symphonic roar until the sound receded. It had been a truck, she guessed, passing overhead. They were in the middle, right under the road.

'We have to go to the end and see,' she said, swinging the torch to Peter's face. He blinked. 'Come on.'

They walked, Peter in front. Soon they had to clamber over small mounds of broken rock and at one stage the gap above their heads narrowed as the rough ceiling lowered to meet the tips of their fingers if they reached up. The thinning space was cold and Olive was about to say so when another truck started to approach, the same eerie boom accumulated until it was a giddy roar above their heads. They yelled in unison again, and even though this time she was ready for the whole-body invasion of noise, and told herself she wouldn't scream, the caterwauling barrelled out against her will. She shook with adrenaline and knew Peter would want to turn back.

'Let's keep going,' she said.

They shuffled on and in a little while Peter said, 'Look,' and she could see a light glowing faintly that marked the end of the tunnel. After a few more slow minutes they got there. There was a fence at this end too but, unlike the other, no gaps were visible around it and it was bolted flush against the cement edge with just a thin lip of light marking the joins.

'Okay,' she said. 'We can't get out at this end so we have to go back.' She shone the torch into his face again and he told her to stop it and she did, but she'd already seen how scared he was.

They started walking back, her in front this time. The torch crawled over the walls, the roof and the rocky way ahead. They were back at the middle and had gone over the two humps of rocks when again she heard the slow approach of the booming noise.

'I'm not going to scream this time,' she said. 'It just makes it worse.'

'Makes what worse?'

'Everything.' As they'd passed along she'd started to feel more and more uncomfortable. She told herself it was her imagination but as the sound built, a cold breeze gathered around her legs. Maybe there was a vent somewhere, a funnel for cool air from outside.

The noise started once more in the tunnel but grew into a crescendo of such intensity. It was much louder than the previous times and Olive realised that the other times had been cars and *this* was a truck. She was about to say something when Pete's hand moved to hers and knocked the torch from her fingers. It fell with a crack and went out. The truck passed overhead and all went quiet once more.

'Don't,' he said.

'Don't what?'

'Scratch me.'

'I didn't.'

The torch was broken.

'This is why you should of remembered. I really hate it when you forget things.'

'I want to go out now,' Peter said.

'Olive?' he said, when she didn't say anything.

'*Okay.*'

They felt with their feet, shuffling forwards, and only let go of each other once they got close enough to the growing white circle of light and, behind it, the scout hall. Once outside, Olive shook the torch and it rattled. She looked at the head. It looked alright but had to be busted inside.

'It's too noisy,' she said. 'We won't be able to do a séance in there. If there was a time when there were no cars or trucks, maybe in the middle of the night, it might be okay.' She stopped and Peter's eyes were on her face. 'I need to think about it, if there's somewhere better.'

'What?' Peter said. '*Ol?*'

'We're still going to do it, just not there.'

He didn't call out things to her as they rode home, or pull faces or point out dog poo. Once they got to the turn, when she called out goodbye, he rode on to his place without replying. She watched him go then walked her bike up the driveway. He'd be alright and she was sure the séance would work. It had to. She went to her room and lay on her bed to think. They needed somewhere quiet, somewhere adults wouldn't interfere. A place they could camp so they could talk to the spirits at midnight.

This must have been how Lenore felt, setting out from her home all those years before, to travel to a place so far away where not only was everything different, nothing was even close to being the same. She had to be brave like Lenore and push ahead. She had to find out what happened to her sister. It had to be her, *she* had to do it because no one else would. No one else had. Life was not like detective books, where the writer made everything fit in together, maybe even worked backwards from the end to the beginning. She was working forwards and it was hard but she would solve it in in the end. They would put the newspapers in the grille outside the newsagency and the headlines would read: GIRL CRACKS CASE AFTER POLICE BAFFLED and: TWELVE-YEAR-OLD GIRL DETECTIVE MEETS QUEEN.

She turned off the light and just as she was about to fall asleep it came to her: Of course. *Ganger's*. They would have the séance at Ganger's.

THE SCHOOL YEAR was ending. It was the last week of grade six and they were making Christmas cards and red-and-green paper decorations to take home. Olive was sitting at her desk holding a coloured paper lantern in her hands. It was really bad and she wished she could make things better. Snooky's was perfect and even John Sands had done one better than hers. At the back row of desks, Luke and Mark were trying to glue paper to each other's heads.

Olive sat with her glue and paper. She'd made the cuts, she'd tried to twist it how the teacher had shown them but it wasn't working. She didn't care so much because she was going to find out what happened to her sister and that was more important. She, Olive Lovelock, child sleuth, smart kid, adventuress, reader. Imaginer, cryptologist and conqueror of high places. Keeper of bones, rocks and feathers. She would show everybody how clever she was and they'd say to each other: 'Here comes Olive Lovelock. Did you know she solved the case of her sister who drowned? She's going to meet the Queen.'

For the next few nights, as she tried to sleep, she forgot about wishing for her usual things—the pony, the baby owl and to be magic. They were the fancies of a child. In her mind, as she dropped away from the realities of the day, she had a picture of herself in clothes like a girl guide outfit, it would be her detective outfit. She focused on that picture and pushed away the memories of the real at school.

The final days of school had been the worst. People signing each other's autograph books, hugging and giving Christmas presents and cards. Talking about how they would have sleepovers in the holidays.

She pushed away the moment when she'd gone into the girls' toilets on the last day and seen Snooky in the middle of a circle of her friends talking excitedly about something and how they'd gone quiet and watched Olive go into a cubicle. Later, when Mrs Barton had got out her guitar so they could all sing together for the last time, the song was the Beatles' blackbird one, and even though it was her favourite it had made her eyes start to hurt. And then at home time, when Megan Vickers was handing out invitations to a picnic in her back garden to celebrate the end of school, Olive had lingered at the bag hooks outside the classroom pretending she was still getting ready to leave so that it would give Megan enough time to give her an invitation but she hadn't.

•

That Friday night Olive sat in the hallway on the phone to Peter. The small lamp was on and it was still light outside. She could hear the fan whirring in the other room where her mother sat on the couch. There was a game show on television.

'Yeah, smee. "Uh-*oh! Razzamatazz.*"

'So, do you think you can come? Tomorrow?'

'What? What is it again?' She heard him bounce his ball on the wooden floorboards of the hallway where his phone was. Another couple of bounces and his mother would say something from the kitchen.

'The séance. Remember?'

The ball bounced.

'I thought we said no. Dead Girl's was too noisy.'

'What are you chewing? Is it bubble gum?'

Bounce. Then, 'Yeah.'

'Save me some, bring it tomorrow.'

Peter chewed and bounced the ball once more. Olive could hear his mother's voice in the background. The ball stopped. 'I'm talking about Ganger's. For the séance. You say you're with me at the farm, that we're camping there, testing out a new tent or something, just make something up, and I'll say I'm with you, that we're in your backyard. Testing out *your* new tent. And instead we meet at Ganger's and stay the night there.'

'I don't get it. Whose tent is it—yours or Seb's?'

'It doesn't have to be a tent, just work out something so you can stay out.'

'I don't think my mum will believe me. She knows when I lie, even about the littlest thing.'

Olive remembered the story of the time Peter had tried to lie to his mother. He'd eaten all his Easter eggs before his parents were even awake but tried to tell his mother he hadn't. He'd been little, too little to know that he should have got rid of the wrappers better, that she would see all the foil scrunched up into little balls in the drawer beside his bed.

'Don't worry, you were younger then. You didn't have me to help you. Now you know better.'

'I don't, not really.'

'Don't worry about the adults. They don't notice stuff, they don't really even think about us,' she said.

Peter breathed out a long, low whistle.

'Okay.'

'Good. I'll tell the others to bring the ouija board. You need a sleeping bag and maybe a lilo, we can use them to sit on and sleep on. It'll be fun. We take sandwiches and things to drink. Maybe make a fire. Have some tins of food, I don't know. Do you think you can bring some tins?'

'Where are we going to go to the dunny?'

'In the bushes of course.'

'Sebastian's definitely coming?'

'I reckon.' She still wasn't sure about Sebastian but they needed one other person at least for the séance.

'Alright.' He didn't sound alright.

'*What?*'

'Nothing.'

'If you *really* don't want to—'

'I said I would, didn't I?'

'Bring your torch tomorrow, mine's busted. Meet you there at seven o'clock.'

They hung up. She needed to make the connections. And the only way that could happen was to talk to people. No one alive would tell her anything more so it had to be dead people. She had to ask the ghosts—see if she could find out anything. She was ready.

THE NEXT NIGHT she waited at the turn-off to Ganger's. She wasn't sure if both her cousins would come. Sebastian had been reluctant on the phone and she wasn't sure if he would care enough. She hadn't told them the reason for the séance, just that they were going to try. Archie had been very enthusiastic, saying he'd bring his pocket knife and two cans of baked beans. She kicked at stones while she waited. It was about seven-thirty she guessed because it took about an hour to ride. After a few minutes she heard the far-off sounds of Archie's voice coming down the road and she straightened. There they were, on their bikes, Sebastian too. He was in a bad mood, though, she could see that by his mouth. He never laughed anymore.

Behind the two boys came Grace, flying down the road to the marker where Olive sat. There were a few blurred grasshoppers in the air, so fast that she couldn't track them with her eyes, where they came from or where they went.

As they rode on to Ganger's, her eyes rested on the dry country, the faded green and nut-brown scenery. She stood and shouted to the boys that now it was a race and they all sped down the road.

Peter was waiting for them at the silo. They got off their bikes and Olive gathered the others into a circle. Peter gave them all a piece of bubble gum and Olive spat out her chewie and it lay pink and wet and slug-like on the ground. She wiped her hands on her shorts and told Sebastian and Archie what Thistle had said, that she had a baby sister who had died from drowning.

'So my plan is I'm going to find out who did it. Then I can let my mum know what happened to her.'

Archie said he didn't think it was a very interesting secret and asked when were they going to do the séance. He wandered over to the rail lines and lay down with his ear on a track. Sebastian picked up a stick and went and sat under a tree in the shade. Grace was nearby on the silo railing and as Olive started to cross the clearing to go to the hut, the bird flew over and hopped onto her foot and pecked at the lace of her runner. Olive walked a step and Grace hung on and it was a new game. She shook her off.

'No, Grace. We're busy.'

Archie was visible through the trees, standing near Soldier's, looking over the fence into the paddock. Sebastian was peeling the bark off the stick and Peter was at the window of the ganger's hut. She called to the others, saying that they needed to get ready. Archie ran into the clearing and started stamping on a drink can, trying to crush it flat. Olive asked him for his windcheater to put over the broken glass along the bottom frame of the hut's windowsill.

'Why does it have to be mine?'

''Cause you're the youngest.'

When she hoisted him up and pushed him through the opening he fell to the floor.

'Ow, my arm.'

He pulled at the jammed door with his left hand while Olive karate kicked it from the outside. Archie started to carry the empty beer bottles out of the hut.

'We can put these around the outside in a line, like an alarm for if any animals come while we're sleeping.'

'Okay,' Olive said. It was a good idea.

They found magazines which showed not just the hair but everything. Olive said they were disgusting. She left the boys' tight circle and went outside to find something she could use as a broom. Back in the hut, the magazines had disappeared and Peter was picking up cigarette butts and putting them into one of the beer bottles. There was a spring-bottomed bed with no mattress and she planned to put her lilo on it. She reckoned it would work well but Archie was lying down with his arm across his middle. He was staring at the ceiling in a rare moment of stillness.

'That's mine,' Olive said. 'I bagsed it, and 'cause I'm a lady.'

'You're not, you're just a kid like us.'

'Well, I'm the boss then.'

Archie got off the bed. 'I'm going to start blowing up my lilo because it's gonna take forever.'

Sebastian had cleared a space and was squatting, working at his own lilo. He had gone red in the face.

'What about the window?' Archie said. 'I saw some stuff, we could stretch it across—it's like material. It could be a sort of curtain.' He went running outside and came back with a piece of gauzy fabric. To Olive, it looked like it was from a summer frock.

'Let's try,' she said. 'It might be too see-through.'

It was starting to get dark. Grace was gone. They did all sorts of tests with the material over the window. When Olive was outside, shining Peter's torch on it and the others shut off their torches in the hut, it was an opaque screen and all she could see were the printed designs on the front. But when she turned off her torch and Sebastian shone his on the window from inside, she could see their faces.

'Can you see out?' she shouted.

They couldn't.

'It's no good,' she said. 'I can see in. We have to find something else.' They found a bit of cardboard and it worked better. Then she said it was time to make a fire.

'A low one,' said Sebastian. 'In case it gets out of control. Our dad will kill us but I'll get in the most trouble.'

'And people might see it from the road,' said Olive.

They agreed to make only a small fire, on the other side of the hut.

They got rocks and made a circle. They brought broken branches which they piled against the wall of the hut. Sitting on their lilos, they compared torches. Peter's was the biggest and the strongest.

'We can share,' Olive told him.

Next best was Archie's, then Seb's. Archie said his was like the one on *Columbo* but Sebastian said it looked like the one from their shed. Sebastian's was one he had from his cubs days. It was small and weak but he'd brought a kerosene lantern as well. He lit it and they all admired the power of the light. When he set it by his feet, Olive said it should go more in the middle.

'I brought it,' he said. 'I want it near me.' Olive decided not to fight, but he was really starting to annoy her.

'When will we eat? And when should we have the séance—before or after the ghost stories? *Johnny, JOOOOHHHNNYY, I've come to get my livvverrrr baaaack.*' She held the torch under her chin so that it pin-spotted her nose.

'It's not even that late yet,' said Peter.

'Ol,' said Sebastian.

'What?'

'I forgot to tell you, we didn't bring it. I couldn't find it.'

'It's on top of the cupboard in Mandy's room. I told you. You have to stand on my bed to reach it.'

'I did, it wasn't there. Mandy's been playing with it. I keep catching her. I take it, put it on top of the cupboard where she can't reach it, but it was gone again today, I swear.'

'We needed that.' Olive held her hand out for the lantern and Sebastian handed it to her. 'Well, I guess we can make one from paper. Thistle said you can do it that way. For the moving thing, we'll have to use a rock or something.'

They went to get the food supplies. They had a tin of tomatoes, some baked beans and Heinz Beef Stockpot soup. They had a loaf of bread but nothing to go on it and some tomato sauce. Peter had a drink cooler with cordial inside and twenty-four plastic cups.

'Are we having a party or something?' said Olive. 'Look how many cups Pete bought!' She showed the others and Peter flushed.

'I just bought them all,' he said. 'What's the big deal?'

'It's "brought" you two.' Sebastian was shaking his head.

'Who cares?' said Olive.

'Yeah,' said Archie.

Peter had some marshmallows so they set off looking for the best toasting sticks. Then it took a long time to get the fire going because there wasn't much paper. They found one old newspaper behind the door of the hut, tucked into a crossbeam, but it wasn't enough. Olive suggested they burn the magazines from earlier.

'I'll get them,' she said, standing up.

'No way,' said Archie. 'You don't know how hard it is to find them.'

'I don't know why you even like them—they're so off.'

Archie said that was where she was wrong. They were interesting. Scientific.

'Who even knew it was like that?' he said. 'Did you?' He was looking at Peter and Sebastian.

Sebastian got up and went into the hut. Peter just sat there, staring at the unburning fire.

'It's like a . . . like a—not a hole, but a cut?'

Olive threw her stick at her cousin and it struck him on the shoulder.

'Hey, you almost got me in the eye.' He started hitting her foot with his, then she showed them how to inhale the smoke from matches. After that it was time to open the tins, but no one had a can opener and they didn't have a saucepan anyway, so they spread sauce on slices of bread with their fingers because they'd forgotten a knife as well. They drank cordial and discussed how scary it might get later, how quiet. Someone asked what would happen if a killer came, or an escaped prisoner wanting some food.

'We'd stop him,' said Peter.

'What would happen if a raper came?' Archie said. They all looked at Olive.

She held her marshmallow stick and scratched her thumbnail along a bump on the surface.

'No one would hurt a girl like that,' she said.

They agreed.

They made bets about who would get the most scared, and what they would do when they got the most scared. Olive spent a long time doing facial expressions of how she thought everyone would show their fear. They all laughed except Sebastian.

The main road was about a football oval's distance away and no cars had passed by since they'd been there. At eleven o'clock they had their sleeping bags out and were lying on their lilos in front of the fire. Olive was worried the others would want to go to sleep before it was time to do the séance so she kept prodding everyone with her marshmallow stick.

'I think we need more wood,' she said. 'Let's go look. Nobody touch my stick.'

Olive held the torch as she and Peter walked away from the fire, to the darkness beyond.

'When you die, what do you think happens?' she said.

'I don't know, but I don't want to be buried. I don't want the worms eating me.'

'I do. I want them to eat me until I'm bones, but also it's because I want to have a place where people can come and see my grave.'

'You can do that when you're burned. You can have a wall like my poppa, or a tree that they plant.'

'I want to be inside a tree,' she said. 'Standing up, where it's hollowed out. They can put me in there and eventually I would join and mix with it. They could carve a face into the trunk at the same height as where my real one is.'

'Would you be wrapped in bandages?'

'I don't know, I'm saying maybe. That's not the most important bit, though. Do you think they could carve my face into the tree?'

They sat on a log.

'Have you noticed how some people look different at night from how they do in the day?' Olive asked. 'Their faces?'

'Not really.'

'It's hard to know which one is real when that happens.'

'Maybe both are.'

They gathered wood and carried it back, dumped it, and went to the trees again but this time ranged a bit further and came to the fence along Soldier's Paddock. Olive's torch picked out a tree with a snake looped over a branch, its head crushed open.

'Over there,' she said. 'Another one.' The torch picked out a second shape threaded in a tree. 'Look.' Dark forms with smooth folds and pale underbellies. She moved the beam away to the fence of Soldier's.

'Did they tell you never go in there?' Olive said to Peter. He nodded. 'Come on.' She held one of the fence wires up so he could climb through. They cut across the paddock on the diagonal. Olive kept the torch on the ground and whenever they came to a shadowed patch they skirted it wide, knowing that even going near the edges of the mines could be dangerous.

'We should go back,' said Peter. The grain silo was outlined, black and mountainous, against the grey sky.

As well as digging mines for gold, the soldier had made a bunker, cutting it into a small rise of land and creating an almost-horizontal duct that stretched into the ground. There was a door at one end and a stone bulwark at the other.

'Don't you want to know what it looks like? You're always talking about the war,' Olive said.

'I suppose so, but I'm not going inside and I don't care if you say we are. You can.'

'Imagine if we looked in and saw a skeleton,' Olive said. 'A skeleton holding a gun.' She leaned against the door. 'Or a skeleton with a knife sticking out of its head!' She moved the torch across a tattered flag that was affixed to a tree stump. It was the marker of the bunker's entrance. The trunk of the tree was splashed with paint, the slogans and end words of a man alone in the bush. Town talk was that he'd been planning for the next war when he died and according to Peter's father he had created 'quite the system', which was what Peter told Olive now.

'He put things in there too. Supplies, my dad said. They had to leave everything because it was too dangerous to try and get it out because of the walls. My dad said some are rock but some are more sandy stuff? So they couldn't be sure if someone went in there, you know, that it would be . . . If someone went in there to get out the things, that it would be safe. That it wouldn't. It might collapse on them, and . . . and . . .'

'Bury them alive.' Her voice was cold and glittery.

'Yeah,' Peter breathed.

'But there might be a can opener in there, we should check.'

'I'm not going in—I'm serious, Ol.'

'You always say that.' Olive moved her hand to the doorhandle. 'You know who should go in there? Luke Sands. That's who should go in.' She pulled and the door opened. The torch moved into the entrance and around it, on the small hillock, across the grass growing there. The old soldier must have been short, Peter said from behind, and she agreed. A tall man would have to bend over to go inside. She saw how the first part of the tunnel angled downwards so you would be going under the ground. After about twenty metres you were all the way under and that's where the torch beam cut out. She squatted in front of the opening.

'I wonder what it's like in there. Do you think there are bats? Maybe someone lives in there—who would ever know? It looks like exactly the place a raper would go. Or there could be foxes. It could actually be a den.'

'What? I can't hear you.'

She straightened and walked back to him.

'Ghosts. Maybe the ghost of the soldier.'

'I'm going back to the others,' Peter said and started walking to the fence. Olive followed. Back at the fire they put more wood on and sat and watched as it burned. Olive said they should start the séance. She had her notebook with her and she ripped out some pages from the back and tore them into smaller pieces of paper. On each she wrote one letter of the alphabet and the digits 0–9. She wrote YES, NO and GOODBYE on others.

'What can we use for the pointer? A rock's too heavy.'

'Too heavy to push, you mean,' said Sebastian.

'Nobody's allowed to push, everybody has to promise. We can use a plastic cup, they're see-through. Get the cardboard from the window and bring it here,' she said to Archie, who was almost asleep. He got up, complaining that he was tired. She sat back on her lilo after placing the letters and numbers and words in their positions on the piece of cardboard. 'Okay. We're ready.'

Peter checked his watch. 'Almost midnight.'

'I'm really tired,' Archie said.

'Me too, I don't think I'll play.' Sebastian had his arms around himself.

'You have to, Seb,' Olive said. 'We need four people. And it's not playing. It's—'

'What?'

'I don't know. It's just not playing.'

'Who are we going to talk to, though?' Peter asked.

'Let's just see who's there, I guess.' Olive sat cross-legged and moved the cardboard so that the words faced her.

'In the middle,' shouted Archie. 'Like that.' He moved the board so it was on an angle but Olive reached out and righted it again. 'Leave it.' She put her forefinger on the inverted cup. 'We have to treat it seriously because it's not a game, so promise.' She waited for Archie to draw his finger twice across his chest. 'And the last thing is we always have to say goodbye.'

'Who to?' Archie said.

'To the spirits, of course, when they come.'

'Real ones?' Archie's bottom lip moved behind his top teeth. 'I thought it was pretend.'

'Of course it's real. Even if the spirit doesn't want to say goodbye we have to force it.'

'Force what?' Archie said.

Olive pushed the plastic cup across the board to the GOODBYE piece of paper.

'Like that. We make it go there.'

'But you said no pushing.' Archie pulled his finger away. 'I thought it was just a game.'

Olive told him to put his finger back.

'Only pushing at the end, when we want to finish, if the spirit's not cooperating. Just do it, alright? Okay, we're going to start.'

They all placed a single index finger on the plastic cup. Immediately it moved and Archie pulled his hand back.

'Don't stop,' Olive said. 'It's working. I'll ask the questions.'

Archie touched it again. 'I don't like it,' he said. 'It feels weird.'

'Hello. Is anyone there? Hello,' Olive said.

They waited but there was no movement.

'Maybe we need candles or something?' Olive said to Sebastian. The cup moved to NO. 'That was you—you pushed it.'

'It wasn't,' said Sebastian. 'Who are you? Are you friendly or evil?' The cup slid across to the YES.

'You're confusing it,' said Olive. 'One question at a time; I'm asking them.' She started and her words were slow and clear. 'What is your name?'

The cup moved quickly across the board. It spelled out S-T-R-E-T-A-R-E-A-S and came to rest in the middle.

'How old are you?'

The cup stayed still.

'When did you die?'

The cup didn't move.

'Maybe it can't do numbers very well. Maybe it's still a kid.'

'How did you die?' The question came from Olive, though it didn't feel like she had spoken aloud. It came out of her and hung in the air and the words had the colour of silverfish.

There was a pulse as the cup spun around the board.

M-M-A-M-A-D-D-A-D-D-M-D-M-D-M.

Sebastian took his hand away and sat back from the group with his arms folded across his chest.

'Someone's pushing it,' Olive said and took her finger off too. 'I don't want to do it anymore, it's boring.'

'I wasn't,' Sebastian said. He had bags under his eyes that she'd never seen before.

'Well, I pushed it.' She felt sick. 'There's no such thing as spirits or ghosts. I'm going to bed.' She got up and stood there, not wanting to go by herself. 'We should all go, it's late.'

'You can say you're scared,' Sebastian said.

'Yeah,' said Archie.

Olive wheeled around and dropped onto her younger cousin where he sat on his lilo. She twisted his arm, saying, 'You. Don't. Get. It. Do. You?' She clambered off him. 'I don't get scared.'

'You're mean, Ollie. That was my sore arm.'

She sat down and gazed into the fire. After a while, Peter said it was twelve twenty. Archie was asleep so they woke him up. They put the cardboard back in the window and got into their beds. No one had pillows but no one cared because everything had grown large and still around them and all they wanted to do was go to sleep so that the morning came sooner. Olive said goodnight. She reached over and turned off the lantern. The last thing she did was feel for the matchbox, to make sure she could find it in case she needed it during the night.

SOMEONE WAS SHAKING her.

'Ol,' said a voice. 'Ollie.' A harsh whisper. What was Archie doing in her room?

'There's people outside.'

She struggled to get up and realised she was in a sleeping bag. She reached for the zip and couldn't find it because it had twisted around underneath her. She wriggled out, making the cot springs move.

'Shhhh, they don't know we're here.' He was at her side, his hand on her arm.

The two of them stepped over Seb, who was asleep on the floor. At the side of the cardboard was a crack and through it she saw figures moving around, some in front of their hut, others over near the silo ladder. There was a spotlight on top of a car and someone was up there, directing the broad white beam around the area so that it fell in turn on gatherings of people, some in twos, kissing, some in larger groupings, smoking and drinking from bottles. Light flooded the hut in a sweep, cutting in through the badly sealed window.

Peter started moving in his sleeping bag.

'What is it?' he said.

She could see forms of people moving in a way that made her think they were being silly, playing around. One of the torchlights swung upwards and across a face.

'Gary Sands,' she whispered. Peter was beside them now. 'What time is it?'

He held up his wrist and the shining green hands showed almost ten past three. Archie's face was tilted upwards, his eyes locked on hers. She was about to whisper something else when an object flew inwards, punching the cardboard out of the window. They tried to find their torches but no one could. She went over and squatted to see what the thing was. It was a face, with long eyelashes and a tongue sticking out through thinned black lips.

'Come out,' a voice yelled. A bare arm reached in the window. Olive grabbed the hand with both of hers and dragged the inside of the forearm back and forth across the edges of the broken window. Shouts from the other side but she hung on, pulling at the arm, forcing it down with her weight. She collapsed into a crouch and lifted her feet off the ground.

'Stop, stop,' the voice shrieked. 'Jesus.'

She let go and stood with the others at the back of the hut. Peter had found his torch and shone it through the window. Filling the space was the squinting, rage-filled face of Gary Sands, a halo of light around his head.

'It's kids,' he shouted to someone behind him. 'Come out or I'll shoot you.'

'You don't even have a gun,' said Olive.

'*Come out, I said.*' Gary stepped back from the window. The door flew inwards as he kicked it open.

'Stay here,' Olive said to the others and went outside.

'Look, it's Olive Tree,' Gary said. He took off his t-shirt and wrapped it around his bloody arm and reached a hand out to Luke, who was standing there. Luke passed his brother a bottle of drink. Gary's eyes were wide, sclera visible, and his chest was thin and bony. Olive saw his nipples.

'We were here first,' she said.

Gary's expression twisted with something she couldn't read.

'You've got some nerves on ya.'

'I'm going to tell Mr Stonehouse about you throwing the kangaroo head. And the snakes.'

'He can get stuffed. Weakest copper ever, that's what my dad says.' He came closer. He lifted his wrapped arm. 'But I reckon he'd be interested in this. Maybe you'd even go to jail—juvie for sure.'

'Ollie, co-come back,' Sebastian stuttered from the doorway.

Everything happened quickly, then. Time accelerating and slowing simultaneously. Luke and Mark Sands moved to block Sebastian and Peter while Gary Sands grabbed Olive's shoulders and marched her around the side of the hut. Then somehow she had turned and he was walking her backwards towards the pipes, pushing her so that she lost her footing and fell over. She wrenched her head around and scrabbled away from underneath Gary Sands and got up and ran. She reached the big pipe and started to crawl in, got halfway, but he came after her, grabbed her legs and pulled. He slammed onto her and her lip hit a tooth. His breath stank of alcohol and there was a flurry of torches from outside, beams running over each other. She could hear Peter's voice coming from far away, his voice muffled. She couldn't move, couldn't even think about what was happening. Her teeth were clamped shut and to keep quiet meant to stay present in the moment. Something was close and she breathed over his shoulder and her eyes looked in the darkness but saw nothing as the cement pipe encircled the two of them. Gary's mouth was on her. Was this kissing?

His nails were scratching her skin so she clenched her limbs, turned her head to the side, and now there was something heavy on her neck and she thought about spitting if she could just manage, but she had no liquid in her mouth, there was nothing there. She managed to wriggle and tried to spit at him and a light spray, maybe even just air, must have reached his face because he released a little and said, 'What did you just do?' Then he said a word that she had never heard before and it was hate-filled and violent and it shocked her.

The others' voices again, closer now, at the end of the pipe. Gary had an arm up, he was wiping himself and she scrambled out from under him down towards the other end, away from him, on hands and knees. Once more he caught her and she was half out and half in this time. She screwed her head around to the side. Beyond the weight of him on her back she saw the moon rising and while most of it was still below the horizon there was a thumb's worth that showed a hazy burnt orange.

Then Peter was there and it must have been him who grabbed Gary by the hair and pulled him clear off her and there was nothing where he'd been but a curl of breeze at the place where her thighs joined her shorts. She tasted salt as she blew air from her lungs and tried to slow her mind. Turning onto her back she lifted her hands and touched the rim of the pipe. It was still warm.

Then the sound of cars starting, of voices calling, and they were leaving and Peter was there asking if she was okay. She came out on her hands and knees. Archie was at the edge of the shed, watching, not coming close, his face white and suspended in the night. Sebastian was there now too, helping her up.

They walked to the front of the shed to watch the red tail-lights disappearing. Archie was holding the lantern and Sebastian was shaking.

'Why didn't you do anything?' Peter was asking Sebastian.

'They're real dickheads,' said Archie.

They went back into the hut. Peter and Sebastian got the kangaroo head out, pushing it with their shoes. They moved it over near the rail tracks while Olive watched from the doorway. She saw their bouncing torches, heard their voices as they returned. They were very far away from her now, had left her or rather she them. They wedged the door shut once more and put the cardboard back into the broken window and sat, all of them lined up on the bed, staying awake until dawn started to show in the small hut. They didn't want to pack and get their bikes and ride home until the sun was all the way up, so they waited for it to be time. Peter had taken his watch off and kept holding it up to his ear and shaking it.

'I think it's busted.'

Archie leaned sideways onto Olive's shoulder as she held herself upright, not allowing herself to relax onto Peter. The others fell asleep as sun washed inside making everything glow. Olive lifted her hands and saw that they were golden too.

THEY GOT READY to leave. Squeezed the air out of the lilos. The bread was finished and Archie tried to cheer everyone up by tapping sauce into his mouth straight from the bottle. He told Olive about some scratches on his arm and back that were hurting him but she told him it was nothing, it probably happened during the fight. He tried to tell her that he wasn't even in the fight and that they were really sore and had been stinging all night but she told him to stop complaining. He wandered off as she tried to stuff her sleeping bag into its case.

A car was coming down the road. Maybe it would go past and not stop, but the instinct was to hide so they ran behind the building nearby, away from the hut. The car pulled into the loading area. Peeking out, Olive saw Archie was on the rails, walking along with a stick, hitting the wooden slats. She pulled back.

'It's Jethro Sands,' she said.

'Where's Archie?'

'Over there.'

'Fruit,' said Sebastian. A figure stepped into their sightline and Archie got up and came running toward them, shouting something about another dead snake. Behind him came the slow walking, sunglasses-wearing Jethro Sands, swinging car keys around his fingers.

'You kids still here?' he said. Olive had never been this close to him before. He was a man and she could see he could grow a beard if he wanted to. He spoke politely, probably a trick to make people trust him.

'So, my brothers—' Jethro pointed back at his car. They were there, faces at the windows. 'They said they had a problem with you last night. My brother's arm is cut up pretty badly. And there was some sort of problem at the pool?'

'Yeah, well if Luke told you I pushed him in that's true but he definitely deserved it. And Gary attacked us—he tried to get into our hut last night. We were here first. He should pick on someone his own size, they're bigger than us.'

'Jeez, you've got guts. You're right, he probably does deserve it.'

Olive continued.

'Luke was going to push me in so I just did it first.'

Jethro smiled.

'What?' Olive said. Her palms were wet.

'I suppose you don't know anything about flirting.'

'It's not.' She was horrified.

'Well, it's dangerous here. You're too little to be playing here.'

'We don't care,' said Archie. He picked up a stick and swung it in the air.

'You don't remember me, do you?' Jethro asked Olive.

She didn't know what he meant. Of course she knew him, but so did everyone. Jethro Sands, in the distance, crossing the street from pub to car, cruising in his car, the flash of his sunglasses as he motored past, window open, elbow resting on the sill, fingers tapping on the door.

'How'd you get that scar?' Sebastian said.

Jethro touched his eyebrow.

'It was a dog in truthful actuality. Your bloody dog.'

'Shaggy?'

'I don't know what its name is.'

Archie started to say something.

'Shut up,' said Sebastian. 'He's not interested.'

'How did our dog bite you?' Olive asked. 'He never goes into town. Nobody takes him off the chain, not since he bit Archie.'

'Doesn't matter how,' Jethro said. 'The thing bit me, bam. Twelve stitches.'

Archie opened his mouth again.

'I said shut up.' Sebastian pushed his brother on the shoulder.

'So, my brother's arm has glass in it, I reckon,' Jethro said. 'My mum has to take him to the doctor once it's open, which'll cost money. Bit over the line I reckon, Olive Lovelock.'

'But he attacked us first, we weren't doing anything.'

Jethro studied her.

'We were just asleep,' she said.

'What have you heard about me?'

'Some bad stuff.'

He acted as though he was thinking about that.

'You shouldn't believe the talk.' His scar was purplish at the hairline. 'Wanna smoke?' He held out the pack to Peter and Sebastian, who both said no.

'I'll have one.' Olive reached out a hand. Her mind was empty of thought other than how to light the cigarette. She took one from the pack and put it in her mouth. Jethro held out the lighter and Olive shook her head and held out her hand. He passed it to her and she took a few goes to make it work. Her fingers were jittery, shaking as she gave the lighter back. She coughed on the smoke, took one more drag, her heart thumping like a fist behind her breastbone.

Over at the car, one of the windows was wound down. Gary yelled across, 'What's taking so long? It's getting hot in here and my arm's hurting.'

Jethro held up a hand but Gary got out of the car and walked over.

'What's she saying?' He pushed his way into the group, looking at Olive. 'Want to know what's wrong with you, what people say?'

'Yes,' Olive said, but Sebastian said, 'No, Ol.'

Jethro told his brother to shut up.

'But, Jeth—'

'I said shut it.'

But Gary swung on Olive and started ranting. 'Everyone knows you're freaks. All of you. You're chi-chi-chicken,' he pointed at Sebastian, 'and you,' he swung around to Archie. 'You've got a tail, and you—' now he was pointing at Peter '—you're just a freak, you're Lurch, but you—' now it was Olive '—you're the worst.' He said something but she started talking over him.

'No, *you're* the worst.' Her voice surprised her. 'Everyone knows you're the ones killing all the kangaroos and snakes, everyone's saying it, so *you're* the killer.'

Sebastian walked away with his hands on his head. Things started to tip and become fuzzy. Olive sat on the ground, watery with dizziness. The look Peter had on his face, she'd never seen it there before.

'You okay, Ol?' he asked.

Gary was holding up his half-finger and it was pointed at her.

'My mother knows,' Gary said.

Jethro was standing with his hands on his hips, head bowed, slowly shaking it from side to side. He kept telling his brother to shut up but Gary was too far gone.

Olive sat on the ground trying not to be sick. They'd planned it like this, Jethro and Gary. It was like one of the cop shows on television where they take turns.

'Your mother too.' Gary was pointing the terrible finger at Peter. 'Everyone does. They all talk about it, at the supermarket, in the chemist, in the street. But the one who talks about it most is your mother.' He was pointing the finger now at Sebastian. 'At our house, in our driveway. You might just be a skinny kid with a weird family . . .' Gary turned to Olive 'But—'

Jethro hawked and spat into the dust. He stepped forwards and grabbed his brother by his sore arm and it made Gary stop. 'I said shut up.'

'She spat in my face.' Gary wiped his eyes.

'I didn't,' Olive said, still on the ground. 'Not properly.'

'Gary's crying.' It was Archie. He'd been watching the scene. He didn't have a tail, Gary Sands was a liar about that, and now he was starting to cry. 'Look,' he said to Sebastian. 'What a crybaby.' His head tipped back in glee. Sebastian stepped back from his brother just as Olive got to her feet and moved in between Gary and her younger cousin.

'Don't hurt him,' she said to Gary Sands. 'He's just a little kid.'

'You can talk,' Gary said softly, sniffling.

There was a noise behind them, car doors slamming. The others were coming over.

'I told you to stay in the car,' Jethro said.

'What's taking so long?' Luke called to Jethro. 'I gotta go to the dunny. Are you retarded?' he said to Olive. 'Don't you know he's been to jail?'

Olive stood, thinking. What could she say that would distract them? She'd seen the sisters do it, Rue and Thistle turning on each other in an instant, a spark of emotion flaring up from something seemingly small. Standing there, Olive conceived it and spoke it in the same moment.

'Luke kissed Cindy,' she said, watching Gary.

'What did you just say?' Gary said.

'I saw him. With these.' She held up her binoculars. 'He pashed her.'

Jethro brought his face right in close to hers. His eyes were a kind of bluey green, a pretty colour, not at all how she'd imagined.

'I heard him say she tastes like Coke and her boobs are as good as Penny Martin's.' Peter was pulling her away. 'He said it,' she finished. Penny was the waitress at the petrol station who wore tank tops with no bra.

Luke retreated to the car, his hands in the air. He was denying, calling back to them that he'd never done anything and that Olive Lovelock was a liar.

Jethro shook his head at her. 'What are you doing?'

Gary's face was screwed with rage and Jethro reached out and held the back of his brother's neck.

Olive opened her mouth to speak, not really knowing what she was going to say, but she would have thought of something because here was an opportunity, but then there was the movement of wings in air as Grace flew into the circle and alighted on one of Gary's runners. White laces in the morning sun. The new game. Grace put her beak to the end of a lace and pulled. Gary looked down.

'Gaz,' said Jethro. 'Gaz.' He took his hand away from his brother's neck and Gary shook the bird off his shoe and Grace was thrown to the dirt where he broke her, using one foot and then the other. He stomped her and the only thing Olive could think in that moment was how noiseless it was. Jethro got his brother's sleeve in his fist and pulled him away from the mess, the bent feathers and broken body on the ground.

'You!' Gary screamed at Olive. 'Don't even look at me again or I'll put you on the track and hold you down until a train cuts you in half. Same with you.' He pointed at Archie, who nodded so hard his chin hit his chest.

'You killed her,' Olive said. Her whole body was shaking.

Gary emitted his wild, chortling sound. 'It was just a crow.'

When she saw how Grace's beautiful body had got destroyed she vomited a cascade of liquid onto the dirt. Jethro walked Gary and the others to the car. Olive picked Grace up but she was gone. There wasn't much blood but she was definitely dead.

A cloud came across the world then and everything went dark and it was the coming of a sudden babel. In the air, glottal clicks as a heavy mass of grasshoppers passed through, ricocheting among them as they stopped moving in the clearing. They stood with heads bowed, lips and eyes closed, hands up to ears. Frozen in place, all anybody could do was wait. Olive felt the insects on her bare legs and arms, they knocked against her chest and the back of her neck and her cheeks. They flicked against her knees and her forehead. She wanted to scream but she couldn't open her mouth. Her hands were full of Grace so she couldn't lift them to her eyes. She stood there, stuck, while all around her, scraping and whirring filled the air. The mass thickened and she squatted and ducked, her face hidden, her hair swinging with the grasshoppers.

No voices, no calling. Just a feeling of aloneness.

The insects left. Everyone began to move. The Sands brothers went back to the car. Olive and the others went to their bikes, got all of their things ready and started to ride, Peter to his house and the two other boys and Olive to Serpentine. Grace was in her front basket and Olive kept looking at her as she pedalled. She couldn't see the road properly. It was as if a screen had come down on the outside of her eyes. She felt the insects dropping off her hair and clothes as she rode. After a few minutes she heard a car coming and it slowed as it passed. Gary was in the passenger seat, hands flapping like wings, his tongue out and eyes crossed. Next to him was Jethro, his face hard and cruel. At the back window as the car pulled away in front, two-thirds of the triplets, middle fingers raised. Olive kept wiping her eyes but the tears wouldn't stop.

She'd worried Grace would leave them. For almost three months she'd worried about it, that she'd grow up and go away—and in the end she had gone but not on a breeze up in the sky. Olive had thought it was the worst thing she had feared, that Grace would fly away, but now she knew there was an even worse story for Grace. The bird had gone, had been taken from her on the ground, a place where no bird should end.

They rode to the farm and it seemed to take a very long time because everything had slowed. Sebastian said something and she didn't hear. Archie also tried to talk to her, his lips making the shape of *Are you alright?*, but she shook her head. She kept pedalling, knowing nothing and everything. Something new had started for her the moment that Grace had been extinguished.

She'd stopped crying by the time they got up the driveway. She lifted Grace out of the basket. Lying on her back, her little claw-feet were raised to her middle and her head was wobbly under Olive's palm. Her cousins surrounded her and it made her feel even worse, their silent pity. She told them she knew what Peter's middle name was and that it was Dewey.

'No it's not,' said Sebastian. 'No one has that for a middle name, it's only in the comics.'

'Ask him yourself. It's the truth.'

She walked down the hallway, unsteady in the crushing space. It took forever to get to the back of the house and all the way, the only thing she could think was: Where had all her breath gone? She'd seen no one inside who could help her so went and found William working out the back. He was doing something with wire. She asked him if he could please help her. That Grace was dead and she needed a hole but didn't think she was able to make one herself. It needed to be a deep grave so nobody could ever dig her up. So even the biggest rainstorm and flood wouldn't wash her bones to the surface.

William said he would help her and went and got the spade.

She hadn't wanted to ask him because he hated Grace but he was kind about it. He told her to choose a place she liked, away from the house, and she did. She pointed to a spot behind the shed in the shade of an old apple tree. He dug the hole for her and each time he stopped and looked back she shook her head and he kept digging. They put Grace in the bottom and William gave Olive his hanky for a covering.

Once they'd finished and the grave was filled in he held her hand and told her not to cry, but she couldn't help it. He asked if she wanted to say a prayer but she said no. It didn't matter. Grace was in the ground. She was safe. She was hidden. No one could find her and hurt her any more.

JETHRO PULLED INTO the driveway. From the back, Luke started to speak, leaning forward, saying he hadn't done anything, that Olive Lovelock was the biggest liar he'd ever seen and that was saying something. Gary reached back and twisted Luke's hair. Jethro slapped them apart.

'Stop it,' he said. 'She's playing with you, alright?'

'Of course you're going to say you didn't do it,' Gary said.

'But I didn't,' Luke said. 'As if. Cin wouldn't, not ever.'

'Cin?' Gary swung around again.

'Sorry, Gaz. I promise.'

'Of course you'd want to, anyone would.' Gary scratched his head.

'Leave it,' said Jethro. 'He didn't do anything, it's her. She's the one making trouble. She always has been, she's—' He opened the door.

'What?' Gary got out too. 'She's what?'

Jethro kept walking to the back door. Once there, he stopped on the step, near the gully trap.

'She's bad luck.'

They sat around the kitchen table. Their mother was still in bed, so Gary boiled the kettle while Jethro got the mugs out.

'Get the milk,' he said to Mark. John was still in bed, probably reading if he was awake.

Jethro dug his teaspoon into the International Roast.

'Jesus, this family.'

He spooned sugar and motioned for Gary to pour. Milk in, stirred and slung the spoon back into the sugar bowl. He sipped his coffee.

What the hell was she doing?

He went outside, and backed his car into the garage. He put the dust sheet on. What a beauty. He'd bought it with money he'd saved since he was a kid. Birthday money, chemist-round wages, all the jobs he'd done. He'd saved most of the earnings, careful to hide it after his father asked to borrow some but had never paid it back. He'd been nine then and knew better now. Then his grandmother had died and left them some cash for when they each turned eighteen. He'd got his the year before, around the time his father had come back. It had been hard, keeping that money in the bank, with his dad saying how he owed him, that a good son would help his father out. In the end, he hadn't managed to keep it all but he had been able to buy the car he'd wanted.

He didn't like anyone touching the Charger and no one was allowed to drive it. He was saving to convert it, get the roof taken off and a soft-top put in. After that, he would get it spray-painted 'Ferrari red'. He'd taken a long time choosing the colour.

'What are we going to do about Olive Lovelock?' Gary said from behind him.

Jethro rubbed his hands on a rag.

'She's a smart-arse and she's also a snoop. Did you see those things around her neck? And that big kid that was there with the blond hair, sort of surfie?'

'Yeah?'

'That's the cop's kid.'

'So?'

'What if they tell, about the animals? I've already got warnings and you've got a record.'

'Those things have got nothing to do with me and I told you to stop it. But you never listen.'

Gary went to Jethro's esky and got a beer, opened it, took a sip. He tossed the ring-pull onto the bench. Jethro watched him. He put a hand on the bonnet. *Gayle.*

'They're just old roos—most of them, anyway,' Gary said. 'The other things, who likes them? Who cares about snakes?'

Jethro threw the rag on the bench.

'We have to stick together,' Gary said. 'Especially against the Lovelocks.'

Jethro didn't want to talk about Olive Lovelock or her family.

'Man, those teeth. If she was my sister I would have bashed them straight by now, right?' Gary pressed his fingers until they cracked and Jethro stepped outside the garage and motioned for Gary to follow. He shut the garage door with a clatter. Gary hawked and spat a glob out to the grass. He wiped his mouth on the back of his hand.

'How's the arm?'

'Sore.' Gary finished his beer and cracked his neck with a quick side-side movement. Jethro stood and watched as his brother went up the back steps and into the house.

IN RUE'S KITCHEN, Olive tried to eat a tomato and cheese jaffle but all she could do was break it apart into smaller and smaller bits, twisting the crusts into fragments and dropping them onto her plate.

People spoke to her, they kept saying, *Olive, Olive*, but she didn't hear them. She couldn't eat, not while Grace was dead. There was something inside her that filled her body and stretched into her fingers and toes. It lined her back and chest and was thick and painful. From the kitchen drawer she got the cooking string and made lines in Mandy's room, stretched between furniture, tied around knobs and shooting off in all directions. From the chair to the bed to the dresser and back to the chair again. Frantic white highways that crisscrossed the floor. She lay under her bed. She lay there for hours.

'Olive?'

Rue stepped in and made her way across to the bed. The springs above dipped a little.

'What's wrong?'

'Grace died,' Olive said. Her hand was pressed to the skirting board and her eyes wandered over the springs under her mattress, the diamond shapes of the wire base. There was a small loop of thread hooked over one wire. It was red, as fine as a hair. She stared at that piece of cotton, seeing the way it was twisted.

'It's time for lunch, we've got sausage rolls. And then I'll drive you home.'

'I'm not hungry.'

Olive stayed under her bed against the wall, not interested in the flaking pastry and steaming meat, not caring about the sweet red sauce. The boys were sent to tell her to come to the table. They squatted in turn but finally Rue came and pulled her out by the arm. It left a salmon-pink mark.

She went to wash her hands. In the bathroom mirror her eyes shone pale and her grown-out fringe flopped to her chin. She found some bobby pins and put her hair back and looked at herself again in the mirror. She'd always hated her hair being back, she liked it on her face and across her eyes, no matter what Rue said. She looked again closely, bringing her nose right up to the glass so that her breath fogged it in small puffs. Her eyes were hollow and round, and when she pulled back she saw she had a wide cavity for a mouth, her lips pulled into a new shape. *How did it get like that?* she wondered. She tried to smile, but it made her look like a hungry animal.

At the table her eyes were sunken.

'I know you're upset,' Rue said, reaching for her wrist. 'Everything will be fine, you'll see. You'll be sad for a while and then it will fade away and you will feel better.'

Olive pulled her arm away. Rue was always trying to feel people's pulses as if the small beats could tell her something important.

'Grace is dead. Nothing will ever be alright.'

Later she heard Rue say to Thistle 'that girl is becoming hard work'. It made her go to her bed and climb under again. She cried until her eyes puffed and her face hurt. Her jaw, her neck, her stomach. All of it was gathered in a tight bundle of pain.

When they finally left, she sat in the back of the car. Rue pressed a lamington into her hand to take home, wrapped in a paper napkin. It was still warm and she knew it was her aunt's way of trying to be sorry. But as she was driven home, she let it drop to the floor of the car where it would dry out and crumble over the next few days.

•

Olive's last thought before sleep that night came in a gasp. It lifted her off the bed like an enormous muscle spasm, its attack coming just as her body and mind fell towards sleep. There was a word printed behind her eyelids in large magenta letters and it spelled GRACE.

•

She woke in the morning with a dry mouth, her sheet twisted off the side of the bed. The house was quiet. There were no magpies to be heard, no soft sighs coming from Mandy as she started to wake up. She could hear Mr McCullers next door clipping his trees and the sound of Mrs McCullers calling him from the back door, asking if he wanted another cup of tea. Even though that was all normal, as she'd slept, during the hours before morning, everything had changed.

WORMWOOD

IT WAS A few days before Christmas. Olive stayed in the cool gloom of her room as her parents loaded the car. Her body had been taken from her and she was floating, removed from her own self. She was now in a place—or a not-place—where she existed without knowledge of anything. The same origins, maybe, that babies came from. It might have been a place covered with water, or in the sky so far above that she couldn't see the earth anymore. Wherever she was, everything had been taken from her. She didn't care what cereal she had for breakfast and didn't care either that she hadn't seen Peter for days. With nothing to anchor her—no school, no companionship—she stayed suspended in the new place, noticing only noise and finding no comfort in any of it.

It was easy to make it seem as if she was still there, where she was meant to be. Say yes to cornflakes and yes to cartoons. The old books she pulled off her shelf, books she'd already read and reread, the people and countries and adventures she'd known and lived already. Familiar friends that she'd liked very much who couldn't reach her now. Even *Heidi* was a stranger, a girl grown cold.

Asleep she was whole, but awake, in parts. Every morning, as soon as she opened her eyes, she thought of Grace. Sometimes there was a moment of forgetting then things returned, visions and memories that had mostly been emptied out by sleep. She remembered Gary's feet, his shoes, the way Grace's feathers had bent in the wrong direction. It had taken her days to let herself know that the worst thing had been that Grace was *playing*. She'd made games and brought presents and shown her love. It was what hurt the most: that Grace had trusted Olive to not let any harm come to her. She had failed in the worst possible way.

Her parents put the presents in the car as well as some cut-crystal bowls and extra salad serving spoons for lunch on Christmas Day. They set off, driving east with Olive in the back, looking at her reflection in the car window. She hated what she saw.

On her lap in the car was her school certificate and report to show Rue and Thistle. Mrs Barton had written that she was 'stubborn' and 'intense' and needed to think about her attitude before Year 7. She'd received the certificate for finishing grade six but it wasn't anything special because Snooky had got dux. Olive knew she could have been dux if she had really tried.

A dirge played in her head as she sat in the car, staring out at the land. Low and constant, the notes that she heard didn't exist in real music. The effect was like the bagpipes on one of Thistle's cassettes, wailing and unpredictable. Thistle loved the bagpipes, Rue called them 'hideous' and her mother 'intolerable'. Her father would clench his jaw in mute resistance, but William would get up and leave the house, take himself off for long walks, announcing he would return once the caterwauling had ceased.

In the car, Olive didn't look out for dead animals up ahead.

She had done her part but wouldn't anymore.

•

They arrived. Rue came out to meet them and Olive walked towards the house with her aunt's arm across her shoulders. Could Rue feel the change through her clothes? Her mother was ahead of them, fanning herself with a brochure. By the time Olive reached the verandah she could hear Audra's shoes moving down the long hallway. Olive went to the back of the house and looked out to the peppercorn tree. Underneath was Cleg's car, the Holden Premier covered in tape, the caravan parked once more in the same place. Why was he always here, anyway?

She leaned against the window for a while then went to the kitchen to get herself a glass of milk. Her mouth felt like there was acid in it and her stomach was sore but none of it mattered. She would never be happy again.

•

She was sitting on the kitchen stool when Archie ran in and announced a dingo had eaten a baby. Rue was there too, going through the bin. She straightened.

'Another one?' she said. Archie looked confused and Rue looked confused too and then he was gone.

'Thistle said that mother wouldn't ever hurt her own baby,' Olive said. 'But Mum says she did.'

'Nonsense,' said Rue, peeling the apples. 'Mothers never do that, they love their babies more than anything—it's just that some women can't show it for whatever reason. Sometimes there's a sickness. Sheba, I need the sugar.'

'What's it called? The sickness?'

Rue shifted things in the pantry.

'I don't remember.'

'What makes people hurt animals?'

Rue was moving jars and boxes. 'Oh, blast, where's Thistle? Go to her room, would you? Knock on the door and ask her if she's got the sugar. If she's not there, just go in and see if you can find it.'

There was no answer to her knock so Olive pushed the bedroom door open. It was chaotic. Thistle said it was a sign of a brain that moves fast, with no time for banal activities such as tidying. Any moron can tidy, was what she said.

The first thing Olive saw was the empty packet of sugar pushed down inside the bin. She went in and shut the door. It was better to stay in the quiet of Thistle's room than go back to the kitchen where her aunt refused to let silence just be. She looked around. Newspapers were stacked to hip height and clippings rested in piles on the floor. There were dolls of all shapes and sizes, baby clothes, finely knitted, jigsaws in their boxes and in small jumbled piles along the skirting boards. Easter egg foil, crusts of toast on plates, empty lolly bags and across the whole of it the strong odour of dirty sheets and spritzes of fruity perfume.

The bed was pushed underneath the curtainless window.

'Why on earth do you want it there?' Audra had asked her sister when Thistle had moved in. It had been Mandy's room but she was too little to protest the swap.

'Because of the moon,' Thistle had said. 'I like to sleep with it on my face.'

'Don't be ridiculous,' Rue had said but Olive had thought a bed right under the window was a good idea. She would like her bed like that.

There were drinking glasses that had furry stuff growing in the bottoms. Feathers and stones and bones on the windowsill, and in the corner the sheep's skull. Thistle's room was like an exciting nature museum and library in one. It was a place that you could talk in, walk around and touch whatever you liked.

She walked across the littered floor, over the plates and food wrappers, single socks, lace-edged bloomers, teacups, groups of bird cards arranged in fans ready to go into their albums. There were music tapes, dozens of them, and shelves of books, and more stacked on the floor in piles. *The Beauties and Furies. Hypatia. The Theban Plays. The Bloody Chamber.* Lots of Shakespeares. *For Love Alone. Modern Women in Love. Dark Places of the Heart.* And the strangest cover was the book with a headless lady's suit made of skin with handles on the sides of the hips. The plays, multiple rehearsal copies of the sisters one and the seagull script also. Crossword books and acrostic puzzles, empty pill bottles on the floor, lotions beside the bed. She went to the window, where the glass was fingerprinted, smudged with a milky-brown dried paste. On one of the panes, the words *You-You*, written in groups of two.

Back in the kitchen she told Rue she couldn't find the sugar. Her aunt made a noise and asked her to please get the honey from the larder.

'No matter. Sweet is sweet.'

Maybe it was true but maybe, also, at the same time, it wasn't.

•

Half an hour later Olive roused enough to yell at Archie, who was excited and kept bothering her. He didn't listen when she kept saying to leave her alone, that she didn't care it was almost Christmas. Rue told her off for shouting in the house and asked her to stay away from him, to please just behave. She went out to the tree where she lay, face down, her narrow form squeezed in at the base, arms wide, holding on to the sprawling mass of roots. It might have felt like a hug if she wasn't so sad. She wasn't interested in wrestling Archie, playing their usual game where she would try to punch his bum five times *whack-whack-whack-whack-whack* or bite his ankle as he sat on her head to fart. She lay on the ground and wondered if a person could just die because of nothing.

After a while she heard Cleg moving around inside the caravan. She wiped her eyes and turned her head. To the side was a piece of grass, a slender shoot, green and new. How did it manage to grow in this world? She touched the bark. A tree didn't have to make a journey and there were no places of decision because a tree didn't have to do anything other than just be in the air and face the wind and rain for all of time.

She sat up and leaned against the trunk. Sheep stood close by. Dry paddocks. Tank. Fences all around. Dead Girl's had been a waste of time, Ganger's too. The whole séance idea had been a stupid one from the beginning. If they hadn't gone to Ganger's, Grace would still be with her, up above in the tree right now, or lying in her lap the way she used to, feet sweetly raised in the air, head tilted so she could watch Olive's face. When she thought of Grace's eyes it was awful. She lay back down and clung to the earth and waited for the world to slow its spin.

CLEG SET UP a workstation for Olive to help him with the mother work. He ran a power cord from the shed to the caravan and showed her how to type in the names and addresses of women and hospitals, dates and birth details, from a handwritten sheet. She had to do it using a typing board which was attached at the bottom of the computer box. She would be paid two dollars for one hour and he said because it was still morning they could probably do quite a bit that day. Every hour or so, he explained, they would save her work to a cassette in a small deck that plugged in to the computer.

'That way it won't get lost if something goes wrong,' he said.

It was slow work but she liked it. As she typed, Cleg told her about the women who'd lost their babies. She asked questions, either about the typing or the mothers, and she found she was fine there, that day, in the small space of the caravan. She had a ruler to keep track of where she was on the list, and a red pen to do a tick to show that she had typed in the information.

Cleg found a packet of biscuits that weren't opened and they tasted okay even if they were a bit old. She tapped on the computer and wondered whether this was what it would be like to play the piano. She wondered whether her job when she grew up could be something to do with typing. Maybe she could use her savings to buy a little typewriter. The high school had a typing subject. She could do that and then grow up and be a typer. It could be alright, she thought.

Olive liked being around Cleg. It was Cleg who had taught them the Latin when they were little. Olive's unique phrase was *inter urinas et faeces nascimur*, which Rue hated, saying it was an inappropriate expression for a young girl. Archie's was the *omnia* one he used every time for the dam, which meant 'let it all hang out'. Cleg was very specific. This should always be used with at least one exclamation mark and was to be reserved for occasions when a person was jumping into, onto or from something, preferably nude.

Cleg had demonstrated what he meant about *omnia*. He'd walked the children down to the dam, away from Rue's tight look and his pregnant wife's languid form on the couch. He stripped off his clothes, called out the phrase in an operatic thrill and belly-whacked into the water in a flat racing dive. Sebastian's expression was *quid agis,* translated as: 'What's going on? What's happening? What's up?' This was to be delivered, their uncle insisted, drops rolling off the end of his beard as he got dressed beside the dam, in a cool, finger-snapping way. As if you were from New York.

Mandy had been given her special saying the first time they'd seen him after the car crash. He'd squatted in front of her and given her an easy word, perfect for a small girl like her, he said. *Lux.* Her tongue lisped on the final consonant and Cleg had cried. Then he'd horsed around and they'd all climbed on him, children hanging off various limbs. Archie and Olive slid onto his feet, their legs wrapped around his ankles.

'Goodness, I seem to have put on kid shoes,' Cleg marvelled, lifting his feet. 'What is this? Are my shoes made out of children?'

He'd driven them into town to get Wizz Fizzes, white-knuckled the whole way. That night, Olive hovered in the doorway and overheard Cleg tell Audra and Rue that the *liberi* were wonderful but that he had to leave early the next day, before anyone was awake. Audra had put her hand on his arm and Rue had wept and Olive had stepped back to stand for a moment, wondering at the emotions that had been on display.

They had a break for lunch. She and Cleg went inside and made sandwiches. Olive told Rue about the work, how it was interesting and sad. They took the sandwiches back to the little table inside the caravan and, while she ate, Cleg showed her a game that she could play on the computer. It was called 'The Castle' and she had to start outside in a garden, follow the prompts and find a way into the castle grounds. For half an hour she tried and tried to get through the walls. First she tried to dig underneath them, then she tried to walk around. She looked for doors that would open for her and kept failing, but she wasn't going to give up. The goal, she had worked out, was to collect everything of value, kill everything that was a threat, and then leave. You didn't even need to really understand anything, just try everything, she realised. Push it all, pull it all. Step on top of, climb under or over. *Tap, hit, strike, roll.*

There were twenty-one levels to the game and during that lunch she made it to level four. She liked the game. It was helpful. She was determined to get to the end.

•

'I don't understand why you're interested in all of that,' Rue said to Olive in the kitchen, arms wrapped around herself, Wettex in one hand and tea towel in the other. But Olive was very interested in what Cleg had to tell her about the mothers. He'd had meetings with the women in the city and they'd told him awful things, about the poisons and the drugs and the hiding places for the babies. The tricks and lies and upset that had happened when the women were younger. One mother had been blind for a whole year after her little boy was taken away, Cleg told Olive. Another had dreams that she had a secret baby that she kept in a shoebox at the back of her wardrobe.

'They're really sad,' Olive reported to the family at dinner. 'I feel more sorry for the babies, though. I think that the mothers could have tried a bit harder.'

Thistle asked what she was implying.

'Nothing.'

She told the family how some of the mothers were drugged and some of the babies taken away while the mother was waiting for the after-burn to come out. That was when Rue said to Cleg it was really too much.

'But it's wrecked their lives, some of them,' Olive said, and Cleg nodded.

'Compassion is important in situations like these,' he said to his sister-in-law. Rue looked at Thistle whose head had dropped, her chin almost to her chest.

'I really don't think she should be hearing all this,' Rue said. 'Olive, that is.'

'In the report it says one has got a really bad scar,' said Olive. 'One of the mothers. From her belly button to her . . . thing, and it's crisscrossed like a railway line but with white dots at the edge like Archie's heel, where Shaggy—'

Archie pushed back his chair and started to take his shoe off.

'Not at the table.' Rue started to fold her serviette. 'You showed her pictures, Cleg? Please, it's Christmastime. Can't we just have a nice time?'

'The doctor said he was making sure she wouldn't be naughty again so that's why he sewed her up like that, but I didn't see anything, it was just words, in the report.' Olive hurried the last few words out and shut her mouth in triumph. The whole thing was surprising to her, but what was most interesting was learning that the world could be hard for adults. They could have bad things happen to them too.

'It's just not appropriate, Cleg, I mean really,' Rue said.

'But I'm helping,' Olive said. 'And I'm getting pocket money for typing on his computer. All the names and numbers, making a databank.'

'Base,' said Cleg.

'It seems unnecessary for a young girl to be exposed to all that misery. Sad for anyone really. I mean it's happened, and I wish them well, but what do they expect can possibly be done now, all this time later? It can't be undone.'

'They want to retribute,' said Olive.

'Retribution,' said Cleg. 'Not the same as—'

'Revenge?' said Olive.

'See?' Cleg said to Rue. 'She's learning other things as well. It's good for her general knowledge, her vocabulary.'

'I just don't think a young girl should be hearing these sorts of stories. Especially not the physical things—it might put her off.'

'Off to what?' Olive said.

'Having a family yourself one day.'

'But I'm not ever having one.'

Rue reached for her napkin ring.

'You're just saying that now. You'll change your mind.'

'I won't,' Olive said under her breath. 'Not ever.' She slumped in her seat.

•

Coming out of the bathroom, Olive found Mandy.

'Christmas is coming. The reindeer are going on the roof when I'm asleep. Is there any real magic in the world? Thistle said there isn't.' Her cousin looked as if she was about to cry.

'What presents do you want?' Olive said.

'I want my tummy ache to go away.'

'What?'

Mandy smiled and Olive saw the crenellations of her teeth. The centre bottom two had already gone and a top one had fallen out a couple of weeks ago.

'My dad did shout at me before.'

'What for?'

'For nothing at all.'

'Go and tell your mother.' She gave Mandy a push and sent her walking down the hall, then went back out to the verandah to get her binoculars. She was about to open the door but heard voices and stopped. Thistle and Cleg sat together on the rattan couch. Cleg was holding her arm. He talked to her in a very low voice. Their heads were close together. He was saying she needed to give him some more details and a bit of time.

Olive crept back to the bathroom. It was a startling thing. To know that Cleg could be tender with Thistle, the sister he seemed to like the least. Standing in front of the mirror it was as if there was an opening inside her mind. A plant, a tall one, with a green stem that was thick all the way around. At the top of it, a tightly bunched bloom, an enormous head of closed, wrapped petals. She didn't know the colour of the flower yet but it was bright as if illuminated by special lights, and inside the head of the flower was a quavering, shimmering sensation of coming movement and understanding.

AT THE CARAVAN she did the work for Cleg and played the game. She tried to lift the third stepping stone outside the castle's massive wooden door with the stick she'd picked up. The message blinked on the screen: YOU HAVE ENTERED THE CASTLE. CONGRATULATIONS.

She sat back in her chair. Finally, she was in. She explored the grounds, found gold and other valuables inside a metal chest. She discovered an armoury, and a kitchen with delectable food. In the castle itself there was a mouse that became a sidekick, and there was an evil cat, as well as ghosts and a floating head that had a black beard and an eye patch.

But she had become stuck. There was a rigged doorway, and no matter what she tried she always ended up decapitated. Her mouse friend Bobo was too little to get hurt by the swinging scimitar that rolled out of a hidden crevice as soon as you opened the door with the chicken bone left over from feasting. Bobo could run in and out but it was no help to her. She lay in bed that night, trying to think of ways to get past that swinging curved blade. How to keep her head and make progress. Tomorrow was the last time she'd be able to try because it was Christmas Eve. Soon Cleg would be going back to the city.

After lunch the next day she had completed entering all the information and she'd almost finished level twenty-one of 'The Castle', the final stage. She had her quiver, complete with arrows. She had her canteen, filled with water. The wolf was beside her with Bobo on its head, and her cloak of invisibility was in her backpack.

Everything was perfect. She knew it would work, and once she had everything in place she made her final move.

It didn't work. She tried a second move. Still nothing happened. By the time she tried the third combination, her hope had disappeared. She kept trying different things but couldn't work it out. She'd been positive she had it. Why hadn't that first move been the one? She kept getting sent back to the last place she'd saved the game. She tried again and again. Through the locked door and rickety staircase that collapsed behind her as she went up it. She was about to give up when she tried one more time and it worked. A shudder of satisfaction and power went through her. She smiled.

'What's that?'

'I've finished,' she said.

'Well, that deserves a cup of tea?'

She nodded and went to the little cupboard to get a mug. She made herself tea and sat down at the table. There was a small stack of books near the window and she looked through the pile. Robert Ludlum, Dick Francis. But then an interesting-looking one: *The Book of Lists*.

'What's this?' She held up the book.

'Oh, that, just a bit of fun. I don't remember where I got it but it makes for good reading. Lots of interesting and obscure facts.'

She opened a page. It was about Ivan the Terrible and it described how terrible he really was. She turned the page. Jack the Ripper. A list of still-alive Nazis.

'Can I borrow this?'

'You can have it if you like.'

She put the book to the side and went back to the computer. All the lists of women and their disappeared babies. Maybe Cleg was the person to ask about her sister.

'I know about the baby,' Olive said. 'My one.'

She wasn't sure if Cleg had heard her, he was still in the kitchenette making his coffee. She waited until he came back and sat down.

'Your mother couldn't get out of bed,' Cleg said. 'Thistle took her lunch on trays.' Olive guessed it would have been bowls of soup, butter-and-sugar sandwiches and glasses of flat lemonade. That was what she had when she was sick.

'But Mum and Thistle hate each other. I don't even know why we always come here.'

'Thist is good in a crisis and your mother had no choice. She needed the help. You wouldn't know this but in the early days your aunt looked like a model in her little angora sweaters. It annoyed Rue but, boy, we all took one look at her and were goners. Rue was lucky there was a brother for her, Thistle would have taken whichever one she wanted, but of the three of us, she always thought William a little too ... I can't remember—well, something. Their mother was tough on those three but hardest of all on her, on Thistle. It might seem difficult for you to believe it now but your mum was Thistle's supporter in those early years. They didn't hate each other. And later, Billy—just children we all were, really. All of it is pretty complicated.'

'But what about the baby?'

Cleg sat down and wouldn't look at her. He opened his mouth three times but no words came out. He looked at the window. He looked at the door. He looked everywhere but at her. It was further proof that no one knew the truth about Aster.

'Mum doesn't even know what happened,' she said.

Cleg breathed in and held all his air in his body for as long as possible. It made her want to hold her own breath, as if they had fallen into water together. There in the caravan she waited for her uncle to say something. Finally, he let the air out in a rush. He took a sip of his coffee.

'Why doesn't anyone know? Didn't the police investigate?'

'There were no questions.'

'I just don't get it,' Olive said and put her lips to her mug. She put it down. 'Too hot.'

'Do you want to play the game again? You can start from the beginning if you like.'

'Nope. Is there anything else?'

He showed her a horse-racing one and blackjack. She was disappointed that the horse-racing one was just numbers moving across the screen, not real horses. She played blackjack for a while and Cleg shook out his newspaper.

Olive stopped the computer games and opened *The Book of Lists* again to a random page. Tutankhamun was a very small king. The JRR bit was for John Ronald *Reuel*. Next in the book was a list of unnamed women in the Bible, beginning with Noah's wife. You'd think a woman who set up house in a boat for a whole year with all those animals would at least have her name written down. There was also a woman who was a nun and then left the church to become a bullfighter.

'What's a sobricket?'

'What's that?'

She pointed to the word.

'Oh. A sobriquet. Nickname.'

She read quickly: *Charles the Simple, Ethelred the Unready. Louis the Fat. Charles the Bad.* She turned the page again and saw something about CIA mind-control experiments. She closed the book.

'I think I'll go now.'

She was going to go and lie down to read about the mind-control experiments. It would be useful to be able to control someone's mind.

As she walked to the back of the house she looked up at the sky for movement, then caught herself. It was a habit she would have to break but she knew it would be hard, maybe impossible. Every time she remembered it was like someone was stepping on her heart.

CHRISTMAS MORNING, AND Rue had already started the fans going. William had been out to the fuse board twice and Thistle was walking around in a petticoat batting a large red fan against herself. There'd been another passing cloud of grasshoppers, the brown insects swaying on leaves and clinging to sheets on clotheslines. Phones around town had rung with people wondering if a larger mass was on the way, but nothing more had arrived other than a spike in temperature around 11 am.

In the kitchen, Rue started the mince pies and the younger children were pulling at their stockings when Shaggy started barking outside. The more oleaginous of the two local butchers drove his truck up the driveway of the house and around the back. Rue went to the door, hands floured and hair unbrushed. Pushing open the door she saw Leonard Sands getting out of his van. He walked towards her, carrying a side of lamb over one shoulder that was spattered with epaulettes of blood. He said g'day and carried the lamb into the kitchen. Rue followed, suspicious at the intrusion, the lamb, that it was him there that Christmas morning. Len Sands slammed the carcass down on the bench too close to her pastry. He leaned on a meaty elbow.

'So, love, yer sister about?'

Rue drew herself up.

'Merry Christmas to you too, Len. If you don't mind.' She pointed at the meat. 'Do you have an invitation?'

He fiddled with his fly, casting glaucous eyes around the kitchen.

'I've got a message for her about New Year's. We were going to talk about the party at the club. About the costumes. She said she'd give me a cuppa.' He winked.

'Thistle did? And she bought that?' She considered the contraband. William would be murderous.

'She didn't buy it, as such. I'm not here in an official capacity, it's more a social visit, you could say. She rang me and the lamb's for the tea.'

The butcher looked through the window.

'You got someone staying out there in the van?' he said, smiling. His mouth looked slippery. 'One of the kids?'

'It's Clegworth,' Rue said, shaking the tin of Ajax.

'Cleg's here? Well.' Len pushed himself up from the bench and said he'd better be off but could she pass on a message to her sister. Before Rue could say that might be best there was a noise at the back door. It was Thistle in her floral housecoat.

'Le-yen.' She leaned an arm in a vertical flourish up the door-jamb and held the position before efflorescing across the kitchen towards him. Thistle's latest folly, as Rue called it, was a new speech affectation, her approximation of a southern belle. Rue tried to carry on as normal but William's face had become redder than usual around Thistle, and Audra was incandescent with fury, a sight that made Thistle's voice crisp as she chittered at dinner, complaining about the mighty oppressive heat. She sashayed about everywhere in a slip, rolling a cut crystal tumbler of ice across her forehead, a charm-bracelet noisy on her wrist. Everyone was doing their best to ignore it.

By the pantry door Thistle grabbed Len's arm, twittered about tea and spun to the kettle.

'Sorry, Thisser, but I have to go. You look pretty today, though.' Audra came in.

'Ah,' she said. 'The butcher.' She crossed her arms and stood in the doorway.

Len took Thistle's hand from his arm and let it go and it flopped and hung at her side. 'I'll have to raincheck the tea, sorry, love.' He tipped his finger at her and went to the door. 'But the message is that Mavis wants fancy dress for New Year's and she's pushing for nuns and vicars. Spooner wants togas but Spooner always wants togas.' No one spoke and Audra cleared her throat. Len said *Merry Christmas* and left.

As soon as he was gone, Thistle swung to the room, her arms aloft in Ophelia's tragic pose.

'You spoil *everything*,' she said to Audra. Their faces were in a cross-fade as first one, then the other, was illuminated by indignant energy. 'You can't bear to think of me having someone for my own. Always had to have the limelight.'

'I don't know how you can even talk to that man.' Rue folded a tea towel, opened it, then folded it again. Thistle swiped at the tea canister, sending it along the bench. It ricocheted off the wall and clattered into the sink, tea leaves spilling.

'Good lord,' Rue said, and sat on the stool. She looked at the lamb, glistening wetly on the laminex, while Audra went to the fridge to get the milk out.

OLIVE WAS AWAKE but still in bed, reading *The Book of Lists*. Mandy had already run in to say she had eaten all her chocolate coins and why wasn't she getting up, it was Christmas. But Olive told her to go away. She wanted to keep reading about the twenty-five things that fell from the sky, including hay, golden rain, black eggs and meat. How in 1977 five hundred dead and dying blackbirds and pigeons cascaded to the streets of California for hours and hours. Toads also fell, and fish. That was in Australia, up in the Northern Territory. The book said fish falls were common, that whirlwinds could create a water spout over the ocean or a lake and then drop the fish down onto the land. She closed the book and imagined all of that. She opened it again. Peaches, too! Falling from the sky. She thought about that for a while. You could catch them in a box. Then she read about eclipses and lightning strikes and a psychic dog called Chris.

She heard a cough outside the window. She was going to go and see who it was—probably Archie, spying—when she remembered the sheep. When she'd been little, she used to think a man came in the night to stand next to the window but Sebastian told her that a sheep's cough is exactly like a human's. That what his dad had said.

•

Later Rue caught her slinking past in the hallway and asked her to come and help with lunch, so she went and did as she was asked. She made the stuffing for the chickens, with Rue directing her.

She trussed them too but didn't do a very good job and Rue had to do it again. Then she carved the ham, also badly, putting the slices onto a platter, wedges of meat thick at one end, thin at the other. She arranged parsley, partly to hide the poor display of ham, partly 'for colour', as Rue called it. She covered the plate with plastic wrap then they made the rice and potato salads.

Thistle came in and Rue asked her where Audra was.

'Still in bed.' Thistle's eyes were on her sister's face.

'Oh, how nice. I'd love to be back in bed with a cup of tea on Christmas morning. How nice to know all the work will be done, she doesn't have to lift a finger.'

'You never let anyone help,' said Thistle.

'What?' Rue said. 'What's that you said?'

Thistle said not to worry and went out again. Rue stood with her hands on her hips and considered the mess on the bench. The baking trays, the spilled stuffing, seeds from inside the tomatoes, the onion skins. She held up her hands. A nice drink would make everything fizz away.

'I might open a bottle of bubbly,' she said. 'Can you get the glasses down for me?' She pulled the stool over and held Olive's legs as she stretched up to the cupboard.

'Careful.'

She gave Olive a third of a glass, telling her not to say anything to her mother. Olive drank it quickly and refilled it when her aunt was setting the table.

Olive carried salads in and put them on silver placemats. Rue came through the swing door carrying two bread baskets and made the time call—ten minutes more she told the family, they may as well start sitting down. Her eyes hovered above Olive's head for a moment then she turned and went back into the kitchen. Olive followed. On the bench was the serving plate with the cut-up chicken

and beside it, a small butter plate upon which rested the two wishbones. Olive always got a wishbone at Christmas but the others had
to take turns. Rue kept a list inside the cupboard door and when
challenged by the other children said Olive got hers just because,
that she didn't have to explain it to anyone. Olive hadn't split any of
her bones yet, she was saving them for when she needed the most
luck. This would be her sixth year and her sixth wishbone.

In the kitchen, Thistle and Rue were standing over the denuded
frames in the trays. The air was redolent with tarragon, the bird
cavities bright with the yellow of the lemons. Without pause, Thistle
stepped to the side to make space for her niece who slid into place
and reached for some skin.

'Hurry,' said Thistle. 'The men will become restless.'

The door opened from the hallway and they all looked up. It
was Audra, eyes fixed on the baking trays. They moved again to let
her in. Olive knew her mother hated the slavering but was drawn
to it, unable to resist the pull of what she called 'the barbarism'.
But she was dainty as she pulled morsels of meat from the bones,
driving a single nail gently down the ridges to lift the meat. They
stood at the laminex bench, mouths working, fingers flashing as
they pulled the oysters from underneath, the thin skerricks along
the lengths of the ribs and the stubborn bits that clung around the
place where the thigh bones had been wrenched from the frame. It
had been minutes already and they had to be quick, because in the
dining room the others would be starting to serve themselves and
if they were too long William might appear at the door asking if it
was to be a vegetarian Christmas this year. He would stand there
with that look on his face and they would all feel the shame of it.

The jostling in the kitchen, though, was warm and compan-
ionable and for Olive, it was a rare spectacle. There was no other
occasion that the three sisters came together in anything even

approximating harmony. No one called anyone feeble or a martyr. No one got huffy and swept from the room in high dudgeon. There was quiet, a hushed sense of almost-giggling as if the sisters might in a bizarre and spontaneous moment hang off each other's necks to laugh about something from their childhood. It had never happened but there was the feeling that it could.

The door opened. Thistle was digging around inside to get at the neck and Rue was nibbling on a parson's nose. Thistle hissed a signal and they left the birds in a single movement: Audra moved out the door, Thistle to the pantry wiping her mouth with the back of her hand, Olive to the sink and Rue to the toaster.

'It's only Archie.' Olive pawed her shining fingers down his cheek. Rue gave Olive some papertowel and she wiped her fingers and mouth, then put the wishbones on the windowsill to dry. Rue picked up the platter of chicken to lead the procession back into the dining room.

'Revolting,' said William as they sat down.

Olive picked at her full plate, ears hot from the champagne. She looked around the table. Was there a fly inside? She flapped her hands in the air.

'Do you want to go to the dam after?' she said to Sebastian. He said no, he didn't. He was going to start constructing the model plane he got for Christmas. Olive said ok, fine. He was being strange lately, as if he was too good for her. And it was like he didn't care about what had happened at Ganger's because he hadn't mentioned Grace even once. He didn't want to talk about anything anymore, he just wanted to be left alone. Olive could remember how interested he used to be in learning the codes—as interested as she was. But now, he couldn't care less.

She looked around the table. Her head felt funny as if her brain was skipping. Her mother and snails. She leaned forward and spoke.

'Mum, did you step on snails when you were little?'

Rue and Audra looked down the table at Thistle. Audra had speared a tiny piece of chicken breast, a thin slice of potato and an eighth of an asparagus spear on her fork and held it aloft. Thistle was layering slabs of butter on a piece of bread. Audra put down her cutlery and picked up her serviette, dabbed each corner of her lips. She carefully folded it and laid it back on the table.

'Did you?'

'Don't be absurd.'

Thistle took a bite of bread. Snails, moving across a path, their trails silver in the rain. Antennae feeling the air, horns waving back and forth.

'What did you say to her?' Audra said, speaking to Thistle, whose face remained closed as she crammed the rest of the bread into her mouth.

'Look at this,' Rue said. Mandy's cheeks were bulging. 'You've got too much in there, spit it out. *Out.*' Rue opened her hand and Mandy leaned over it. A ball of chewed meat and potatoes fell into Rue's cupped palm.

'What a maw,' Thistle said.

'My tummy hurts,' Mandy said.

'And no wonder,' said Rue.

The table fell silent. The fly buzzed. The adults chatted about the usual things and the children ate quickly, wanting to leave and go back to their presents. Toward the end of the meal William began one of his low, rumbling oratories.

'Hate the bunny,' he said.

Cleg got up to go outside, saying he couldn't tolerate one of his brother's 'quasi-mad rabbit operas' just then. Olive too looked for escape, but William had already started. She slumped back in her chair.

'*Oryctolagus cuniculus*.' William settled with hands over his belly. Rue leaned over her husband to clear the plates and he reached a finger to her chin. 'The humble rabbit and one idiot. Thomas bloody Austin, fool and ponce.' He made eye contact with Olive, who looked at the door. 'Wanted to shoot bunnies, he did. Wanted to feel at home. Rabbits love this country, the sandy soil suits them. There's good drainage but a big problem for stock is the tunnels can collapse. Animals get their legs caught, can snap them and the farmer needs to shoot them because a cow or sheep with a broken leg is no good. Horses too.'

The burrows were like underground cities, he said. Mazes of pathways and residences. There was one with a total combined length of more than five hundred metres and one hundred and fifty doors. Olive couldn't imagine that long in metres but she knew so many doors was a lot.

'There he is. It's the 1850s, he's sitting on his estate near Geelong, probably in a white linen suit. He's got his whiskey, he's got his French soda siphon. Land in hand, near the river, shady and green, keeps the lawns nice and posh. But he's missing home, Enger-land. Yessiree, he says, what I need is a couple of bunnies and maybe some game birds to hunt. He doesn't feel at home, you see, without something familiar to crack a bullet at. Shooting roos just isn't the same for this poor toff. He feels sorry for them, probably, sees them as exotics. But—and this is important—the bunnies we had here before, well, they weren't the same as the ones back in England. He doesn't want to hunt *them*.'

Olive looked at the door again.

'Now, don't get me wrong.' William leaned onto his hands, eyes fixed on Mandy now. She'd edged off her chair so only one half of her bottom was still in contact. 'I like a bit of a shoot now and again,' William continued. 'But what we had before were poodles and these ones were wolves.'

Mandy's lips moved as she listened, mouthing *wolf*, her eyes on her father.

'They say rabbits caused the Sahara. Canny mongrels, they know how to survive. They can breed almost anywhere. Their warrens are enormous, dangerous for livestock, it collapses underneath a cow or a group of sheep—did I already say that? The bastards run like the wind and out-breed anything else on earth. Six bunnies will eat the same as a sheep, so when a drought hits, the sheep are rooted.'

'William,' said Rue.

'Warren is at my kinder,' said Mandy. Her eyes moved to the wall opposite, where there was a small picture of a mother sheep standing over her dead lamb which was surrounded by a circle of crows. Mandy didn't like that picture. She'd told her mother it gave her shivers all over and that she'd seen it in her sleep. Once, even, the mother sheep had come inside and stood beside her bed.

Cleg stuck his head through the door telling William to stop his nonsense and come outside. That it was better to sing when drinking, not lecture bored children.

'With my brothers, three men all,' he sang. 'Come, *patrem omnipotentem*. Brucie-boy's already out here.'

Rue tried to intercede but Cleg called her a woman with many regrets and Thistle clapped her hands and Cleg tipped an imaginary hat. Rue retreated to the dishes.

Olive sat in her chair thinking about what her uncle had been saying. There was something happening in her brain. She asked to leave the table and went outside and crawled into the cavity under the verandah. In the house people started to walk ponderously through rooms and she could hear their footsteps. She knew the older members of the family would soon be falling into chairs and on couches, digestion aided by interiority. William would finish his rabbit speech and he and Bruce would soon have hardback novels or cricket books resting on their chests, opened and ignored as their heads began to nod. They would fight sleep and fail, and fall to dozing.

Lying in the cool space Olive felt recast. The sun came through the side-wall slats in wide strips. She heard someone come out to the verandah. It was Sebastian, probably to set up his model construction. Olive thought about getting out and asking him why he was being such a weirdo but then she heard someone else step out onto the verandah. It was Thistle. They sat above her for a while and Olive was almost falling asleep herself when she heard Thistle ask a question.

'How are things with you these days?'

'Alright.'

'How is Olive?'

'She's alright.' Olive looked sideways to the lattice. She was about to crawl out and surprise them—maybe tell them she wasn't alright, that in fact she was pretty awful because Grace was dead and she was starting to have a headache as well but then Sebastian said something else.

'I've been avoiding her. She's always going on about Aster.'

'It seems she has no memory of it. Of the day.'

Sebastian didn't say anything. Olive could imagine him shrugging, or making an expression on his face. He lifted his chin and pushed out his bottom lip. She had told him it made him look dumb but he still did it.

'But you remember, don't you?' Thistle said. Her voice wasn't mean but it did sound a bit sly to Olive, as if she was trying to find out something without the other person knowing that it was significant.

'Was it at the dam?' Sebastian's voice cracked on the final syllable.

'Yes,' Thistle said. 'It was at the dam.'

'And I was there too.'

'You were there too.'

Olive had never guessed that Sebastian really might know something. It was obvious now and she was a *quid nunc* for not thinking of it. She could have made him talk. She *would* make him talk. It was the dam not a bath. Now all she needed to know was WHO and WHY.

'None of you were to blame, not you, not Olive, not even that boy. He might be a fire-starter but something like this, no sir.'

'Gary Sands was there?'

'Not him, though he's the dangerous one. He's like his father and uncle, and you must be careful with him. No. I was talking about the older son with the funny name. You don't remember?'

'Jethro?'

'Yes. Him.'

More muttering as the wire door sounded overhead—Rue coming out to ask if Thistle wanted tea. Thistle said yes and after a moment she went back inside. Sebastian was there. She was there. And Jethro Sands was there too. He was there when Aster died. He took her to the dam and put her in. She knew he had done it on purpose, she was filled with hot certitude. Sebastian hadn't mentioned it to her, probably because he was scared—and Jethro had covered it up. Somehow he'd got away with it. It all made sense. It was Jethro. He told Gary to stomp Grace so of course he killed Aster too.

She got to her hands and knees and crawled out. She peeped up over the side of the verandah and saw Sebastian sitting there at the card table, snapping the plastic model pieces out of the frame. He'd been really pleased that it was a Luftwaffe plane and he said he was going to start collecting them. It had stickers and paint included. His pleasure had seemed too much for just a grey plane. Sitting at their stockings earlier Olive had called him a Nazi for being so happy about the model plane. But now the annoyance toward Sebastian evaporated. Olive went along the side of the house and in the back door. She got the half-full champagne bottle from the fridge and took it into the laundry. It made troubles fizz away—that's what Rue said. Next thing she knew she was standing in the laundry, the empty bottle in her hand. She went and sat in the sunroom and watched the rug and after a while the pattern on it started to move in lines so she went to the hallway but then her limbs began to detach and float off down the hall, her legs heading to the back of the house and her arms swinging to the front. She thought about Thistle and her mother and Rue. Of herself as a little girl standing beside the dam and a bigger boy dropping a baby into the water. She had probably been crying. While she could see how none of it was fair, she didn't understand why any of it had happened *to her* and why she was the only one who seemed to care about it, not just about Grace but about having a dead sister and about finding out what the truth might be.

She went to where the adults were sitting in their chairs. She stood in front of her mother and arched her back and screamed, the noise shattering the brumous fug of the room. The napping adults jerked from their seats, books and newspapers sliding from laps. She screamed and screamed again.

Audra held Olive's arms, telling her to stop. A glossy magazine—*Sweden Cruises*—was underfoot and they almost slipped over on it. Rue came running in but it was William who took his niece by the hand.

'Come on, big girl,' he said. 'Let's get you out of here.'

He steered her out.

'What happened?' said Rue, following.

'I don't know,' Audra said.

Rue started crying.

•

With the door closed, Audra sat on the bed.

'Sit down,' she said, but Olive refused.

'You must tell me what's wrong.'

Her mother's lipstick was fresh and Olive found herself falling into that red patch. The white teeth, lips moving without meaning. The door opened and it was Rue.

'You have to talk to her,' Rue said. She shut the door.

Audra drew her hands into a ball in her lap. There were words coming but they were without force. It was as if her mother was whispering to herself, trying to make herself believe something. She put her hands to her brow, fingers shaking. She couldn't believe it. Her mother's hands were shaking. She was going to tell her now. Tell her mother that it was Jethro Sands who did it.

'Mum, when Aster drowned, it was at the dam.'

Her mother gave the tiniest nod.

'It was Jethro Sands who put her in the water.'

She waited for her mother's face to change. To understand.

'No, Olive.'

'It was.'

'Have you remembered something?'

'No, but I worked it out. That's what happened.'

Her mother closed her eyes and now her face *was* changing. She looked like the mother of Jesus.

'Oh,' Audra said, and reached for one of Olive's hands which was fisted and damp against her hip. Olive coughed twice and clapped both hands over her mouth. She bent forwards with a chymic lurch and spattered herself and her mother, the bed and the floor. Audra called for Rue, for a towel, and Olive sat down and wiped at the puddle of vomit on the carpet. Rue came running. Towels and a wet cloth were produced.

'Have you been drinking?' Audra leaned forwards and sniffed at her daughter.

Olive looked at her aunt, who was behind Audra, but Rue put a finger to her lips and closed the door.

NEW ENERGY HAD arrived and it moved through her in a wave. Her brain was spinning fast, like a flat dish on top of a rod in a circus. When she thought about Jethro her stomach clenched. His arms were so big around the top muscle part. He would be very strong. To get her revenge she had to be smarter than him because she definitely couldn't beat him in a fight, she was certain about that.

Her world had split when Gary Sands had done what he did to Grace. When he did what Jethro had told him to do.

This was the first truth about Jethro Sands.

He had told Gary to stomp Grace. He had held his neck and given him the signal and although it was something she was certain of at the same time she realised it was a slippery kind of knowing, a knowing that came from feeling. The second truth, the new truth, was that Jethro Sands had put Aster in the water. She had to get him back for that, as well as for Grace.

In her note-book she made a list:

1. Guns (too hard, don't now how)
2. Stabbing—bit messy
3. Crash into him with car
4. Make his car crash with snake (alive OR dead)/big rock from overpass
5. Posion from shed
6. Quicksand?
7. Drug him with the pills
8. Bury???????

She wondered how to make quicksand. Maybe she could do it at the golf club, in one of the sand pits there. Or anonymous notes and phone calls to make him nervous and not sleep. A person could die if they didn't sleep, she thought. Or she could try to find a snake, kill it and hang it on his car. Like a threat. She closed her eyes. She knew she couldn't kill a snake. She had the feeling the answer was somewhere very close. Pits that opened up under trees and swallowed boys. Tunnels under roads. Concrete pipes. Holes in sand. Rabbit tunnels collapsing.

She wandered the house and waited. When it slid into place it was perfect. She went to the phone and called Peter.

'Pete?' she said. 'I've got something to tell you. I was there too.'

'What?'

'My sister. It was at the dam.' She wiped her face with her hands. 'I was there and so was Sebastian, and—get this—so was Jethro Sands. I think he murdered her and I blanked it out from being too upset.'

'No.'

'Yes.' He was making noises with his mouth. 'What are you eating?'

'Ice cream.' He smacked his lips. 'Choc-mint chip.'

'I need your help.'

The spoon-scraping noise stopped.

'I'm going to kill him, but in a way that no one knows it's us. It will be the most perfect revenge.'

The spoon clanged into the bowl. He took ages to reply. Sometimes she had to be very patient with Peter.

'Who?'

'Jethro Sands.'

He groaned. 'Don't be crazy.'

'He drowned my sister.' She paused. 'He did it and no one has cared anything about it.' She twisted the cord of the telephone around her index finger. It fitted perfectly. 'Her put her in the dam. Listen. No one will suspect *kids*. I'm still working it out but you have to help me.'

'I'm not sure, Ol. Hey, you sound weird.'

'I got drunk but I have to go,' she said. 'Oh, one more thing. What did your dad say again?'

'About what?'

'About panicking. Remember?'

She could hear him breathing. She knew he didn't want to say but he was powerless against her.

'He said—' Peter swallowed '—he said that's what people do and then they make mistakes.'

'Alright. Write down anything else he's said. For our plan.'

'He said they don't know what they're doing and it's best to take things slowly no matter what. Even if things go wrong, just stick to the plan. That's what he also said.'

'Okay, thanks. I have to go now. Bye.'

She hung up the phone and sat on the little stool in the hallway. She knew how she was going to do it. She was going to make Jethro go in the bunker at Soldier's and trap him in there, make it collapse.

She was going to bury Jethro Sands alive.

SHE NEEDED A weapon. Jethro Sands would definitely have a knife or a gun. She went to the shed, where her grandfather's woodworking tools were. She searched through drawers and stood on her toes to try to see on top of shelves, reaching up with patting hands. She was looking for something to stand on when she heard a noise outside and went over to the window. Archie was there, crouching so no one would see him. She tapped and he looked up. Disappointment spread across his face.

He came in.

'What are you looking for?'

'Nothing.' She opened an old closet. 'Why are you spying on me?'

'Wasn't,' he said. He went to the far wall where the special stone-cutting machine sat, an old army tent covering it, its white canvas marked with rust and old paint rings. 'Mandy's sick,' he said. 'Mum's been looking in her book—you know, the one with the pictures. She thinks it might be epi- . . . ep- . . . something wrong with her brain. I said, "We already know she's got something wrong with her brain," and my mum started crying and your mum took me to the kitchen and said I was a bad boy.' He kicked a box. 'I don't like your mum, she's really mean.'

'No, she's not,' said Olive. She went to Archie and put her hand on his shoulder. 'She's sad.' She turned away to keep looking.

'Hey,' said Archie behind her. 'Look at this.' He was holding up a gigantic knife in a leather holder that closed with a press stud. The leather was brown and the knife was curved, the handle long.

'Give it,' she said. 'I was looking for that.'

'What for?' said Archie.

Olive stood in front of her cousin. She needed help and maybe it had to be him.

'It's something I have to do but I'll tell you later. I'm going to need your help but don't say anything, not even to Sebastian.' She smiled. 'Promise.'

Archie was pleased. He promised.

'Our first secret together,' she said.

Archie raised a clenched fist up near his ear and then the other with fingers crossed.

·

When she was five she asked to sit in the shed with her grandad Fletcher, in the corner where he had set up his knife-making table. He worked in there on Sundays. 'Wood days,' he called them.

She had been hoping for it forever and finally Rue said yes and she would sit with him as he carved the offcuts and their heads would bend together on those happy afternoons, the filaments from the shavings moving in the air like tiny stars. He only carved for her, he said, and explained the different types of woods, their relative hardness, their grains, their hearts.

'Look at this one, little girl,' he said. 'A type of dryland acacia but not as good as the ironwood.' He put it on the bench and took another. She didn't understand, but she was old enough to enjoy how the wood felt in her hands, to look forward to the smell as she studied the tools and repeated their names. The baby was not old enough to be in there and she was glad. The baby cried all the time.

The wood-words were like fairytales, strong magic lodged in things called *gidgee*, *fiddleback* and *beeswing*. These words helped form the beauty of the knives but it wasn't just about the handles,

Fletcher told her. It was about how the handle accepted the blade, the iron taken into the wood. Two substances meeting in a join that created something new.

'Strength and purpose,' he said.

The olivewood was one of the hardest woods on earth and it was from the Bible. Olive sat up straight on her chair when she heard that. She was God's favourite wood?

Her grandfather explained. The dove that went from the ark in one of the stories brought back a broken bit of olive branch. It meant that the water was pulling back, that there was land out there, somewhere to be found. It meant that God was no longer angry. Jesus prayed under an olive tree before he died and he died on a cross made from olivewood. Grandad Fletcher said 'tied to' but Thistle had told her the truth. She said 'nailed to' and it had made Olive stare at the steel nails on the bench in the workshop for a long while.

Olive trees were also called the Sacred Tree, the Peace Tree, the Tree of Light. She loved all those names but especially the last one. She thought about her tree, the peppercorn, but no matter how she stretched her imagination she could never think of that one as anything but a tree of darkness.

And then there were the gemstones, a collection Grandad Fletcher had gathered since he was a boy. Milky ones, heavy in her hands. Smooth jade. Spiky purple amethyst.

'Stones can bruise,' he had told her and she hadn't believed him. She said that he was trying to trick her.

'No, little girl. They can. Alabaster especially.' He showed her a piece that had a discoloration. 'And this one.' A veined green stone, greasy and vitreous. He placed it in her hand. She weighed it in her palm the way she'd seen him do it.

'Serpent rock.'

'But this is a bruise.' She held out an arm. She always had haemat-
omas, as Rue called them. How could it be that such a tough wild
girl could bruise so easily? her aunt had wondered.

'They call it a bruise,' Fletcher said. 'It's the same thing.'

'But it's not the same,' said Olive.

'If you say so, girl.'

'I do say so.' She gave back the stone.

'You keep that one. Green stone for a tough girl. Keep it so you
can remember me.'

'Are you going away?'

'Not anytime soon.'

When Fletcher was dying he lay rigid and sweating on his bed,
reciting poetry and relaxing only when someone brought him a
particular lacquered box. He opened it and one by one took out
the blades, his precious beauties. He talked to each, gave it a final
touch, a loving swipe of the finger, then endowed it to a chosen
family member.

'No more trailing serpent's tooth to fear
Let him who by the dragon's fang hath bled,
On the dire wound serpentine powder spread,
And in the stone his sure reliance place,
For wounds inflicted by the reptile race!'

The sons were embarrassed and without comprehension. It was
Rue who shooed them out and brought wet face washers and sips of
cool lemon water to her father-in-law. For her trouble, she was given
a medium-sized kitchen knife and Audra a neat nail one, for doing
her cuticles. Later, no one would remember which one Thistle got.

'Probably a standard dagger,' Cleg said.

The sons were given a couple of hunting knives each. Bruce put
his down on the kitchen table but William hefted and balanced his
in turn across a finger, checking their lines before sliding them

into his belt. He blew his nose once and then set off to check the perimeters for the rest of the afternoon. Olive got the small knife with the olivewood handle. She was a bit older by then and it made her feel special.

Just before Fletcher died, he slid into delirium and talked about 'polishing' and 'fine grits' and 'Danish oil'. The children weren't allowed to see him as he became more agitated, and the end came with him shouting, 'BURL!' at the wardrobe.

Olive pushed the knife from the shed into the back of her shorts like a mugger on a police show and went to the house. In the sunroom, she took it out and sat, thinking about the sand pits at the golf club. It could be a back-up plan. She swung her legs around and there was a noise from under the couch. It was Mandy Milk.

'What have you got there?'

'Nothing.' Mandy pulled a cushion in front of whatever it was. Olive pulled it from her. It was the ouija board.

'Where'd you get it?'

Mandy shook her head.

'You shouldn't play with it. Come out.' She reached under the sofa and grabbed it. 'Come on, where's the thing?'

Mandy handed her the planchette.

'How long have you been playing with it?'

Mandy looked up at her, her tongue pushed into the gap where a tooth was loose. She moved it in and out.

'You can't play it by yourself anyway,' said Olive. 'It doesn't work just with one.'

'It does,' Mandy said.

'No, it can't.'

'I play with Mr Cracker.'

Olive squatted down beside her cousin.

'What's that on your arm? Those marks?'

Mandy said they were nothing. Mr Cracker said they were secret.

'You should show your mother.'

Mandy shook her head.

'You should. Go on.' Olive went and put the board and planchette under her mattress and lay down on the bed. She had her weapon and she had her plan. She would get him and win. She was a genius, a mastermind, a smart girl the likes of which the world had never known before. Clever and brave and sure.

LITTLE GODS

IT WAS A chance comment that Mrs Sands made at the New Year's Eve party that let Olive know everything was over. They were at the golf club and the night was stinking hot. Mr Spooner was making shandies and serving lemonade and sweet wine at the bar. Tables were arranged outside with umbrellas open for shade, but they were mostly empty as people formed gendered groups, crowding around the tinny evaporative cooler. The women pulled at their necklines and the men stood with red faces and blew their cheeks and licked beer foam from their top lips and talked about the expected cool change of thirty-five that was overdue.

Raffle prizes were displayed on trestle tables set up under the felt pennants strung along the wood-panelled wall. Mr Spooner wore a toga and was meant to be from old Rome but looked embarrassed, Olive thought. Thistle was dressed as Cleopatra and sat on her own, away from the crowd. She had her hair coiled into loops on her head and a snake bracelet winding up her arm.

Olive stood near her mother holding a plastic cup between her teeth like a pig's snout and her mother told her not to do it, that she looked silly. Jethro's mother was there too and she was showing off. First about Snooky with her dux award, and then about Jethro getting a job with a carpenter, in the city. He was staying with Mr Sands's brother, the younger one, and Olive, hearing this, had blinked back strange tears. She'd listened to how Jethro's car had boiled over like a kettle on the trip up to the city, how he'd got three quotations for repairs, how they all said it was the *head gasket* and would cost *almost a thousand dollars.*

'I don't think he'll be back anytime soon,' Mrs Sands had said.

She started to greet another person and Olive and her mother were released to the crowd. Audra had gone over to where Rue was sitting with an intense look on her face, looking up at Len Sands, the butcher. Olive went and sat in the corner, itchy in the frock Rue had told her she had to put on. Her sandals rubbed because they were a bit small and she sat there and hated everyone. She hated Mandy who was excited about the sparklers and walking around in her Jeannie costume with a new puppet—Little Red Riding Hood. She hated Archie who was dressed as a cowboy, standing at the food table with its bowls of chips, kabana and cubed cheese. He was pipetting Passiona drops a few at a time into his mouth with a straw and eating handfuls of food.

Olive remembered being a girl who was excited about sparklers. She remembered being a girl who didn't care what people thought. Someone who just wanted to practise cartwheels outside on the lawn. A girl who, when she came across a bowl of Cheezels, would stand there and eat with commitment until they were gone. She didn't care that adults might tell her off, insist that it was polite to share, or call her from the front door telling her it was time to come in, that they had something very important to talk to her about. She would keep turning on the grass until she could do it perfectly or stand by a table and eat Cheezels in a deeply meditative state until there were none left in the bowl.

She was almost asleep on her chair when Rue came and shook her arm, telling her to come on, come on, it was almost time. She let herself be shepherded outside by her aunt and opened her hand for the sparkler. She stood with the other children as they counted down from ten. She waved the stick in the air obediently until it guttered. Then she watched the other fireworks. The Jumping Jacks, Catherine wheels and rockets. Children were asking for another sparkler, their faces under-lit with white light but there was no joy in any of it for her. She went back inside to sit and wait until they went home. Her mother passed by and said they were going soon and she knew it was a lie, one thousand per cent. Rue told her to cheer up. It was a new year. Thistle said that she should think of her resolution and that it was a good idea to make it something achievable. She knew, from experience, how important that was. There was only one resolution she cared about though. Getting Jethro. But he had left town and there was nothing she could do about it.

AT THE BEGINNING of January her parents took her away to a place near the beach at the island, a holiday spot the brothers used to go with their cousins, when they were little. They stayed for two weeks and camped behind the sand dunes that lay in a straight ridge between tents and surf. It was a holiday Olive would have usually loved but she felt as if she was in costume, playing a part. A girl in summer shorts, eating lollies and trying to bodysurf. Rolling down sand dunes, reading comics in the cool of the tent. All of it would have been fun if things had been different but they weren't. They were real. Grace was dead and Jethro gone and none of the fun touched her because she was away from the place she wanted to be. Home. She worried that Jethro would come back while she was away, that she wouldn't get to do her revenge.

Archie made some friends with other children who had older brothers and sisters and cousins there, a family from Gippsland. One night they'd sat around the campfire, saying which was their favourite Peanuts character. When it was Olive's turn, she said Lucy. The other girls laughed at her. They liked Patty, they said.

Olive argued her point. Lucy was a good character, she said. Interesting. 'And she's a main girl.

'She's mean and has black hair,' said one of the other girls.

Olive wondered what they meant by that. Lucy *was* mean, but she was also funny and tough. Olive understood Lucy. Did that mean she was mean too?

They talked about other things but Olive stayed at the fire after the others went to do their teeth, saying she wasn't tired yet.

During the holiday, other things happened too. She lost her skiffle board the first time she used it. She'd found it hard to balance, had kept falling off onto her bum, and had dropped it down near the water and run to get a drink of cordial. When she went back the board was gone, that green smiling face disappeared into the waves and sand forever.

Mandy had almost drowned in the surf and Cleg had to swim out to get her. Rue had been hysterical. Down by the water's edge, as the mothers comforted Rue, one of them had sat down on the sand, her heaving belly the biggest Olive had ever seen.

'Oh,' she said. 'The baby's kicking.' She looked at Olive. 'Do you want to have a feel?' Olive had shaken her head, saying no thank you. She did not want to touch that huge stretched stomach. She did not want to feel anything inside. Then the mother had leaned over and vomited. She wiped her mouth with the back of her hand and started to cover up the sick by sweeping sand over it. Olive was embarrassed.

She got sunburned and her back peeled twice. They saw a dead shark and she ran—screaming—up the path to the campground, her mouth stretched wide as she cut through a hovering cloud of gnats near the carcass. At the end of the track she bent double and hacked and spat them out.

They surfed on the lilos and made sure they were dry enough to sleep on at night. Put on zinc cream, lost and found and lost hats. Chafed from wet bathers and had jaffles for lunch and it all stretched into an eternity.

And she had a crush—at least that's what Sebastian had called it—on the brother of the family from Gippsland. The boy was older than her and his white hair sat up in a funny wave across his head.

He was kind and smiled at everyone, even Olive. One day he gave her a bug catcher, saying he didn't want it anymore. Did she want him to help her find something to put in it? She said she did, so they crawled around together but really all they could see were some ants, so they got some and put them in. After that she always tried to see where he was because she liked to know if he was nearby. Then Sebastian thought he'd worked out what was going on and he told the boy and teased her in front of all of the others, saying that she loved the boy with the white hair. The feelings had been strong but it wasn't what Sebastian was saying it was. She wasn't able to explain that it was about someone being kind to her.

The last evening they'd been there they got ready to do the night fishing with a net. It was unrolled on the beach and the kids had to walk along the edge and carefully check if there were any rips. One of the other fathers had some twine and a sharp knife and he tied up anywhere there was a hole. If you saw a hole you had to stand next to it with your hand in the air and he'd come along and fix it. Olive found two holes and he put his hand on her shoulder and said *well spotted*. That had made her feel good. The net was the biggest that she had ever seen. It was three big steps wide and much longer than that. She had no idea how many steps long it might have been.

When they were ready some of the adults went down either end and the children all spread out along the length of it. They hoisted the net and the feeling of it lifting was great and exciting. The men went in the end, where it was deeper, up to their waists. They weren't scared of sharks. The mothers and children took the rest of the net and walked along, and no one said anything about sharks, they just angled the net straight out from the beach and walked, not even for very long. Olive hoped they'd catch a seahorse and that she would be allowed to keep it, or a baby dolphin. But they didn't sweep up anything like that. There were fishes—so many different types, including flounders with weird eyes—and back on the shore they divided it all up fairly between the families. Everyone had to help carry the fish back to the campsite, to the eskies that were filled with ice.

Then there were the caves. Down the beach and around a lip of land where a small river joined the beach, halfway up a cliff that pushed out into the line from shore to sea. One was easily visible from the beach and the other two were hidden. The one that you could see was a wide gash in the yellow rock, an opening that loomed even at a distance. As soon as she saw it she knew she wanted to climb up there and go inside.

'Let's go there,' she said to Archie, who was bent over great strings of kelp pulling at the round almost-opaque green polyps they called seaweed eggs.

'These are more like grapes than eggs,' he said.

'Archie. Let's go up there.' She pointed.

He looked, hands on hips, considering the steep climb. They could do it, Olive assessed. They just needed to be careful.

'Is it going to be dark in there?' Archie said.

'Who knows?' said Olive. 'Probably.'

They started to go up the rocks, her leading the way. At first it wasn't so very steep and they didn't need their hands, just had to lean into the incline. Then it got harder and they began to reach and clutch at rocks and plants that were probably not going to hold them if they slipped. There was a small ledge about halfway and they sat for a few minutes. The rock beneath them was rough and in parts very hot from the sun. They looked back along the beach to where the families were, small as they moved around on the sand. Mandy running to the water and back with a bucket, Sebastian on his towel under the beach umbrella reading. The women with their shirts and hats and sunglasses.

'We're pretty high,' Archie said.

Olive looked out at the blue, the waves cresting white as they broke, and beyond that, a calmer field.

'There would be sharks out there,' she said, thinking of the film and how the massive fish had bitten people in half.

'No way I'd go out that far,' said Archie. 'Not even with a surfboard.'

'I would,' she said. 'I would go out, even just swimming.'

'No you wouldn't,' he said, 'that's a lie', but she was getting up and moving on.

They got to the mouth of the cave and walked a little way inside. There were burned stumps of candles near the walls, cigarette butts and empty bottles, the typical refuse of people in places where they shouldn't be. Olive went in a bit further. There was a smell too, of animal, of damp fur and feathers, but that was all there was. No sound, no movement.

'Come on, we can go further.'

In they went and then down quite a way but because the opening was so wide there was plenty of light. At the end was a drop to a broad sandy interior. Olive calculated that if they jumped down they'd be able to get back up. There was a built-up area of rock, like steps. They could come back up that way. She jumped. It wasn't far but as she hit the sand it was hard and jolted her teeth. It hurt. She stood up and told Archie to come down.

'I'm not sure,' he said.

'Why not?'

Archie disappeared. She called to him but he didn't come back. She put her hand on the rocks to climb back up. Archie appeared.

'Let's go to one of those down there,' he pointed. 'One of the smaller ones.'

She climbed out and they walked a little further along the same level and then down a little walkway cut into the cliff. Here were the other caves. This entrance was closer to the base of the cliff. They would have had to get on their hands and knees. She looked over her shoulder at the water. The waves were bigger and it seemed the tide was coming in.

'Not a good idea,' she said. 'We might get stuck if we go inside.'

They stood and watched the cave. In less than five minutes a surging messy cascade of water rushed inwards and was sucked back out through the hole. As the water rushed out of the cave Olive imagined she could see the open eyes of a small face being carried along in the water. Archie said let's go, but she stood until all the water had gone to make sure.

SCHOOL WAS STARTING and Jethro wasn't back. Olive went with her mother to buy her textbooks and new uniform. She stood on a chair as her mother took up the hem, managing only a lukewarm battle about the length. She dutifully covered her books with contact, taking ages to get it right, and wrote her name inside the covers, inventing new ways to do fancy Os and Ls. She made space on her shelves for the thick maths book and the English one, the German one too. She packed away her childhood books into boxes: her pony books and English girls' boarding school books, the child investigator books. All her Beatrix Potters. *Heidi* and *The Guinness Book of Records*.

The Book of Lists and *Unexplained: Things You Just Won't Believe* stayed on her bedside table and she read a few pages each night before going to sleep.

She ran through her mental lists after she turned off her lamp and as she lay there her mind went to Jethro and the plan. He would come back, he had to. Jethro Sands was the reason she managed to perform all the things she needed to do. Getting ready for school, beginning Year 7. The unbearable routines were made tolerable only because she could feel her rage as it shifted inside of her, alive and hot and ready.

The first day at school was nothing special. All the kids were the same and she'd come home disappointed. She had thought maybe she would find a new friend, but it didn't matter. In class, more than one of her teachers told her off for staring out the window and they called on her to answer questions when they knew she hadn't been listening. She was sure they did it on purpose and that made her angry too. The way they picked on her wasn't fair.

She said no to her mother when Peter rang.

'Have you two had a fight then?'

'I just don't feel like it.'

'If you could listen for the phone,' her mother said, 'maybe you could answer it sometimes. You know I like to lie down in the afternoon.'

Olive said okay and went to do her homework.

TIME HAD STOPPED and the moon had been full twice in a month. It was rainy and clouds skidded across grey-washed skies. The entire state had been hit with thunderstorms, weather that Rue called 'biblical' and Thistle 'sublime'. It was the wettest it had been since 1910, since Lenore and Edgar arrived in their dray from Melbourne. The adults talked about how odd it was for March—or any month, they said—and all after a ten-year drought.

William kept reminding everyone that it had only been last winter that the widespread frosts had killed the banksias, rupturing their cells across wide areas. And the previous month there'd been the big dust storm that shifted all the topsoil to Melbourne, and then, just the week after that, the fires where people had died. But Olive didn't care about the drought or the weather, or the stupid Al Neenyo or whatever it was that William kept going on about. She was thinking about Jethro Sands. She was thinking about him all the time.

As it rained Olive thought about the banks of sand pushed up by the wind against dead trees. She thought about the bunker at Soldier's and the empty mine holes slowly filling with frothy brown water. If the bunker collapsed on its own her plan was definitely over.

She rode her bike home from school down streets that smelled of wet leaves. At night in bed she listened to the cracks of thunder rolling across the sky. Sometimes she crept out at night and went to the park, drawn to the dark streets. She enjoyed being alone out on her bike in the night air, her raincoat flapping as she rode. On the few dry days she went to the silo and climbed to sit cross-legged on the waterlogged platform. Up high she found a cleaner type of air where she could steady her breathing. She listened for the determined mosquitoes and slapped at them, wiping their crushed bodies away, leaving a smear of blood on her jeans.

THE LAND WAS becoming green from all the rain. Cleg had returned to the farm from the city. He had come to talk to Thistle and everything happened dramatically after lunch one day.

Olive's cousins had finished and left the table and it was only Olive who remained, struggling to eat her sandwich. Rue had told her she wasn't allowed to leave until it had all gone, crusts included, but Olive wasn't hungry. These days she was finding it hard to swallow anything.

'There's a woman speaking at a conference later this month,' Cleg began. 'She was a district officer in Bendigo and did the placements.'

Thistle looked up. 'Tell me.'

'Shall we go in the other room?'

'Why?'

'For privacy?' Cleg gestured to Olive.

'I don't care about privacy. Olive can hear. Let them all hear.'

Cleg moved his chair. 'The woman from Bendigo, she's written a book.'

'What kind of book?' Thistle put down her glass. 'Where is the conference? Will the babies be there?' Thistle's voice was loud.

God, Olive thought.

'Tell me.' Thistle was preparing to stand.

Cleg went and sat next to her, and took her hand. She let him.

'What is her name?'

Cleg took out a note and checked it.

'Wendy Davis.'

'I remember. Short, round. Orange hair.' Thistle dropped her chin and she placed her hands wide on top of the tablecloth in the position of a person playing a very forceful song on a piano.

'She took one of my client's babies and told her he died when he was alive. But yours she took home for herself.'

God, Olive thought again.

Thistle's face had tipped forwards and Olive could see the roundness of the back of her neck. The Nash hump, the sisters called it. She hoped she wasn't going to get one of those when she was old.

'She kept my boy?'

The white collar of Thistle's dress was half in and half out and there was a smear of Vegemite on it. Olive could hear her cousins' voices, carrying through the wire door at the front. The clock ticked.

'The book is about her and him,' Cleg went on. 'There's nothing in it about her time as a district officer, no mention about the ethics of taking a child for herself or of giving babies to friends and relatives. We know it's the right woman and we know she had your boy. We've got hospital and agency records under FOI.'

'I don't need records, not FO anything.' Thistle said. 'The book tells about him? How can she write about him? how dare she. The mother is the one, who writes, about her baby, how can she write— how is it possible, that this person can steal— It's my baby.'

Cleg shook his head as if he didn't understand the question.

'Can we find him?'

There was a piece of egg stuck to Thistle's eyebrow.

'I'm sorry, Thist, he didn't survive,' Cleg said. 'His name was Steven. He died four years ago.'

The crumb dropped to Thistle's lap.

'Well, that explains it. He was sick?' She sounded as if she was at the drycleaners, asking why her coat wasn't ready.

'Sort of,' said Cleg. 'He killed himself.'

Thistle was folding and rolling her napkin. She reached for the pewter ring and slid it on.

'Where is this book? Do you have it with you?' Her voice was bright, a playful reed melody but blown by a piper running out of air. It was a voice Olive had never heard emerge from this aunt. Rue was the one who forced cheer, not Thistle.

Cleg went and got it. On the front was a photograph. Thistle held it up to them.

'Look at her. The same eyes, smiling at the camera as if she were someone normal. A woman with nothing close to, to sadism, in her, standing in her lovely garden, in the garden. With her white shirt and brown slacks. I remember the hair, the same hair, cut short back then too. Look at her, that meaningless smile. Look.'

Olive wondered if Thistle was about to cry.

'It will be hard to read,' Cleg said. 'She's trying to get people to feel sorry for her because her adopted boy didn't turn out the way she expected. She talks about his asthma, his wheeziness. And how his "angelic" white hair belied a stubborn instinct. That he was "overly needy" and "pathetic". Unfortunately, it will sell very well.'

Thistle took a long time to get to her feet. Cleg helped her.

'I hate to think of her smiling like that at my boy,' she said at the door. 'But thank you. Thank you for finding this out.'

'I'm not sure we've done the right thing,' Cleg said once Thistle had left. Olive sat very still. 'Surely not knowing must be worse than hearing even the most terrible news?' He looked at her. 'Surely?'

Olive nodded and Rue came in.

'What have you said to her now?'

'I found out what she asked me to, Rue. That is all.'

Rue stacked plates, sniffing, until Cleg told her she should get a tissue.

'I've got one,' she howled. 'It's in my sleeve.'

She went back into the kitchen and Olive finally put down the crust she'd been holding and slid back in her chair.

OLIVE WOKE AND listened. Surely it was only a minute after she'd turned the light out. The room was lit from outside and she went to the window. It was still raining and the sky had a wild maroon overlay filtered across it, the clouds electric and full. Paler shapes hung like lanterns, the sheep huddled against the rain. Again and again sheet lightning illuminated the paddocks in a sweeping flood. Before she could think to count for the clap, before the world returned to black, she saw a figure lurching across the grass. She turned away from the window and the next flash of light showed that Mandy wasn't in her bed.

Olive found her in the hallway, near the kitchen door, walking but still asleep. She took her back to bed and put the covers over her. She went to her own bed and sat wondering what she should do. She didn't know so she got in, right under the covers. The sky boomed. She was unsure. She didn't want to be a dibber-dobber like Mandy. Thistle was a woman of independent inclinations. Finally, though, she decided. She went out into the hallway and opened Rue and William's door. Rue was quickly awake, turning on the bedside lamp asking what was wrong. Olive told her that Thistle was outside in the rain.

Rue pushed William. 'Wake up.'

'I'm awake. I'll go.'

He went down the hall and pulled on his boots at the door, as well as his hat and raincoat. Rue came forwards with a torch and Bruce arrived in his pyjamas. They waited while he too got his shoes and a coat, then he and William went out into the night, towards the dam.

ON THE FAR side of the dam, Thistle sat on the edge, puffing. She should have brought some sweeties—Rue had some hidden in the pantry, on the high shelf behind the big canister of rice—but it was too late to go back now. The risk of meeting sisters in the night, one mordant the other pernicious, no. Too late now. Besides, the sugar gave her reflux, another thing she'd had to abide far too long.

There was nothing left for her. He hadn't come, hadn't come. They thought they were dulling her into submission with their doses of opium, sassafras and treacle. Thinking them disguised with modern-day names, but she knew. They were treating nothing. Her lability was manufactured by circumstance. Her mind, there was nothing wrong with it. They thought she was *exzentrisch* at best, *übergeschnappt* at worst but she wasn't, she wasn't. She was from a family of liars and secret makers but she had been a truth-teller and she should have used a real dagger not just tried to speak one.

'We can be so hurtful to each other.' She spoke the words to the night and took off her slippers. The little barbs that prick and pull at another's skin. How they settle into the flesh and start to rust over time, especially with the swill foaming over them. Once this happens, even a person's breath becomes toxic. You can breathe in and out and not utter a word but those hooks have done their damage. The poison seeps in and everything becomes ruined. 'So unkind.'

There was no rush, plenty of time now.

The level was lower than usual but it didn't matter. That thinning was not important here. She had failed the young girl, the one she used to be. She had failed her boy too but she could taste change and it subsumed the bitterness and became golden on her tongue.

Here she was. She looked up to the sky. He was coming, on the clouds! Everyone would see him, including those who took him. A white horse, a rider. The conqueror. Then the sixth, an earthquake. The sun already gone, the night around her coarse and black.

She took off her first skin, dropped the wet cardigan. The joints in her shoulders rotated and she could hear their crepitus. She was not so old but her teeth were cracking and food would get caught. Sometimes she suffered the most dreadful toothache. The wet was a good thing she supposed, for the farmer, but it had been an interminable wait and she was relieved of everything except her pain. She struggled to take off her second skin but her arm caught in the sleeve of the cotton nightie and she decided there was no point removing it. What had she been thinking? That her final gesture would include the revelation of her bloated body to men? There was more dignity in being found clothed.

All that was left to her now was to go.

How poor are those that have not patience.

She turned an ear heavenwards and listened for the trumpets. They would scale across the sky with brassy flourishes but there were no swoops or moans. Not anymore. The water was quickly at her waist. She didn't look to see if there was a moon but no matter, its pale pull had never affected her even when the colour of blood. She was too smart for madness and entirely unknown to all. That person who collected bird cards and completed jigsaw puzzles was just her outer shape. Her real self was a sensualist, sleeping with sheets twisted around her body, a girl who had seen the flashes in the sky too, their bright vertical tails, just once she'd seen them.

Pushing forwards the water came to her chest, a sea of glass mixed with fire. She raised heavy arms and let out her hair, dropping the pins into the dam where they spiralled into the oily depths. She spread her limbs and the dam started its work. Her ears filled and it came across her eyes. She remembered the hospital room, her own strong self in the bed, what a girl she'd been. Magnificent. She had felt her strength deep in her bones. She wasn't going to let them take him. People hadn't been happy but she didn't care, did not care. She'd hidden it until it was too late for her mother to do anything. Had got the baby started under her loose dresses and managed to grow him before anyone noticed but still she'd tried, the old bitch. Wanted to make him slip out of her with a long walk on a hot day and after that laxatives and finally a bucket of cold water thrown over from behind, but nothing had made her clever foetus loosen its grip.

She told Gladys she didn't know who the father was.

'What do you mean you don't know? There was more than one?'

She had enjoyed seeing that look on her mother's face, as if she had her fingers on a switch turning it this way and that, making her mother's knowingness dim up, dim down, and out.

In the hospital, things were different. While she didn't care about their talk of moral deficits and turpitude, in the end powerful men and women held her down and gave her needles and, while she was sure she didn't sign any papers, in the end in the end she returned home alone. Forever after that in her imaginings her baby remained at the hospital. Perpetually there as if stuck behind glass, swaddled and mute in a distant nursery down a sterile run of corridors. Silent and stopped. Fixed like a butterfly on a pin. In the end, she'd had no choice but go home, go home.

The noise registered, minor tremors as if from far away. In the cold dam her arms drew her downwards and her final thought was one of a parade of babies trying to find their way back to their mothers, endless numbers of them moving like small clouds across skies, following roads, through cities and over country pathways. The men went into the dam but it took them too long to find her and by the time they hauled her out nothing could spoil her dark rapture.

•

Olive refused to go back to bed and Rue sat with her while the others went to make phone calls.

'Poor *vulner bilis*,' Cleg said.

'Her clothes must have pulled her under,' Rue said, crying. Audra cried too.

They found a note, a piece of paper that had, down at the bottom in tiny handwriting: *Olive. Don't let any* quid nuncs *take your baby away.*

Olive couldn't stop sobbing and it was Cleg who finally pulled her onto his knee and bear-hugged her until she calmed. No one would answer her question about Thistle's soul and what would happen to it. She asked and she asked but eventually she stopped and became still.

•

Before they left the next day Olive leaned her cheek against the peppercorn tree. She put her arms around its girth and listened to the beat that came from deep below. The message was that she was right to get revenge, that the Bible said so. It was her duty, for her sister, for Grace. Thistle had said not to let them be taken. It was the right thing to do.

How poor are those who don't have any patience.

That's what Thistle always said but she, Olive, had patience. She was very good at it. She would wait as long as she had to for Jethro to come back.

OLIVE WAS CONFUSED about how someone could do a suicide. How a person could destroy themselves, especially someone who talked so often about life the way Thistle had. But neither parent would talk to her about it so Olive read her books and lingered once more over the spontaneous combustion section, studying the stockinged legs in front of open fires, half-bodies propped in armchairs, women who'd been reading, knitting or dozing before bursting into flames, a pinpointed conflagration that left the rest of the rooms untouched. Had these women's lives been so unbearable that they simply exploded out of sadness? Had they sat in chairs in front of fires, sewing buttons for so long with their insides heated by such despair and anger that their bodies shuddered one final time and burst into flames? Maybe the same had happened to Thistle.

She thought about the milk bar family. She had been too young to remember any of them properly. The story had been that one of them, the middle son, had made a fist and looked inside it. He saw a demon and told someone at school and then a week later the whole family died. Then there was Peter's story of the boy in his old town who was found hanged in a tree, from a skipping rope, in his back garden. Olive had been surprised to learn that children really could die. That something so bad could happen to them like that.

Olive asked her father if she could stay up to watch *Tales of the Unexpected* and he said yes. There'd been several phone calls during the evening. Audra had sat on the stool in the hallway for more than an hour, first talking to Rue, listening mostly and saying, 'mmm, I know' and 'yairs', and talking about quiches and scones and when the funeral might be. Then they talked about the weather. The only thing they didn't talk about was their sister and how she was dead.

After that, Mavis Sands had rung and Olive heard Audra agree that it was very sad, and after that she talked again about funeral food. Olive sat up on the couch when her mother said something about Jethro but around the time of the click of her mother's lighter and the wafting smell of menthols, she fell back on the couch. In a few more minutes she was asleep, even before *Tales of the Unexpected* had started.

THE DAY BEFORE Thistle's funeral Peter came over.

'Where have you been?' he said at the front door. 'I've been calling you.'

'Here.'

'But when I ring your mum always says you're not at home.' He held up a present. 'Sorry about your aunty. I got you this.'

They went and sat on the back step. The gift was wrapped badly in Christmas paper, the corners folded and refolded where he'd tried to get them even.

'I didn't get you one.'

'That's okay. My mum got it ages ago, when she was doing the shopping. I kept forgetting to give it to you.'

She ripped the paper open and inside were a sketchpad and three bottles of ink and an old-fashioned pen. There was a card which said *To Ollie from Pete* around the printed greeting.

'Your writing is still like a spider's.' She put the present on the step beside her.

He was wiping his hands up and down his legs and saying he got a magic set for Christmas.

'Magic is for kids,' she said.

'It's a professional one.'

'Maybe.'

When they were younger and on the seesaw at the park, Peter would sit at the bottom and she would be up the top, her legs gripping the wooden plank to stop herself sliding. She felt like that now.

'I don't know how she could do that.' She pulled at a little weed that pushed up between a crack in the steps.

'What?'

'I know why but I don't understand how. I would never want to die.'

'What about being buried inside the tree? What about that?'

'That's for when I'm very old and I die from age.' She plucked the slender green shoot from the ground.

Peter was lifting his wrist to his ear. Shook it, and listened again.

'I really think it's broken,' he said. 'It keeps stopping, since Ganger's.'

'Give us a look.'

He hesitated, then took his watch off and passed it to her.

'I'm still going to do it,' she said. 'The plan. He'll come back eventually, he has to.'

'I don't get why Jethro Sands would even put your sister into the dam.'

'That's what I have to find out. I'm going to make him confess and then do the revenge. My detectivising will get the last piece of the mystery. Why he did it.'

'That's not a word.' He put his head on his knees, looking at the watch in her hands.

'Anyway, I need your help.'

'I told you, you can't just decide, Ollie.'

'What?'

'Well . . .' He swallowed. 'I was going to tell you anyway.'

She stared at him.

'It's about the group pressure.'

'You told your mum.'

'I didn't.' But he wouldn't look at her. 'Are you serious about it?'

'Say yes.'

'It's okay for you—you just do things without thinking.'

'No I don't.'

'Like last month when you ran into the middle of the oval during the dust storm when everyone was freaking out, even that teacher? She was shouting about the grasshoppers and saying it was the end and you came back and your face was just covered, all red, and you were laughing.'

'So?'

'And when you drank the milk? With tomato sauce, chocolate sauce and chilli powder. And what was it . . .'

'Soy sauce.'

'You always pick dare, never truth. It's like you don't care if something is dangerous.' He looked at her through his hair. 'It's like . . .'

'Like what?'

'Nothing. I've got to go.' He sawed his arm across his eyes and stood up. 'I just wanted to give you the present.'

She passed the watch back to him and he strapped it to his wrist.

'Maybe it'll be okay.'

'I don't think so. I think it's stuffed.'

They walked around to the side of the house and he picked up his bike. 'I don't think you're psychic or whatever they call it, not even a little bit. Maybe you're a good guesser but only sometimes. You don't know what people are thinking, you never guess what I'm thinking. I dunno, I can't explain it properly.' He touched his bell hammer.

She didn't say anything.

'And it's normal to get scared. My dad said he does all the time when he sees it, when people die. If they get squashed by tractors or drunk in their cars, he said it breaks the families and the mothers cry and not just them, the kids cry and the fathers, they cry all the time. He goes to say sorry, you know, he goes back to see how they are, to ask if he can cut their grass or wash their car and they're still crying and it can be weeks after even, all of them crying, all the time.'

'My family's not like that,' Olive said. 'No one cries in my house.'

Peter got on his bike. 'I used to want to be in the police but I think I'm changing my mind. It sounds too sad.'

'Yeah, but it's just this once and I won't ever ask you to help me again. It's important, more than a watch or some family your dad's met because of his work. I'm your friend.'

He readied the pedal.

'Your best friend.' Peter's face stayed closed, his eyes on the hydrangeas.

'What?' she said.

'You don't listen. You say one thing but you do the opposite, like a hypo- . . . hypocritical. And when people want to say "no" you don't let them. You always have to be the boss and everyone always has to do what you want. Sebastian got sick of it too.' He got onto the seat, one leg planted. 'I feel sorry for those families,' he said and rode away.

'I got sick of Sebastian first,' she shouted after him.

She sat on the verandah steps. She stretched her legs in front of her, her knees knobbled and brown, the four pink gravel scars. She cleaned out the gunk between her toes and went into the house. In the hallway, she put both palms on the wall and felt the stretching within.

At the phone, she opened her mother's teledex to S. The first time it was Mrs Sands and she hung up. She waited ten minutes and rang again. That time it was John, his voice quiet on the phone.

'Hello?'

'Hi,' she said and hung up.

Half an hour later, she rang again.

'Hello?'

Bingo.

'Is Mr Wall there?' she said.

'Listen, bitch, I know that one. I know who you are and I'm going to get you. I don't care if you're a girl.'

She heavy-breathed into the phone but Gary Sands made his goofy laugh, puffy and light.

'Wanna root?' he said.

'Tell your brother I'm going to get him back as well as you. For Grace and for other things.'

'Who's Grace? Is that your cousin, that girl?'

She hung up. He didn't even know who Grace was.

EARLY IN THE morning it was dry and there was hope for the day, that the burial hole wouldn't be sodden, its bottom turning to mud. They were gathered at Olive's house, her cousins sitting glumly in the lounge room because Rue had told them not to run around, to just sit still and be quiet. Olive couldn't remember the last time they had been at her place. They sat and looked at each other with discomfort.

Rue was walking around, peering at framed pictures, at the displays of objects on the sideboard and the mantelpiece. When they were at the farm Audra did the same, mostly pausing in front of the two paintings: the seascape and the matriarch, Lenore.

'Was this Mum's?' Rue asked, holding up a small vase.

Audra flicked her menthol at the ashtray. 'I don't remember.'

Just when the optimistic Rue thought the weather might hold, a new downpour came, rain running off the gutters to spatter and foam in the hydrangea beds.

'Cold enough for a fire later,' the adults said, but Olive worried about what might be happening at Soldier's, to the bunker. Was water battering the roof, seeping through and washing inside? Was the rock and sand crumbling and falling? Would the whole thing collapse before she could even get Jethro Sands inside?

•

It was the same church and the same position they'd sat in as a family all those years earlier. Audra and Rue had spoken about it only once, soon after it happened, and had fallen into an undignified, scrappy mess. That day at Aster's funeral, it had been Rue playing the secondary part of grieving aunt who cried and clutched, while Audra—tragic mother—remained dry-eyed and stood, passing tissues and patting her sister's arm. Bruce was there, redundant at the side, shifting his hands from pockets to hips and back again, his usual phlegmatic self.

As the minister walked to the front to begin the service, Thistle had pushed her face forwards, in between Audra and Bruce who sat in the front pew. Olive wasn't there, of course.

'What happened to the baby?' Thistle asked, but Bruce put his arm around his wife's shoulder and tried to mask her from her oldest sister. It was no use, though, because later Thistle went to Rue. Unable to parry the forceful questions and dismantled by her own grief, Rue began weeping and unburdened herself. She told Thistle what had happened.

'But you can't tell anyone.' She reached for the damp tissues balled in her sleeve. As she pulled them out a small flurry of white beads dropped to the floor. She was upset also, truth be told, that Sebastian had regressed. He was stuttering and wetting the bed again.

'I knew it.' Thistle inhaled, satisfied. She'd always had a nose for disappeared babies.

And now it was Thistle they gathered for at the Scots church. The place was half full, the sightlines clear. There were people from town and some even from Geelong. To Rue's distress Cleg was wearing a kilt and as he slid into place next to Archie, he whispered, '*Omnia extares*,' which Archie told Olive later he thought meant Uncle Cleg wasn't wearing any jocks.

Audra sat next to Bruce, her back straight and lipstick muted. She wore an immaculate knit suit, grey with black trim, and her single strand of South Sea pearls. Her tweedy elegance contrasted with the unsophisticated Rue, who wore her dated pants suit and clumpy shoes. Olive could smell her mother's perfume. Pink musk, undercut with the scent of tobacco and talcum powder.

The organ started to play and they stood for the first hymn. It was Thistle's favourite: 'Jerusalem'. When they got to the line about the bows of burning gold Olive leaned forwards, wanting to look at her mother and Rue, to see if they looked sad, but all she got was the side of William's head, mouth in a firm line, eyes down, not even pretending to sing. The hymn finished and William went up the front. He was dressed in a blue suit with a tan-checked shirt and brown tie. He coughed into the microphone. Cleg walked to the front to join his brother and Olive saw him mouth 'G'day, Blondie'. William seemed unsure about having Cleg with him at the front of the church.

'I'm not sure what to say,' he began. 'My sister-in-law was a complex person, so perhaps if I remember her when she was young. She had a good sense of humour and was someone who knew her own mind. She didn't care for herd thinking and she had a waist the size of Liz Taylor's . . .'

The minister looked up. Cleg moved William out of the way of the microphone and stepped forwards. He put both his hands on the top of the lectern and spoke too loudly, causing feedback.

'*Aqua vitae.*' His tongue snuck out a little then was retracted. 'Thistle had spirit, she was filled with it. As a young girl, as Bill said, she was determined. No one could tell her a darned thing.' He winked at the minister. 'I admired her but at times feared her, and feared for her. When we boys first knew Thistle Nash we were falling into all sorts of usual childhood scrapes. One time our old yellow dog died and I was a bit upset, and even though she was only a girl it was Thist who came and found me to try and make me feel better. She drew a picture of that old dog for me. She had a gentle nature and for most people it remained unexcavated. That's not to say she was always a saint—who the flock is? Sorry.'

The minister waved an airy hand.

'I guess that's all,' Cleg finished. 'We should be kind in our memories of Thistle.'

The minister approached the podium. Cleg managed to say, '*Requiescat in pace*,' making the microphone shudder again. The brothers started to walk away but William stopped and went back to the lectern. Cleg followed him, hand on his brother's shoulder.

'There's one more thing. What's happened, well, in some ways we expected it years ago, but I think it's because of my wife's tolerance that we got this far.' William wiped his eyes. 'It was a struggle for Thistle but she had a good heart.' William kept wiping his eyes with his hanky, then he blew his nose.

Olive looked at Rue, who had tissues pressed to her lips and was weeping noiselessly.

William held up a finger, pointing it out at the church congregation, at his wife and stiff-backed sister-in-law. 'You're all invited back to the house.'

He and Cleg returned to their seats, William clearing his throat all the way. They had a final prayer about grace and how God blesses even those who do not deserve it, and that mercy was about Him not punishing humans even though they usually deserved it. Finally came some words about forgiveness and then the service was over.

Olive stood outside the church and waited for her parents, who were talking to other adults. They always took ages. They would say they had to be going, get on back to the house to prepare for the guests, but they wouldn't move even a little but would continue to stand and talk. She got sick of waiting and went to sit on the steps, but it was windy and cold out there on the street. She was thinking to go inside again when Peter came pushing through the crowd and stood in front of her. He didn't speak, just planted his feet wide and put his hands on his hips. He was smiling at her.

'What?' she said.

'Guess.'

'Just tell me.'

'Jethro's back.' Peter pointed across the street.

Olive saw the car, parked in a small side street near the fish-and-chip shop. Inside the shop, Jethro Sands was sitting with his back to the window. Olive left Peter and ran across the road, keeping away from the shopfront. She walked around the car. The aerial wouldn't work but as she stood in front her eyes went to the grille and she saw what she was looking for. She ran back and found her parents who were saying they were ready to leave and where was she, they'd been looking for her. Rue was saying they had to hurry up, they had to go to the cemetery and then back to the house so she could get the teacups out. She hadn't managed to do that and was worried people would be turning up too soon after the burial.

Olive followed her parents to the car and across the street she saw Jethro come out of the shop and walk to his car. Their eyes met and she looked away.

EVERYTHING WAS STILL and wet and the rain made the eucalypts smell oily and sweet. At the drenched plot, they put Thistle in the ground, people slipping a little on the edge of the grave, shoes sliding in the slaggy clay. Rue had stopped crying but her eyes were puffy and rimmed with red. Audra's face was tight and empty.

Olive took note of the trees, the rocks and the view off the slope of the hill. It was a bitter thing, this new taste, that seemed it might be about growing up. The jolt of time passing hurt so much. She was in between with her childhood at the back of her and something illogical and confusing that loomed in front.

After the burial, they went back to Serpentine. The magpies called words from the trees. *Broooo—ooooos, brooo—ooooos. Will-will, will-will. Cleck-cleck-cleck.* Out in the paddocks, small lakes had appeared in the grass and the sheep stood in circles with noses pointed inwards. Someone started a fire and Olive sat on the couch in the Green Room, staring into the flames as they surged and dropped. Audra came in, gave Olive a small smile and sat close to her. For a moment Olive thought her mother was going to take her hand. Then Mavis Sands joined them with her crêpey décolletage, sitting on the other side of Audra.

'William was quite philosophical in the church, wasn't he?' Mrs Sands's lipstick had bled into the lines around her mouth. 'Thirty-seven, so young.'

In her politest voice, Audra said that yes, he had been and it was.

'But Clegworth, with that kilt, not appropriate. Still, she's at peace now, finally.' Mrs Sands's voice showed that she didn't believe in peace like that and was just saying the words because everyone said them.

'Mmm, yairs,' Audra said.

'And you're looking a little peaky, dear,' said Mavis, biting into a lamington, shreds of coconut falling onto the tops of her bosoms.

Audra didn't seem to hear.

'It's really good Vanessa got dux,' Olive said to Mrs Sands across her mother.

'Thank you. Are you happy with your new classes and teachers? Maybe you'll be friends with Vanessa again, that would be nice.' Mrs Sands put the rest of the lamington in her mouth, smiling. What a liar. Olive didn't care about her classes and she and Snooky would never be friends again.

'Why did Jethro come back?' The question slipped out without Olive thinking.

'Oh. I didn't think you had anything to do with my Jethro.' Mrs Sands made her eyes small and turned her head on a slight angle as if considering a too-hard sum.

'Mum said I had to be polite. Like a hostess.'

Audra stirred on the couch beside them.

'It's true,' she said. 'I did say that.'

'Well . . .' Mavis Sands drained her glass. 'The job was going well, but it just didn't work out with his uncle.' She looked around. 'Which was a shame. But he got his car fixed so he's happy and says it was worth it.'

Audra leaned forwards. Her usually pale cheeks were florid, despite the powder. Two hectic bright spots of pink. 'Did I thank you for the scones, Mavis? It was very good of you to bring them.'

Mavis's sharp eyes moved back to Audra.

'Such a shame about Thistle,' she said. 'Odd, how families have their runs of bad luck. And there, again. What is it about that place?'

Olive wasn't listening. Whatever was coming, she couldn't avoid it, and whatever it was would pass right though her. She was on a pathway and had no choice other than to push forwards. She stood up.

'Can I get you a cup of tea?' she said to Mrs Sands.

'Oh no, dear, but thank you.' Mavis Sands clutched at her wine-glass, which was rolling empty in her lap.

·

The guests were gone. Olive found her mother at the back door. She looked tired and small.

'Where's Dad?' Olive asked.

Her mother said she didn't know.

Rue had a red blotch on her neck and was holding out a small bowl of French onion dip to William, who was shaking his head and growling that he would never eat that muck.

'You need to eat something and it's really quite nice,' Rue was saying.

Olive sat in the sunroom on her own as the land slowly darkened outside. She could see the tree and Cleg's van, the shed, the clothesline and the stepping stones in between. It was quiet and the chilled evening air began to pass through the flywire of the windows, air that was cool and fresh. Still she sat, unmoving. Cleg came out of the van and walked to the house. He came in the back door, saw her and smiled. He'd trimmed his beard for the funeral but still looked like one of the bushrangers.

'Milo?'

She nodded.

'Why doesn't Mum have one of your sayings?' she asked.

'She does. *Pulchrum est paucorum hominum.*' The words came easily but they were ones Olive had never heard before.

'What does it mean?'

'It means "beauty is for the few". Rue's was "pick, girl, the roses", and I used to sometimes make it "prick", just to make her laugh. She laughed more easily in those days.'

'What was Thistle's again?'

'I don't want to say what hers was because it wasn't too kind.' He was in the kitchen now.

'Was it *vulner* something?'

He came back to the doorway. 'Yes, it was "*vulner* something".'

'Did Thistle try hard to keep her baby?'

Cleg sat down again. He had a teabag in his hand.

'Bloody hard, but they still got him from her. Poor Thist.'

'Were you a lawyer? Did you help her try to get it back?'

'No, I was just a kid, hadn't even finished school. She didn't want our help anyway. "It's not your concern" is what she told me, and I believed her. They told her that it was in the baby's best interests to go to a married couple.'

'They?'

'The adults. And later, once we were older, I said it too. Rue said it, we all said it. It's what you said in those days but it was a mistake.'

'Did Mum know?'

'Of course she did.'

'What about William and Dad?'

'Everyone knew. She wasn't ashamed about anything.'

'Do you know who the dad was?'

Cleg looked at the teabag. He started to pull the string open. 'She never told us that particular piece of information.'

'Why didn't Thistle live in her own house?'

Cleg put his hands over his eyes and went quiet. His shoulders started moving up and down, so she looked out the window and sat with her hands making fists. He kept his hands over his face and she was scared he was going to cry and then he did cry. She couldn't move. All she could do was keep her hands in her lap and wait for him to stop.

'I'm sorry. I miss my wife.' He pulled out a hanky and wiped his eyes. 'Any time it was suggested she get a place in town Thistle was firm, saying she had to be here.'

'I'm going in with the others now.' She got up.

'Sorry,' he said again. 'Not what you expect from your uncle, is it?'

She shook her head.

'Yes, you go, I'll be in soon.'

She went into the hallway. How often adults were intruders, moving across rooms from left to right, distant in the background, or if not in motion, fixed in place, sitting in a particular chair, perhaps, or the front seat of the car. They stood on the street, at the shops, called you to dinner from doorways, interrupted the play and halted the swell and flow of the day's business that for children happened under beds, astride bikes, on roofs and roads, in parks, up trees. The high places. The closed spaces. Adults didn't pierce the membrane other than when they were getting in the way. But like rabbits, questions made more questions, and now that Thistle was gone, no one would be able to answer them. How did Christmas start? How deep was the dam? How exactly did the boy get sucked into the sand hole in America? Could the peppercorn out the back get hit by lightning ever again? What is a soul? Thistle had done her best with that one, but it was the only question Olive hadn't received a satisfactory answer to and also the one she most desperately wanted to understand.

Though she and Thistle had spent a lot of time talking about these things, other adults were never interested. They folded into themselves like socks, became lumpy balls and shut you out. They might answer your questions but what they said was always the fewest words that they could give you, and inside those answers were messages, like codes, that told you to stop even asking.

It occurred to her at that moment that she and her mother and father were always at the farm because it was comfortable for them there in the same way that she didn't want to stay at Peter's for dinner, but even so she still didn't understand why Thistle had stayed. If she was Thistle she'd want her own house where she could have things how she wanted them and be free. She would cook dinner however she wanted or not have it at all. She would watch television all day and drink jugs of cordial. And she would read her *Book of Lists* all night, without anyone telling her to turn out the light and go to sleep.

•

In the Green Room the fire was so hot that people had started to take off cardigans and jumpers. Bruce and Audra had gone to bed and when someone suggested a game of charades, Rue said everyone was tired.

'I think we've all had enough,' she said, but nobody moved.

Cleg came in and stretched out with his eyes closed in one of the big chairs. Olive moved to stand in front of the fire.

'Careful, those logs can roll,' William said. His voice was thick and he didn't make the sounds of each word properly. He'd had a lot of wine but he hadn't talked about rabbits, not even once. 'One would take off your foot at the flocking ankle.' He stretched in his chair. 'A decent Mallee root can burn for a week, you know.'

Cleg said that he was a decent Mallee root as well and that was when Rue said it was definitely time for bed.

Cleg told William he was going to move on from the mother work, that asbestos was where it was at.

'There's some real money in it.'

'Money's not important.' Olive had moved a little distance from the fire but was in front, facing her uncles. 'That's what you always say.'

'No?' Cleg said. 'How's that sixteen dollars feeling in your pocket, then?'

Olive flushed. 'But helping people and fairness is more important. That's what the law is for.'

'You're a smart girl but you don't understand. You will when you're older.' Cleg crossed his legs. Cleg always crossed his legs when he was going to talk about the law. 'It's how the law works. It's not about whether someone did it or not. It's not about *justice*, it's about systems. You'll see, it's just life.'

'But you can tell, can't you? If someone did it?'

'They tell me if they've done it, usually. But even so, you have to know when to go back and forth about something, how to be okay with not knowing the truth, thinking it could be this, thinking it could be that. If you make up your mind too soon you could be wrong, but the time comes when you have to stop the swinging back and forth and just pick one way. You have to know that guilty people act innocent and innocent ones can seem guilty. All the time. You need to be able to put all these things together. If something doesn't fit, *maybe* it doesn't belong, but remember, for a long time it might not seem to fit and then it just does, so if you rush, well. Problems. Most people find it too hard to sit for a while, not knowing.'

'But what about the other things?'

'Like what?'

'Like what is fairness, what makes people bad. What is good punishment.'

'All that stuff is for other people. Not lawyers, not really.'

'I don't get it.'

'Guilty is something the court decides. It's not a real thing. What you're asking is whether I think they've done it and I'm telling you *that doesn't matter*. Those coppers aren't idiots, they don't waste their time on a case they won't win. Most people aren't bad but they can do bad things. There's a difference. That's what you will eventually understand.'

'But the guilty ones have to go to jail,' said Olive. 'In the Bible it says that people are the little gods, which means they have power to do things, like make baddies pay. That's what Thistle said. That you should do whatever you can to make things right.'

'Here we go. Enter the childhood philosopher slash theologian slash women's liberationist with her firm convictions intact before the travails of adulthood overwhelm her and shepherd her towards corruption, cynicism or confirmed and permanent denial.'

'But all criminals should go to jail or pay money. They have to fix the problem and pay things back.' She could feel her face going red. Why was Cleg being mean, especially when he was so sad before? 'It's not true, is it?' she said to William. 'Does he help bad people?'

'He has and does,' William said. 'Like your uncle said, you'll see when you're older.'

It was the wrongest thing she had ever heard. She wouldn't 'see', and it wasn't 'life'. Rue's refrain of 'it will all be alright' was a lie. If lawyers weren't the ones making the decisions and making sure people got paid back, made sure people did the right things, who did? The police just cleaned up the messes. Who fixed things? Maybe it was judges. Alright, she'd be a judge then.

'That's so stuffed,' she said and stalked off to bed.

She slept well and woke early in the morning. She ate corn-flakes and read her book until her mother told her it was time to go home. Often, when it was time to leave, she couldn't be found. There would be many delays followed by much fuss. But this time she was already packed and went and sat in the car with her seat-belt on while her parents were still gathering everything together. Rue asked her if she was feeling alright but Olive didn't say a word.

Bruce drove them home in silence. Once in her own bedroom she spent the rest of the day thinking. Jethro was back and it was time to start the final action. If she didn't do it she would combust into a million pieces of bone and ash.

She had to get it done.

IT WAS REMEMBERING Thistle's strength, the way her aunt said that they were the same, that made her wait until it was late and go to get the screwdriver from her father's toolbox. It was thinking about what Cleg said, that he helped criminals, and her decision to become a judge, that made her put it in her pocket and get her bike out from the shed.

She pedalled down the street on the footpath, cut across a driveway and went right at the school. It was two in the morning and she was headed to Farkham Street. Farkham was long and spinelike and ran from the old highway at the north of Stratford to the main road. It had shops on the south side and a football oval on the north. About halfway along, it intersected with Hopetoun, a broad avenue which bisected the town into two west and east halves, one side with the church and the other with the pub.

As she rode she realised Jethro's car might not be out the front. Maybe it would be in the driveway, or even in the garage. She would stop a few houses away, dump her bike on the nature strip to creep along and have a look.

She really hoped it would be parked on the street.

It wasn't. She got off her bike at number seventy-one and put it under a bush. She walked along the fence line towards seventy-five, where the Sandses lived. Approaching, she could see no lights on at the front of the house, a compact single-storey weatherboard. The exterior was neglected, with peeling green paint and rusted gutters, an overgrown garden and gates off their hinges. The interior, though, was always neat and clean, the surfaces shining as best as Mrs Sands could get them. Olive had liked the house when she was friends with Snooky but now it sat with a toxic glow in the night, round as a toad as if waiting to hurt her.

She peered around the edge. The car wasn't in the driveway either. This was a problem. At the end of the drive was the garage, narrow with one of those pull-up doors that made a noise and the only patch of light was a small spread falling out of a window at the side. Was it the kitchen? She couldn't remember. It had been a long time since she'd played at Snooky's. There might be a separate door on the right side of the garage but with people still awake inside it was a big risk. She had thought three o'clock would be better, but the idea of being out even one hour later scared her.

She stood at the fence, listening. She was almost certain there wasn't a dog. She'd never heard about Snooky having one and she tried to remember if Jethro had said anything at the ganger's hut. She thought he had said he hated them when they were talking about the scar on his face.

She looked down the drive. She was sure she'd be able to bend and scurry underneath the sightline but found herself powerless against curiosity and was drawn to the window. She inched up the side from the bottom. A little more and she was looking into the lounge. It was empty but the TV was on, snow on the screen throwing light into the corner where two windows met. Then she saw them: feet at the end of the couch. Big feet, crossed and still. Dirty socks. Was it Mr Sands or Jethro? Was the someone asleep? Maybe it was John on the couch, not Jethro. If it was him and she got caught she knew he wouldn't hurt her. Hopefully Jethro was asleep and his car was in the garage. Hopefully he wasn't out at a pub or a friend's place, drunk and trying to get with girls. Hopefully he wasn't about to pull into the driveway with his high beams to discover her pressed up against the side of the house. She would freeze and wasn't sure if she would be able to run. At the window she was about to move, or think about moving, when she saw the socks start tapping, the toes clapping against each other at the end of the couch.

She ducked and scrambled further along, under the window. On the other side, she peeped again. The socks were still in the same position but now there was an arm over the back of the couch, a thick arm with man-hair and one of the silver-studded leather straps that Jethro wore. He was clicking his fingers. He was awake.

She moved down the driveway. Past some pot plants lined up along the cement, the sweet dusty smell of geraniums in the air. Around the corner came a cat. Orange, big, back arched with its tail up, turning in front of her, threading between her ankles. It miaowed and she patted it. She went to the side of the garage. There was a door and she put her hand on the knob, looking back over her shoulder. She pulled a little and it didn't move. She pulled a bit harder and it opened and the cat darted through. She followed it inside, closing the door behind her, glad it didn't make any noise. She couldn't see so waited until her eyes adjusted, the cat rubbing against her legs.

Something big emerged in outline, a pale form looming out of the darkness. Moving with her hands in front, sliding her feet forwards carefully so she didn't knock anything, she passed around the front of the sheet. The cat followed, getting in between her feet, purring. She lifted the sheet and felt down to where the metal grille was at the front. She crouched, peering at the badge. Through a gap in the garage door came enough light for her to see the lettering, the silver metal word: CHARGER. She put the tip of the screwdriver in behind the emblem, in the middle of the word, and started to lever, first with arm strength and then leaning down hard with her whole body weight. Before she could stop the thing had bent outwards in the middle. She adjusted the screwdriver to the side a bit and tried again. It took a few goes but it popped off with a snap. She did the same at the other end, near the C, and that end came off too, though it took a bit longer. The cat was still there, she could hear it purring, and she was glad it was there with her. She didn't want to be alone in the garage doing what she was doing, which was a bad thing.

Then she tried to get the other badge off and luckily that one was easier, probably because it was a more solid rectangle rather than thin writing. She had them. She smiled. She would make an excellent thief.

She put the badges in her pocket with the screwdriver, pulled the sheet back over the front of the car and, still grinning, stepped on the cat. It shrieked and scratched her leg and she ran to the door, knocking over something that was leaning against the wall. Behind her the clattering noise sounded like wood and metal, maybe gardening tools, falling onto the floor of the garage.

She ran out the door to the driveway as the porch light came on. As she turned the corner she heard the back door open. Down the driveway, past the window, she didn't bother to duck but sprinted out to the footpath, to her bike. She rode down the street, crossed to the other side where there were more trees and pedalled to the end of Farkham and around the corner, almost crashing into the fence. She stopped. Sitting on her bike she rolled back and looked through the bushes. Someone was standing in front of the house, looking up and down the street. He walked back in and she stayed a moment, chest sore and legs shaking. She pulled the two badges out of her pocket and held them up to her nose and whispered, 'Howzat.'

Looking through the bushes once more she saw two figures outside the house now, one walking away from her and the other coming in her direction. She set off home, bike wheels whirring.

She put her bike in the shed, crept in through the back door and climbed the stairs, stepping in the right order so they didn't make their creaks. She went to her room, shut the door in increments, and her heart started to slow. She kicked her shoes off and got into bed and lay listening to the sound of her breathing, then put on her bedside lamp and took out the things from her pocket. The silver badge, with the curving 'C' at the beginning and the 'R' lengthened at the end. The snappy shapes of the other 'r's' and the cut-off of the 'g'. It was pretty cool even if it was bent a bit. Maybe she could hammer it flat again. And the arrow-type badge, an oblong with three triangles all nested inside each other; a black one, a white one and a red one. She put them under her pillow and turned off the lamp and went straight to sleep.

JETHRO RAN ALONG Kellda Street. Her house was somewhere along here. Was it the one next to where his old teacher Mr McCullers lived? The streets and houses were quiet. One dog barked a little behind a gate as he walked past but it settled quickly. He thought he'd go around the block, see if he came across anything.

He knew it had been her. The knocked-over tools in the garage couldn't have been the cat and he was certain he had heard light footsteps, the gripping sound of runners on cement, of feet running away. It was possible he'd imagined it. He had been almost asleep on the couch, after all. He'd been tired from the drive back from the city, and once home he'd had to listen to his mother talking about the Nash women. Then she'd complained about the doctor's bill for Gary's arm being more expensive because it had been a weekend, that she still hadn't paid because next month Luke had to get his plate from the dentist, which would cost such a lot.

He stopped under a tree. There was a light on upstairs in one of the houses. He considered it and, just as he was about to walk on, the window went dark. It was her. He took note of the number, seven, and walked on.

Back at home, he lay a long while before sleep, thinking of Olive Lovelock and wondering what she was up to.

MAVIS SANDS HAD a headache and was trying to rest when she heard loud talking in the kitchen. It was Jethro and Vanessa and when she came out she saw them sitting in the kitchen.

'What's that?' she said. 'What are you hiding?'

'It's nothing,' said Jethro.

'Just a funny picture,' said Snooky.

'Keep it down, please,' said Mavis. 'I'm not feeling well.' She went back to her room.

Jethro got the note out from under the table. He read it once more:

TO JETHRO WE HAVE
WHAT YOU WANT SO
COME TO THE
SOLdIER'S PAddOCK
TOMORROW nIGHT
AT FOUR In THE
nIGHT. TO TALK
ABOuT IT.
FROM SOMEOnE
YOu KnOw

'Who gave it to you?' he asked his sister again.

'I can't say.'

'Snooky.'

'I can't. He told me not to.'

He? Jethro had been certain it was Olive Lovelock. That morning he'd seen the car grille, that the badges were gone, and any reluctant admiration he'd felt had disappeared with the realisation that this girl had touched his car. This creepy kid, riding all over the place on her bike in the middle of the night, camping out at the hut. Reading the note, though, he wondered if it was Bulldog. His sister had said it was a man who gave it to her, but wouldn't say anymore. Bulldog or Nutter maybe—but why would they do it? It didn't make any sense.

He went out to the car again and studied the grille. Maybe she hadn't done it. The removal was a clean job. Bulldog worked at the mechanics and liked to souvenir tags. Jethro was confused. The note said to go to Soldier's so he guessed that was what he was going to do.

'Are you gonna go?' Snooky said.

'None of your business. Now git.'

Jethro knew that it would be a very bad thing if it was Nutter, but he had to go anyway, to see who had nicked his badges. He would get them back or not, but either way it was something he couldn't ignore.

OLIVE RANG THE farm and got Archie. He was sure one thousand per cent that he wanted to help. He suggested trying to get a gun out of his father's cupboard but she said no, could he find some rope? And they needed a spade, too. She told him what his job as part of the plan was. She ran through everything with him twice. He didn't ask why and he didn't say it was a bad idea. He listened, and each time she paused his small breathy voice came down the line: *Yeah*.

'And don't say anything.'

'To anyone, I know.'

She hung up and ate a bit of toothpaste and got into bed. Soon she was going to find out exactly what had happened. She felt excited but also worried, with a small flicker of something in her chest.

That night she dreamed that her mouth was filled with dressmaker pins and beyond, lodged in her throat, were clumps of cottonwool. First she had to pull out the pins. Then she had to reach in, past her teeth, reach for the round white balls that were stuffed in there. In her sleep, she was practical and calm, making herself breathe steadily, in and out and in, as her hands did their work. She knew that to panic was to lose control, but it was almost impossible to keep calm as she sensed herself edging closer to something dangerous.

SHE WAS ON her bike in the meeting spot at the bottom of the driveway, waiting for Archie's signal. She'd ridden there with her torch, her backpack and, most importantly, her tape recorder. She waited a bit longer but he still didn't appear. There was no torchlight moving from house to shed. Maybe he hadn't woken up yet. Maybe he was still working out how to balance the spade on his bike. She put her things down, left her bike and backpack beside the fence, and walked up the long drive, careful on the rocky gravel. She didn't want to put the torch on and there was not much light in the sky. But she could see enough. Beside the driveway the pines towered, black on black. She probably should be scared but was so fixed on her purpose, she realised, that she hadn't even thought of what would happen if a murderer came out from behind one of the trees and tried to get her.

She went to the back of the house and was about to open the door when Archie appeared. Mandy was with him.

'She was in the hallway but I think she's still asleep.'

'Shhh,' Olive said. '*Whisper.*'

Mandy's eyes were open like in a horror movie.

'Mandy?' There was no reaction. Olive waved a hand in front of her face and then pinched her. '*Mandy.*' Her cousin's eyes tracked around Olive's face, blinked and settled back into an empty stare. She pinched her again. No response.

'What's wrong with her?'

'I don't know. I didn't know what to do, so I told her to come and she followed me.' Archie sat down on the step to tie his runners up. 'I've got the rope ready, like you said. And the spade.'

'What are we going to do with her?' Olive said. 'She has to go back to bed.'

Mandy spoke in a normal voice.

'What are you doing?'

'Shhh. You have to go back to bed now,' said Olive. 'It's late.'

'Where are you going?'

'Nowhere.'

'I want to come too,' said Mandy.

'You can't. I'm taking you back to bed.'

'I'll tell.'

It was a night empty of sound and very still, a time for ghosts. Thistle said wind blew the ghosts away but Olive had started to realise that while some of the things her aunt had said were true, many weren't.

'You can't come. I'm taking you back to bed and you can't tell anyone afterwards. I'm really serious. If you do, I'll bash you.' She felt bad because it was something Gary Sands would say. Mandy arched her back, throwing a shadow that reared up along the wall. She was about to tell Mandy to go back to bed again when her cousin opened her mouth and started keening. It started low and Olive clapped her hands across Mandy's mouth.

'Okay, shush. You can come.' She turned to Archie. 'What are we going to do? We can't take her on the bikes.'

Archie thought a minute.

'It's like with the fires, when I said we would drive to escape them. They said we couldn't do it but I know that it would work. We have to drive now too,' he said. 'You can drive there, in the ute.'

It was a crazy idea but they had no choice. If Mandy wouldn't go back to bed, it was the only way.

'Get the keys,' Olive whispered. 'They're in the bowl, in the kitchen.'

The hardest part would be getting the ute down the driveway without anyone hearing. Maybe they could roll it without turning on the engine. She'd seen her father and uncles do it and was sure she could manage it.

Archie came back with the keys and they walked along the path to the rear of the shed.

'Get in,' Olive said to Mandy, guiding her cousin into the back seat. 'Stay there.' She shut the door. Archie got in the front passenger seat.

'Do we need to put our seatbelts on?' Mandy said from the back.

'Of course!' Archie said. 'It's dangerous if you don't.' He clipped his in and they sat, then Olive realised they needed to get out again, to push. The engine would be too noisy starting up. They both got out and tried but it wouldn't move.

'Wait here,' she said to him. 'Don't talk. Keep the doors shut and the torches off.'

She went in the back door and crept through the house, working out in her head what she would say to her aunt or uncle if a door opened. Rue would be surprised to see her and ask lots of questions. She made it to the boys' bedroom and crept over to Sebastian's side, to his bed. She stood there a moment, wondering how to wake him up without him yelling. She was about to bend over and gently push his arm when she saw that his eyes were already open.

'You need my help, right?'

She nodded.

'I want all your birthday money and the money from Cleg too. The sixteen dollars.'

She started to say no, that it was more than a hundred bucks. He turned in his bed to face the wall.

'*Alright.*' She thought about the typewriter and it made her heart hurt.

Back at the car Mandy was sitting upright, staring out the window.

'What the hell?' Sebastian said.

'She was sleepwalking, she followed Arch. She wasn't in the plan and I think she's in a trance, but don't worry, she'll be fine. Heidi was alright.'

'Yeah, she'll be fine, 'cause I'm taking her back in with me once we roll the car.'

'That's not *fair*. You *have* to come with us for that much money.'

He didn't say anything.

'Peter chickened out too. I can't believe neither of you will help me.'

Why was everyone against her? It would be so easy just to forget it. She was tired and it all seemed so hard. But she had to keep going, she was so close to the end. She took a deep breath. 'Okay, it's not chicken.' She'd never apologised to Sebastian. 'I'm sorry.'

'You're scared, aren't you?' Sebastian was smiling.

Archie came around from the other side of the car. He pulled his hand out from behind his back. He was holding one of William's small guns. A pistol.

'We don't need him,' he said.

'No way.' Sebastian stepped forward. He held out his hand to his brother but Archie didn't hand him the gun. He stepped backwards.

'We don't need him,' Archie said again.

'Arch, come on,' said Olive. 'We can't take that—it's dangerous. And we do need Sebastian, it's better if he comes.' She hated that he was right but at least she didn't have to admit it. Not properly.

'The whole thing's stupid,' Sebastian said. He opened Mandy's door and undid her seatbelt. 'Come on, I'm taking you back to bed.'

Olive held onto his arm. She promised she'd never be mean to him ever again. She said he could have all her future birthday and Christmas money. All her Easter eggs, anything he wanted, just to please come with them. From the corner of her eye she saw Archie make a movement, swinging around on his feet and putting his hands to his head. She didn't care what he thought. She had to make her plan happen and this was the only way. Sebastian stopped what he was doing, straightened and looked at her.

Standing there in the garden the colours of the night seemed to pulse. She didn't have time to try to interpret Sebastian's expression. He was getting so weird anyway. Rue said it was the hormones.

'Alright, but only because I have to make sure my brother and sister will be safe.' Sebastian did Mandy's seatbelt up again. 'And you have to give me the Colt Navy.'

Olive told Archie to give it and he did and Sebastian put it on the front passenger floor of the ute. With Mandy sitting in the back, Archie now at the other rear door and Sebastian at the open passenger's side and her at the driver's, the three of them pushed. It was hard work and the ute moved a little forwards and backwards before they could get it over a rock. Once cleared it started to move better and they jumped in and coasted down the driveway with the doors still open, soundless and smooth even though Archie almost fell out. She rolled the car past the trees and all the way down to the gate. She stopped there and got her backpack, then started the engine and they shut the doors. She got the car going smoothly and turned right onto the road. It was a good sign she thought. That things would go well.

'How do I put the lights on?'

Sebastian reached over and pulled out a knob on the dashboard.

'Half a click for parking, all the way for full. The high beams is a button on the floor, I think, but I'm not sure. We don't need the strongest ones if you just go slowly. We can see.'

They crawled along with the land spread outside the windows. She was aware how tightly her hands held the wheel and how far forwards she was sitting on the seat. She was in second gear now and they covered the distance slowly. There were no other vehicles on the road.

At first, no one spoke but then Archie started to chat, quietly at first, about levitation and whether the others believed in it. Next he asked whether identical twins could feel each other's pain, and then wondered whether they believed some people could move things just with the power of their minds. Olive didn't answer. She didn't speak the whole way. She was concentrating hard on making sure she steered properly while looking out for the turn-off to Soldier's. It was the one before Ganger's. It didn't have a sign, just a white-painted stick with a little reflecting square of tin that shone red. She waited for that marker. It was the same one that Grace had stopped at the time they went to Ganger's.

'There.' Sebastian raised his hand.

'I know.' She took her foot off the accelerator and the car shuddered as they went around in second but she managed to keep it moving. They drove the last few hundred metres to the spot where there was a wider verge at the side of the road. The car came to a stop and stalled. Sebastian leaned over and pushed the knob in and everything went dark with the trees packed together in complete blackout. She put on her backpack with the tape recorder inside. She'd done tests. She needed to be as close as possible to Jethro Sands when he confessed what he'd done to Aster, and she had to keep the zip open along the top of the bag as well.

'Should we take the pistol?' Sebastian said.

'No way. Give it here. You're being a *quid nunc* to even think that, Sebastian.' She put the gun in the glove box.

'I don't think you know what that means.' Sebastian turned to the bush. 'Where is he?' he said. 'I bet he won't turn up.'

They walked along the narrow path. Mandy had wanted to stay in the car and sleep on the back seat. She was very tired, she said, and didn't want to walk but Sebastian told her she couldn't stay, that she might get kidnapped. She had to go with them, he said, to be safe.

They went through the fence and got to the entrance of the bunker where they sat on a fallen branch to wait. The air was fresh in the night. Olive breathed it in and let herself believe that it gave her some sort of power. Across the top of the trees the inky shape of the silo loomed, the megastructure fixed against the darkness, solid and immutable and outlined with stars. A branch creaked and it made her think of 'Hist!' and she was just wondering what a mopoke actually was and was going to ask Sebastian if he knew when Jethro appeared. She couldn't see his face so she swung her torch up and saw that he was smiling. He squinted and held his hand across his eyes.

'I knew it was you.'

Here he was. She forced herself to take a step forwards.

'I have the things from your car but I have a question that you have to answer before I give them back.'

'What's stopping me from just taking them off you now, without answering anything?'

She pulled out the knife from her backpack and unclipped the press-stud of the case. She pulled out the blade and held it up and gestured with it at Sebastian, who sat nearby with Mandy on his lap. Sebastian looked surprised, shocked even, and Olive knew it was not by her and the knife. It was that Jethro was there at all. Mandy was shivering, hunched over with hollow eyes and Archie was nearby on one of the low branches.

'Okay,' Jethro said, holding up his hands. 'What a crew. Your henchmen have me scared.' He wasn't taking her seriously but he would. 'Okay then. What do you want to know?'

Olive swung her backpack around to her front and stepped forwards. She unzipped it, reached inside.

'I want you to tell me what happened to my sister, at the dam.' She was speaking in a loud voice and it sounded strange even to her. 'I want you to tell me what you did to her, Jethro Sands.'

His smile disappeared—here was the proof. He looked like he knew something, he was guilty. She was right.

Sebastian was making some kind of noise to the side.

'Ollie,' he was saying. 'Don't.'

'What makes you think I know anything about your sister?' Jethro said.

'I know you were there because people told me you were.'

'But they didn't tell you everything, did they?' He folded his arms and scuffed his boot against the ground. 'You sure you want to know?'

He was bluffing. Trying to use reverse psychology, which she knew about. But he couldn't trick her. She said she did. She definitely did want to know. She looked at Sebastian. He was shaking his head and mouthing *no*. Archie had stood up and was holding his hands apart in question. What about the plan? He was right. She'd forgotten the plan as soon as she saw Jethro. She had to get him into the tunnel to do the second part. She didn't know how she could manage it. Maybe she could say the badges were there, and if he wanted them he had to go in with her.

'Alright,' he said. 'I'll tell you, but not here. It has to be just you and me.'

She got it, he was clever. He didn't want the others to be witnesses.

'We can go to our clubhouse,' Olive said. 'I'll give you the badges there.'

'You have a clubhouse?'

'Of course, we're kids.' She pointed at the entrance to the bunker.

'In there?' He walked towards it and she followed, ignoring Sebastian telling her it was a really dumb idea. He didn't know the plan because she hadn't told him. Archie started to follow.

'You aren't scared?' Jethro said.

She shook her head but her mouth was dry and she felt she might faint from terror. They went inside, Jethro gesturing for Olive to go first. She went down the passageway, holding the backpack to her tummy.

'You kids really come in here?' Jethro said, looking around.

'All the time.' She shone her torch on the roof to check for bats. There were old burned-down candles set into niches in the walls.

She walked around Jethro to shut the door. As she did she caught sight of Archie. He gave her a thumbs-up. She showed her cousin a thumb then closed the door.

She faced Jethro Sands. He looked unsure, worried even, which was how she knew he was going to confess.

'Tell me,' she said.

He started the story a couple of times and his voice was tight, but once he got going, it came quickly. He had been at her uncle's farm, helping with the fences. He told her how the dog had bitten the boy—the small one out there—and the adults took him to the doctor.

'It's Archie,' she said.

Mr Lovelock had told him to wait, Jethro said, that he'd either be back in time for them to finish the work or to drive him home. Mrs Lovelock had told him to go ahead and find something to eat in the kitchen, to just help himself. Olive watched his face. He had been there. And he wasn't even trying to hide it.

Jethro had gone into the house, but instead of looking for the kitchen, he went and looked around.

'Kids are nosy,' he said. 'Right?'

She shook her head. 'I'm not.'

'Anyway, you were in the lounge room, playing with some kind of toy, with that bigger kid out there. Mrs Lovelock said your mother was in the house but I didn't see her. I said hello but neither of you said anything back. You just stared.'

'How old were you?'

'Almost thirteen.'

He had gone to the kitchen and found some bread and made a honey sandwich. There was a baby crying and he thought the mother might come, so he got an apple from the fruit bowl and went into the back garden to find somewhere to sit.

'Our apples always get eaten the first day at home,' he said.

Jethro said he found a spot under a big tree. He'd seen a beetle walking across a leaf and he watched it for a long time. Then, near the house, he saw movement and it was someone on the path, Olive and her cousin, the big one.

'Sebastian,' she said.

They were walking through a paddock, away from the house.

'You were carrying something between you, a basket, and you had a bucket and spade. You know those little kid ones, from the beach?'

It was as if wings were flapping near her face. She could hear the tape deck turn inside the backpack with a tiny whirr. Jethro kept talking and it took her a while to stop him.

'I don't want you to say,' she said and reached into her bag. She switched the recorder off.

'It was the same day the dog bit me,' he said. It had come right at that moment, as he sat, panting and wet and almost hysterical on the edge of the dam. It jumped on him and bit him on the face. He held his face but the blood was thin and dripped through his fingers and splashed his shirt bright red. He took off his t-shirt and held it to his forehead and waited. He didn't know what to do, he said. It had taken a long time for her older cousin to stop crying. 'You were really upset about your hands. You wanted to wash the mud off. That's what I remember too.'

'I said I changed my mind.' She turned off her torch. 'They still have Shaggy,' she said. She could hear him breathing. 'They keep him on a chain.'

'It was an accident.'

'But he bit Archie too.'

She switched her torch back on. It hurt her to see the look on his face.

'You have the same colour eyes,' he said. 'I remember it. Exactly the same.'

'I'm going back.' She opened the door and walked out of the tunnel. Archie was outside with his torch and the rope but she shook her head at him as she pushed past. Sebastian and Mandy were still in the same spot, Mandy asleep in her brother's lap, her hands clasped around his neck. Olive moved her torch to Sebastian's face and saw his tender look before he squinted away from the glare.

'What happened?' he said.

'Nothing. Let's go.'

'Do you want a lift?' said Jethro.

'It's alright, we have our own car,' Sebastian said.

Jethro laughed. 'You kids really are nuts.' He lit a cigarette.

Olive started to walk away, back to the fence. There was a sensation in her ears, a pressing of air that made a high-pitched sound.

They walked through the trees and around the holes. Everything was bending. All the sounds including the others' voices were reaching across space to her and almost disappearing in the wide space of the night. The air smelled new, not oiled eucalyptus but something sharp.

She walked first, followed by Archie, then Sebastian carrying Mandy. They all had torches except for Jethro, who was behind. She looked back only once, her eyes finding Jethro's. It was terrible to know that Jethro Sands felt sorry for her. Archie started to ask about whether there had been any bats in the tunnel and why did she change her mind about the rope. Why didn't they do the *plan*?

She told Archie to be quiet. They climbed through the fence, Mandy grumbling because Sebastian said she had to walk the rest of the way.

'What about the plan?' said Archie.

'I changed my mind about it,' Olive said.

They got to the ute and she knew she wouldn't be able to drive so she gave the keys to Sebastian. Jethro walked into the trees, his cigarette end a small glowing spot moving in the night along the track. Sebastian got the car going and took about five tries to get it turned around. Back on the main road as they crawled towards Serpentine, Olive rested against the door, her eyes closed.

'Look,' she heard Sebastian say. It was Jethro's car, still parked. Jethro was leaning against it. He lifted a hand in farewell and Olive remembered she hadn't given back the grille badges.

•

It took them a long time to get back to the farm because Sebastian drove even slower than she had. It was almost quarter to six when they made it into their beds. Her aunt would be unhappy that she was at the house without her knowing but there was no way she could ride home. Rue would get into a state and say Audra would be worried sick but she didn't care. She should knock on her aunt's door and tell her she was there but it would cause a fuss and a phone call to her parents right away and she didn't want to think about things until the morning.

She thought back to herself only a few hours ago. She'd been like that girl doing cartwheels just before her parents told her something very sad. She went to the window and the moon was gone, the horizon a pale line. To see that pink streak in the sky was painful. She wanted to go outside, to the tree, and see how the branches looked like big claws against the brightening sky. If she went there and climbed she could think about how it was that the places and people that were meant to make you safe could make you feel so wobbly. How it was that you could believe one thing about yourself but for the truth to be completely the opposite.

'I wish I was a girl again,' she whispered.

She stood at the window, listening to Mandy breathe.

IT WAS DAWN as she walked past the tree. She went to the dam and waded in because this was the place Thistle had gone when she was hurting, into the cold and wet. She waded out and lay on her back and let herself drift to the middle.

If she tried would it hurt? Her clothes would suck the water in and become heavy and pull her down. The pondweed would cover her face as she sank but she would make sure to keep her eyes wide so she could reach for the open white spot. If she kept her ears open too she would hear the sound effects, a chortling blend of magpie and child. She would close her eyes and search for something and, if she found it, it would make her free. But she wasn't doing that. She wasn't doing anything like that. She was floating on her back, imagining.

But William had been up unable to sleep. Standing outside the back door, he'd seen her walk across the paddock and followed, keeping at a distance. When he saw her go in he sprinted to the dam, his legs and arms pumping. She felt the vibrations of his flat racing dive and lifted her head to see him swimming towards her, his mouth gaping. He pulled her out and put her on the edge. His tree-trunk legs with the hairs on them were near her face and he was only wearing his underpants which were wet too.

'No, girl, no,' he said, breathing hard.

•

Rue made her get undressed and she sat in the kitchen with a blanket around her while her aunt called her mother and then went and found some dry clothes. Rue said very little and when Audra and Bruce arrived there was a short, brisk conversation about why she was there in the first place. They hadn't even realised she wasn't in her own bed until Rue's phone call. They decided to take her to the hospital.

'But I'm okay,' Olive said.

'You're not,' said Rue, lifting Olive's chin. 'Better for them to check you over. You might feel fine in your body, but . . .'

Olive said she was definitely fine in her body, whatever that meant. She said she'd been sleepwalking but she let them take her. She had no choice but to lie on the back seat of the car with her head on her mother's lap. Even though Audra was angry and looking out the window rather than downwards, Olive felt the sensation of the hard muscles in her mother's thighs lengthening under her neck.

She knew what it was now. What she'd been missing all along.

She was a girl without her mother's love.

Her father said something and Audra leaned forwards.

'I beg your pardon?'

'I said it's enough now.'

Audra looked out the window. 'She seemed alright.'

Olive didn't understand who they were talking about, but one of her mother's hands crept into her hair and it was not unpleasant. She lay limp, eyes shut so she wouldn't see her mother. She wanted to tell them she hadn't tried to do a suicide but that would make her mother's hand stop so she kept quiet.

The doctor had wild eyebrows and a purple nose which he put too close to her face. He checked her ears and throat. He listened to her chest and pronounced her fine.

'Why did you go for a swim so early in the morning?'

'She won't tell anyone what's wrong.' Audra smoothed her skirt down the sides of her legs. 'My sister tried to find out and if Rue can't get anything out of her, well . . .'

'Can you tell me?' The doctor kept looking at Olive.

'I was hot.'

The doctor waited but she kept herself hard.

'Keep an eye on her,' he said, turning to Bruce. 'It's not usually something that children attempt, but they can.' The doctor wrote something on a pad.

During the drive home, Olive found her reflection in the window. She was a blob in the glass, her features almost gone. The lines on the road were flat like her. The wire fences at the swimming pool, the oval, the two schools, some connecting others running alongside each other and never meeting. Her mother sitting in the front seat now and her father's profile occasionally showing as he looked across at the back of his wife's smooth head. All flat. All finished. Gone.

THE BOYS SAT swinging their legs in the tree.

'I wonder if it was on purpose,' Sebastian said, picking at the rubber strip coming off along the edge of his runner.

Archie was across from him.

'She wouldn't go for a swim with her clothes on,' Sebastian added. 'That bit, I don't know. So maybe she was trying to—to—'

Archie leaned out of the tree and let his dribble go down a bit. He sucked it back up and let it lengthen again.

'I wonder if Jethro did something to her in the tunnel.'

'How could you get a saddle up a tree?' Archie said, after recalling his spit three more times.

Sebastian told his brother it was a stupid idea and to forget it but Archie said it was Olive's idea first.

'She said Snooky had one up her tree and she said she was going to get one too. At her house. In the back.'

Sebastian ripped at his runner some more. He remembered now. It had been her idea, one in a series of things she kept going on about. The tapping code, then the saddle up a tree, and after that it was the book with people burning in their houses. And once she'd even been sure there was a secret room at Serpentine and he'd had to help her look for hours until exhausted, yet unwilling to admit there wasn't, she'd had a tantrum and thrown a small key at him.

'Well, I don't know, go ask Dad,' he said to his brother.

'*Pffft,*' said Archie. 'Dad doesn't care. You always say you don't know. *You never help me.*'

Sebastian swung at him but his brother was already shimmying down the tree and swinging to the ground, to run back to the house with his hair flopping long as he ran up the serrated driveway.

HER MOTHER WAS sitting in the chair beside the bed, dozing with an orange in her hand. Her chin had dropped to show between her lips a sliver of pearly teeth. The skin on the backs of her hands was translucent, shades of lavender and grey, and her nails were curved and polished with a frosted pink. Her shirt was open at the neck to the second button and the hollow at her throat shaded, like a bruise. Olive could see the ropy tendons at the side of her mother's neck, how the bones of her clavicle were sharp against her skin and framed a tiny pump of movement.

Olive was caught in those few seconds as dust motes float suspended in nothingness. She half closed her eyes and continued to study her mother and that's when the noise began. She could see from the front that her mother's face was falling into a hole. Her jaws worked, her eyes squeezed and her mouth formed the opposite of a smile. This was her mother crying.

'Oh, you're awake.'

'Why do you have an orange?'

Her mother told her she had decided to stop smoking so she planned to have a mint or an orange any time she wanted a cigarette.

Olive sat up and said she was thirsty. Her mother handed the glass across and passed her a mint. They sat together, sucking the lollies. Olive wondered whether her mother had dozed off because her eyes were closed again.

'I didn't mean it, Mum.'

'Maybe it was wrong, not to talk about her. People gave contra-dictory advice. They always do. It was hard to know what was right.'

Olive kept still a while longer. She was going to ask. She was going to be magnificent. Her finger searched for her thumb. There were things in the room that had been just out of sight and hearing, always ahead as her mother had been, turning corners and passing through doors. The sound of a felt-soled slipper on the stairs, or turning out of sight on the landing. At the front door pulling on tan and mustard golf gloves. Closing her bag clasp *snip-snip-snap* and calling out to the empty hallway: *I'm going to the shops, the petrol station, the bank.*

'Why didn't you ever hug me when I was little?'

Audra put the orange on the bedside table and repositioned a tissue at her mouth.

'I did try but you pushed me away.'

This was an impossibility to Olive and she shook her head.

'It's true,' her mother said. 'I tried not to feel hurt but you've always gravitated more to your father, to Rue and Thistle. Cleg even.'

Olive lay flat on her back. Maybe they had given her some medi-cine. Here was her mother speaking in a gentle voice, patting her with soft hands, refilling her water glass and saying that she had to go downstairs to start dinner. She left, quietly shutting the door behind her. Olive lay stiff with her mother's ministrations on her skin like a fine coating of oil, her legs and arms stretched into straight, well-boned lines.

•

Things settled like a bedsheet that has been lifted and falls through the air. All she wanted to do was sleep. The first day her mother had carried in toast and milk on a tray. A bowl of cornflakes for breakfast the second morning. The third morning porridge. She stayed in bed and played solitaire and did some of her Knitting Nancy.

Rue visited and brought yellow roses but they were too bright for the room. She also had some of Archie's *How and Why* books, and a jigsaw, one of Thistle's favourites. Venice. Thistle had liked the idea of a sinking city, had thought it romantic but Rue laughed at that. She said that Thistle was a woman with some odd ideas and handed over the bird cards in tall stacks, rubber bands holding them together.

'I took them out of the albums.'

'Are they in order?'

'Of course.'

Olive knew they wouldn't be.

Holding the cards made her sad. Rue said she knew that Thistle would want Olive to have them out of everyone but Olive knew she didn't deserve them out of anyone.

'Are you feeling much better?' her aunt asked from the chair. 'I've got a card from the boys.'

Olive took it out of the envelope and it was a funny card, designed to make her laugh, so she did. Rue and Audra both leaned forwards with their hands out and Olive held it in the air and Audra took it first, read it and passed it across to her sister.

Olive sat and drank her Milo. The ghosts felt very close. She wanted to ask why she felt so altered and why she had an ache deep in her stomach. She had been thinking about her new name—her *sobriquet*—and she had it now. She knew what it was, the only thing it could be: *Olive the Bad.*

•

She dozed and woke and the light was different. Her mother and aunt were talking. Olive made her eyes into fuzzy slits. Her mother was by the window with her back to Rue who was in the chair, searching her pockets. She pulled out a tissue and another and put both hands over her eyes and began to weep, the sounds small and hushed.

'She couldn't have kept him, not with her temperament,' Rue said. 'Fanciful and meddlesome. Says it all, really.'

'We could have helped her, I told you that.'

'I couldn't.'

'Doesn't much matter now, does it?' Her mother turned from the window. 'I don't know what to do with her.'

Through the line of her lashes Olive felt her mother look at the bed, at her. They were talking about her now.

'Has she had it yet? You know, her . . .'

'No.'

'That would explain the—all the—'

'I suppose.'

'Hormones. They have a lot to answer for.'

Audra started to open the blinds.

'I'm going to wake her up for lunch in a minute,' she said.

'Do you remember the card he wrote?'

'Who?'

'The Sands boy. How he wrote that card, saying sorry. That he had tried so hard, managed to get Olive but couldn't find—'

'I don't remember any card.'

'It was very sad, that card.' Rue blew her nose. 'Mavis said he wants to go back to the city but not stay with the uncle next time. Get his own place. She said he liked it there. Felt there were . . . what did she say? Opportunities. And I said what type of "opportunities" and she said no, not like that. That he had told her he wants to straighten out but she didn't use that term. Was it distance? I can't remember. She said he told her he wants to have a good life and feels he can't, here. With the *influences*, I suppose. Again, this isn't her language, it's my *interpretation*.'

Audra moved to the door. 'Can you wake her? Would you like some soup?'

Rue said no. She gave a brisk double-tap on Olive's shoulder and said lunch would be soon then followed her sister downstairs. Olive heard her aunt's chatty voice disappear then got up and went to the toilet. She could hear them talking in the kitchen. She walked all the way back to her bed with a noise clanging in her ears.

•

Hot soups. Tomato and cream of chicken. A bath once her mother thought she had rested enough. She let herself be guided into the bathroom and immersed. Her mother wanted to keep the door ajar and called to her every five minutes.

'Olive?'

'I'm fine.'

She kept quiet and cooperated, and on the fourth evening, Audra let her up to watch some television. It was strange to be permitted what she'd taken for herself previously. She begged to be allowed to watch *Dallas* but her mother said, 'We'll see,' which usually meant 'no'. Olive didn't care so much because Audra was doing something else. Tucking her into bed. Checking she'd done her teeth properly. Asking her how she'd slept.

At times she lay in bed and drifted before she remembered and called for her mother, thinking she might vomit. Her mother came with a bowl and sat with a feathery hand on her back, then left to heat more soup. The bowl remained beside her bed with a towel over it. She hadn't been sick but the nausea was real.

She sat in a chair by the window with her knees all the way up to her chest in the way her mother hated but let pass unremarked now. She was bored with the puzzle, the Knitting Nancy and the books. It was true what Thistle always said, that trouble is around a person like air is, and you breathe it in. She made sure to sleep with her jaw clenched and woke in the mornings, wrenched out of her sleep, heart throbbing with a dream-fear so thick and real it was as if she might make everything come true just by imagining it.

•

She went downstairs to the phone.

'I've been calling you,' Peter said.

'I've been sick.'

'Every day I tried, but your mum said you couldn't talk.'

'I didn't want to talk, especially not to you.' Her head was sore.

'Did you do it? The plan?'

'Why do you want to know?' She heard a voice in the background, it was a girl. 'So you can tell Snooky?'

'She wants people to call her Vanessa now.'

'You've been playing with her. Is she there?'

A shaky 'um' from the phone.

'It's not really playing,' he said. 'We're in Year 7 now.'

Olive thought of the bird cards on the blanket hills of her bed. The Knitting Nancy, her Spirograph set. Her slinky.

'But she's there.'

'Kind of.'

'I have to go.' She hung up.

She went back to bed. It was all wrong. Who cared about high school? It didn't matter anymore. She lay in her bed staring at the ceiling. The ache in her tummy got worse so she turned on her side and tucked her knees up, closed her eyes and tried to sleep. She had stolen the things off his car and she would get in trouble. Maybe go to juvie. She got the badges out of her jewellery box, the ballerina rotating on her single plastic leg. She didn't want to go to juvie. She hadn't done the plan but still she'd done things that were definitely wrong. She was sitting on her bed when the door opened. She put her hands behind her back.

'Peter's here,' her mother said. 'I told him no more than ten minutes.'

He sat down on her bed.

'Why'd you hang up?' He dropped his voice to a whisper. 'You have to tell me. *Did you do the plan?*'

She stared at him. He was asking her if she'd trapped Jethro Sands in a tunnel and left him there to die.

'You owe me.'

He'd been closer than a brother, closer even than Sebastian or Archie. If anyone owed anyone, he owed her. She counted to ten in her head. She was trying not to do things so quickly these days.

'I didn't,' she said. 'I didn't do the plan and if you'd asked *Vanessa* she'd tell you he's fine.'

He got up. 'There's a show about sea turtles on tonight, you should watch it.' She heard him running down the stairs and, in the distance, the sound of the front door closing.

She got the tape recorder out from her backpack. Rewound it and pressed 'play'. The first bit was her and Archie mucking around when they were little. She fast forwarded. Now it was her voice, slightly older, but high and thin, singing 'A Scottish Soldier'. She heard the flattened sounds of someone who thinks she is a good singer, has confidence. The way her voice cracked on the highest 'green hills' notes made her ashamed for that young girl, made her want to tell her she couldn't sing, to not even try because it was embarrassing. That carefree girl, cartwheeling on a spring lawn, while her parents were inside, arguing about whether to tell her something in five minutes. A girl who wanted to stay in the unknowing place because she didn't want to go inside and listen to what they had to say. It could be they wanted to tell her about someone who died, about a truth that would be hard to hear, so in the meantime, during those safe five minutes she had left, she turned in the air, over and over, across the grass as their loud voices carried from the open window.

She pressed fast forward again and then it was Jethro saying the bit about the beetle on the leaf. She listened to the rest of it, clicked off the recorder and got back into bed.

She realised now that things mattered. *Everything* did, including the smallest flowers, the least valuable rocks and minerals, the plainest woods and the ugliest, most stupid people. The other thing she realised, sitting in her bed with pillows propped behind, her childhood distractions on top of the blanket and her hands over her eyes, was that she, Olive May Lovelock, could be wrong.

•

She lay on the couch. The mother turtle struggled out of the sea onto the beach in the middle of the night and crawled up the sand, using her flippers like arms, pulling her broad-shelled body to a spot where she dug a hole. The mother turtle cried black tears while she laid her round eggs, covered them up then went back to the water. Olive wished for an adult to be with her so she could ask why the mother was crying and how the baby turtles were going to find her once they were hatched. Did she stay nearby somewhere waiting for her children. But there wasn't time to go and find her father, no time to get the encyclopaedia, because now it was early morning and the beach was growing sunny and hot, it was baking and the baby turtles were hatching themselves, cracking out of their shells and digging their way up and out of the sand and trundling madly down to the sea. But oh! No! Seagulls were waiting to eat the baby turtles and some of the babies got taken away into the air. Others made it to the ocean, rushing as fast as they could on their mini flippers to swim away, their little bodies frantic, but still, lots were eaten or got stuck and dried out to death on the beach. The man who was talking said only one in every thousand would grow up to be big.

Olive started crying and found she could not stop and it was worse even than the time her parents told her about Aster, after they'd called her inside from where she'd been playing outside on the grass.

She lay on the couch, her hands made into flippers. Her father came to carry her to bed and on the way up the stairs she pushed her face into his neck. He tried to make her feel better. He spoke her sister's name and told Olive she was a great kid and that everything would be okay. He told her it would all be fine and she had no choice but to believe him.

SHE FOUND THE sketchbook she'd got for Christmas—she couldn't remember who had given it to her—and started drawing, making shapes and doodles in ink, close-up studies of found objects she had. While she was saving up again for her typewriter she would be an artist and so started with a pine cone from Serpentine and a carefully selected sheath of grass with a heavy load of seeds that she'd found in her backyard, down near the fence. She drew the smallest parts of things and it helped her imagine that she was a small girl crouched over nasturtium plants, studying the cups of soft green with their drinks of raindrops.

She remembered how the drops of water sat on Grace's feathers, brilliant and luminous. How a surprising row of delicate feather strands decorated the top of her beak in an unexpected fringe. She let herself draw parts of Grace—her feet, her eyes—and if she could have illustrated life at the atomic level she would have done that too. She avoided the larger frame of things, wanting to keep her registration of the real small and in manageable segments. Tiny doses of reality, the only way she could proceed. She went into the backyard to collect more things to draw. Shreds of bark and cross-sections of beetles, flowers and ants. She would often be down there, drawing, when her mother called to her, saying she'd baked a cake and would Olive like a piece. She wouldn't want to stop her work at night until her mother had told her several times to turn off her lamp and go to sleep.

Other times she sat and looked through her binoculars at the world. She saw the neighbours as they went about their days, taking rubbish bins to the nature strip, mowing lawns, hanging washing. She tracked cars as they moved along from one end of the street to the other, turning into and from roads, and in the distance were the goalposts of the footy oval at her old school.

Once, as she stood in the window in her bedroom looking over all the back gardens, Mrs McCullers from next door spotted her and raised a hand in greeting. Olive waved back, worrying as the old lady tottered along her uneven garden path, carrying the empty clothes basket inside. She watched Mrs McCullers walk all the way up the path to the back door, keeping her fingers crossed, hoping she wouldn't fall over. Then she got the six wishbones from the ledge where they'd dried and, pinkie to pinkie, snapped them all.

A NEW SET of kids were riding their bikes through the streets. Olive had seen Archie in the middle of the group and waved at him. He turned his wheel so that he was facing the other way.

The police didn't come and arrest her and she didn't go to juvie. She'd taken the car badges back to Jethro and he'd said no harm had been done. She watched as he straightened the bent one and walked to his car to reattach them.

She'd seen Peter outside the fish-and-chip shop, talking to older boys who were in the footy team and who stood, blocking the foot-path and being rowdy. They talked about who would play which position that year. They drank Big Ms and ate fried dim sims, laughing with their mouths full and with bits of food falling out onto the ground. Olive was with her mother at the chemist, already embarrassed, and when they exited—she was holding the paper bag because her mother hadn't brought a shopping bag—she and Peter looked at each other. Before he could say anything she walked very quickly to the car.

He cornered her in the school library one day.

'I never see you.'

She looked up from her book. 'I'm around.'

'Not really. I see you in the distance but then you disappear.' He sat down.

Sitting at the table with her textbooks open in front of her, Olive thought about disappearing.

'There's been stuff,' she said. 'You know. I've been at home, reading, plus we have harder homework now.'

'I didn't tell anything to my dad, you know,' Peter said. It seemed important that she believe him so she said that she did. Then he talked a little bit about the grasshoppers, how they were still appearing and people were joking about the end of time. And then there were the fires in the area. His father had told him they were deliberately lit.

'Do they know who it was?'

'Nope,' said Peter. 'But people are saying it's the Sandses. Gary, Jethro and that.'

'It's not Jethro,' she said. 'It's not him and it won't be Johnno either.' She closed her book. 'Did you know? All this time?'

His face flattened. 'Know what? What are you talking about?' He stood up and walked away from the table without pushing his chair in.

SHE WAS STANDING outside the pool, thinking about going in. The weather was back to normal, so hot that the skin inside her nose hurt. It was the last day the pool would be open until the next summer.

'Hey, it's Ollie Lovelock.'

She turned around. Behind her was a boy in a blue singlet with long blond hair sitting on a low wall. He had a towel over his shoulder and his legs were stretched out in front of him. He was clicking his thongs against his feet. There was a chip out of one of his front teeth that she didn't remember and his shoulders were peeling. His freckles were the same though. He made a viewfinder with his hands and looked through them at her.

'Hi John,' she said. She looked over at the car park. More people were arriving. His friends called out to him across the space. He held his hand up, palm outwards. He didn't move.

'How's your mum and the brothers?'

'They're good, I suppose.'

They looked across at the entrance where Peter was standing and Snooky too.

'Are they going out?'

John said he didn't know. Maybe. 'Are you coming in?'

'In a minute.'

He stood up. 'Well, I'm going in. Come and find me?'

'Okay.'

He went and joined Snooky and Peter, merging into the group as it moved through the gate but Olive stayed in the shade outside.

She watched them through the cyclone-wire fence as they found spots on the grass slopes, put down their towels, the girls standing waiting for the boys to go in before they raised their arms to pull off dresses. Peter was taking off his t-shirt and dropping it on his towel and Snooky was standing closest. John was facing the entrance, shading his eyes with his hands. She started to walk home thinking she'd spend her money on lollies at the milk bar, but when she got to the end of the street she turned and walked back to the pool.

The last day of March. She needed to do it.

She took off her thongs and got out of her dress and sat away from everyone else. She could see Peter across the way with Snooky sitting cross-legged beside him. She was talking but he wasn't listening to her. He was lying on his back with his hands under his head.

She lay face down on her towel but soon someone came over and sat beside her. She turned her head and saw the freckled face of Johnno Sands. His teeth were very white. He talked about high school and about permaculture, how he was interested in it, in maybe doing it when he was older. She didn't know what it was so he explained and it wasn't about hairdressing. She listened and tried to concentrate on what he was saying. Then she said she was going in and she ran down the grass and made a little skip at the end onto the concrete.

•

Years later, in the flat near the city beach, there'd be fixed memories for Olive. Thoughts would tap at her in a random series of small images that dropped into her head, without cause. All the smells and shapes of childhood. Here a particular perspective of the schoolyard. The curved lip of the brick back steps. The sound of the kitchen window sash being raised by her mother, that juddering squeal of the hardwood in the frame. The way the light flooded through the green bubbled glass above the back door. How the camellia flowers dropped to bruise and moulder in the garden bed outside the dining room window.

These were the brightly lit scenes she memorialised. The farm with its rustic tableaux of things left on the verandah. The froideur of her mother. The sisters with their rotating, collective umbrage. The silence of the brothers. How you thought you knew yourself when really you were only at the beginning. How right and wrong seemed so distinct but weren't, not really.

Sometimes the past was very close, but there was the comfort of Sunday night fish and chips and sitting on the floor in the new place with high ceilings. Baby Lila asleep in her cot in the tower and she and John Sands holding hands, side by side. But even in those paused moments she thought about the way life caught and spun as quickly as a strobe, how time pressed forwards in a series of flashes of light in a way that made you unsettled, hopeful. And that even though she had arrived in a place that was clean and cool, she had once been a girl who went to the high places. She knew herself—her old self—was still a paper doll within, a girl who was wilful, fanciful and brave.

•

There was no queue so she climbed the ladder and walked without hesitation to the end of one of the big boards. Suspended above the cobalt of the diving pool she thought of the dam. She wondered if it would hurt when she hit. She bounced once and stopped, letting her loose knees settle. Her fringe curtained her eyes but she didn't move it, rather looked through it. She bent from the waist, her upper body perpendicular to her legs. Her back was flat, her neck long as her hands slid down beside her knees. She straightened, bounced again and jumped into the air and came down in a fast roar with both knees tucked under, one hand clasped across to hold her folded legs. Mouth wide open, a soundless scream in a slow-motion bomb, her free hand pinching her nose shut. In the water, the dark-tile lines on the bottom were closer. She rose and lay a moment on the surface, face down, spread like a starfish, then lifted her head and looked around. She got out and went back to her towel. She lay down on her back and kept her face to the sky. The whiteness of the sun entered her thin lids and combined with her insides, the interior of her complete world, and it travelled and pushed through her pipes to all her corners and shadowed places, where she lived and hid and turned and realised. And finally, everything became orange.

ACKNOWLEDGEMENTS

The first thank you must go to Sallie Muirden, early teacher and reader of this story, whose critical feedback and encouragement meant the world (and still does). It was Sallie who made me think I could do this.

Enormous gratitude and thanks once again to Virginia Lloyd for her invaluable professional help with developing this manuscript, and additional support over the last few years. Without her guidance and belief in me this would have been a vastly harder task.

A huge thank you and eternal gratitude to Allen & Unwin for publishing this book, especially the magnificent Jane Palfreyman for her belief in my work. Also, to Siobhán Cantrill and Ali Lavau for their painstaking, professional and patient editorial attention.

For reading and feedback on countless early versions, much gratitude to Pam, Roger, Elly, Erina, Serje, Christina, Athi, Paul and 'Alex'.

And thank you, as ever, to my family, especially Anthony for his ongoing love and support.